MW01487269

A Path of Ashes

Book 1 of The Path of Ashes

a post-apocalyptic novel by
Brian Parker

Baillie,
Thank you for your
support! Good luck
in your writing
career!

BP GeekFest
2015

MUDDY BOOTS PRESS

This is a work of fiction. Names, characters, places and incidents are the product of the author's imagination or are used fictitiously. Any resemblance to actual events, locales, or persons, living or dead, is purely coincidental.

Notice: The views expressed herein are NOT endorsed by the United States Government, Department of Defense or Department of the Army.

A Path of Ashes
Book 1 of The Path of Ashes

Copyright © 2015 by Brian Parker
All rights reserved. Published by Muddy Boots Press.
www.MuddyBootsPress.com
Edited by Aurora Dewater
Cover art designed by Jafet Martinez

This book is protected under the copyright laws of the United States of America. Any reproduction or other unauthorized use of the material or artwork herein is prohibited without the express written permission of the author.

Works available by Brian Parker

Enduring Armageddon

A Path of Ashes, Book One of The Path of Ashes

The Collective Protocol

Battle Damage Assessment

Origins of the Outbreak

Zombie in the Basement

Self-Publishing the Hard Way

Upcoming Novels by Brian Parker

Washington, Dead City Series from Permuted Press:

GNASH, coming Feb 2016

REND, coming Mar 2016

SEVER, coming Apr 2016

The Path of Ashes Series from Muddy Boots Press:

Fireside

Dark Embers

PROLOGUE

Ash drifted across the family's campsite. The old man didn't know if it was from his own fire or if it simply fell from the clouds above. The filth was a constant reminder of what had been lost to human pride and arrogance. The old world died in fire and somehow humanity continued to scrape by in the darkness.

Aiden Traxx leaned back in the wooden chair that his youngest son had made for him years ago when the heavy metal chair from his grandfather's time had finally rusted through. He watched his grandchildren play while they used sticks as swords, imitating their father and older brothers, not even realizing that they were already laying the foundation for training with the weapons that they would soon need. The armaments that his predecessors used to destroy the old world were mostly useless relics now, scavenged for the metal that they contained. Occasionally a working *gun* would make an appearance or be unearthed, but it was a person's ability to use a sword to defend one's family that mattered now, not questionable old world technology.

Unconsciously, the old man's gnarled hand drifted down to the blade beside him. It had been many years since he'd needed to use his own weapon to protect the family perimeter, but he still carried it with him everywhere. His sons and grandsons had taken over the role of defending the family and their meager crops against the Vultures who lived in the ruins of the cities with the creatures of the night. The Vultures were men who'd succumbed to the deprivation of the world around them, more deadly than any other living thing. They lived deep in the wastelands with the other creatures like the demonwolves that had been born after the world had burned.

"Come, children, come. Grandad has a story to tell you," he called to the young ones on the far side of the fire.

The two boys and their cousin, a girl, looked at the old man for a moment. Recognition flickered in his eyes. The children's desire to disobey the feeble old man was almost palpable. Why should they stop their game and sit to listen to him? But the respect that their parents had instilled in them overcame their resentment and they came near to hear his tale.

"Caleb, you sit over here," Aiden said, indicating the space to his left. "Varan, sit on this side with Tanya." It was better to keep the boys separated so they would actually pay attention to the story of their family history.

He waited for them to seat themselves before looking to his left and then the right. "Are you all settled?"

"Yes, Grandad," Caleb, the oldest of the three, answered for the group.

"Good. When I saw the two of you fighting through the flames of the fire I was reminded of a story that you haven't heard yet. It's the story of my grandfather, Aeric Traxx. Have you heard of him before?"

"We're Traxx," the little girl answered proudly with a thumb to her chest.

"Yes, little one, we are. Aeric was the first of us." He leaned down conspiratorially and whispered, "In fact, Aeric's family name wasn't even Traxx. He took the name when the old world burned. He was the last of his family and he no longer had any use for the name that he'd been given as a child."

"Was that when the ruins were made?" Caleb asked.

"Yes, when the ruins were made," he replied and then stared into the flickering flames. A piece of ash separated from the wood and drifted upwards, riding the heat current towards the heavens where it would combine with the rest of the ash to eventually fall back to earth.

Fitting, he thought. The man's gravelly voice filled the space between the Traxx family homes where they sat as he began to tell the story of his grandfather Aeric. It had been told to Aeric's son, who then passed it on to the elderly man when he was young. Now, he passed the family's history on to his grandchildren.

"On the day that the old world ended, ash drifted across the sky, blotting out the heavens and making it impossible to see the sun in the day or the stars at night—much like it does now when we have high winds, children—except this wasn't the way that it used to be. Would you believe that when Aeric was a boy, they could see the sun all day long and people were never cold because of the warmth that it provided? It's true."

ONE

Aeric stared at the ceiling above his bed and imagined life outside of his tired hometown of Springfield, Missouri. He was done with this town and ready to move on to the next phase in his life. In just two weeks he'd graduate from Central High, and then he was headed to Austin, Texas to attend the University of Texas on a baseball scholarship.

He was ready to be an adult, to experience life to its fullest, away from his parents and away from everyone he'd ever known. He was moving three entire states away from his parents, over ten hours one-way. The opportunity to put that much distance between himself, his doting father and overprotective mother sounded like heaven to Aeric.

It wasn't that he didn't love them—he did—it was just…too much. His dad always praised everything that he did, or found a way to put negatives in a positive light while somehow still managing to be headstrong, and not budge on much of anything once he'd made up his mind about a subject. His mother worried that something would happen to her only child, so much so that he hadn't been allowed to go out for football when all of his other friends had. She told him that with all the information about traumatic brain injuries that football players sustained, it would have been criminally negligent for her to allow him to play. So he'd tried out for baseball and earned a spot on the varsity baseball team as a freshman. Four years later, Central High had won three Missouri High School Baseball State Championships and Aeric had a full ride to UT—away from his parents.

He was even looking forward to the summer job that the coaches had helped him land. He was going to spend Monday through Friday coaching at a baseball camp for underprivileged kids. He'd be able to keep working on his own fundamentals while teaching the kids how to perform theirs. It was a win-win for him.

Aeric just had to get through the last two weeks of school and then he could leave. Everything had become complicated once he and Kate, his former girlfriend, had broken up. She was a cheerleader and the Prom Queen, easily the most popular girl in their school and they'd dated since the seventh grade. They broke up over a huge misunderstanding. Katie thought that he was cheating on her with his biology partner. As a result, the past three months had been hell as she'd made it her life's goal to ruin him, turning almost everyone at the school against him. He was just ready to get it over with and move on.

The alarm on his phone chimed once again and he pressed the button to turn it off. "One day at a time," he muttered as he sat up on his bed.

He went to the bathroom and then selected a pair of jeans and his baseball team's t-shirt from his closet. It was supposed to be rainy all week, so he'd have to wear a jacket—another thing that he was looking forward to when he moved to Texas. He hated the rain and knew that it hardly rained in Austin. When it did rain, they had actual storms, not the drizzle that seemed to go on for days in Missouri, keeping his mood sour.

"Honey, time to get up!" his mother called up the stairs.

"I'm up, Mom. Just getting dressed."

"Okay, honey. I made you some breakfast. Oh! It's raining so don't forget to take a change of socks and shoes in your backpack in case yours get wet."

"Be down in a second." There it was again. The constant coddling and over-protectiveness was exhausting. Why couldn't she just give him a bowl of cereal like every other kid in America got before they went to school? He reluctantly grabbed a second pair of socks and another pair of sneakers.

As he jogged down the steps, the smell of fried eggs hit him full in the face and his stomach rumbled accordingly. *Okay, maybe I'll let her cooking for me slide,* he thought. Aeric dropped the extra pair of shoes beside his bag and went into the kitchen. She'd made him an egg sandwich with mayonnaise and tomato. On the side was a bowl of freshly chopped melon and a glass of milk. He liked to complain that his parents were always doting on him, but he was going to miss having a home-cooked meal waiting for him whenever he was hungry.

He scooped up the sandwich in one hand and crammed a large bite into his mouth while he used his other hand to unravel a paper towel. Another bite went in as he dumped the melon onto the napkin. The milk disappeared as quickly as the sandwich had and he yelled, "Thanks, mom!" while he carried the melon down the hallway towards his backpack and shoes.

"Have a good day, honey!" she called after him. "I love you!"

"Yeah, love you too."

He slipped on the rain jacket that his mother had laid out for him and darted out the front door into the drizzle. Aeric was tempted to run so he could get out of the weather faster, but he knew that doing so would only result in him getting soaked from the waist down as the water splashed up from his feet slapping the pavement. Besides, he had more food to eat.

He was still three blocks from school when he finished the melon and used the paper towel to wipe his mouth. It came away smudged with a greasy, gray film.

"What the hell?" he muttered and looked skyward. He squinted against the falling rain and noticed a dark cloud above that trailed towards the southeast side of town where the industrial park was located. Something big was on fire over on that side of town.

The dirty rain dribbled through his dark hair down his forehead and stung his eyes. "Ow! Come on! Can this day get any worse?" he grumbled as he walked quickly towards his school rubbing his eyelids.

Once he got there, everyone in the hallway talked about the big industrial fire to the south of town. First one plant had caught fire and then an adjacent factory had lit as well. The school's resident conspiracy theorists said it was a terrorist attack since the two buildings were separated by massive parking lots and there was no way that the fire had jumped that distance.

Their theory married up with the rest of the attacks happening across the country. Over the last several years, they'd gotten worse. Riots happened almost weekly as the disillusioned youth protested the lack of jobs and rising cost of education while minorities protested the lack of upwardly-mobile positions available to them. Adding fuel to the fire were the religious extremists who'd stayed away from America's shores for decades after getting their asses handed to them in the Middle

East, but had recently begun to return in force to spread their message of hatred and intolerance.

The police had become increasingly hostile as well. They no longer knew who the enemy was since they were confronted on all sides. As a result, they often dealt rapidly and with an iron fist before small demonstrations became full-fledged riots. Their heavy-handed tactics did little more than add to the tension and further divided the nation's residents as seemingly innocent people were injured during melees with the people who they trusted to protect them.

Aeric didn't know whether the conspiracy theorists were right in proclaiming that the industrial fires outside of town had been a terrorist act, but he did know that it was another nail in the coffin of his life in Missouri. If anything, the idea that the troubles might be coming to Springfield solidified his desire to leave the state and never return. Graduation couldn't get there soon enough so he could start making a life for himself elsewhere.

*****

Aeric pulled up in front of his new apartment on San Jacinto Boulevard. He was tired after driving all day from Springfield to Austin and wanted nothing more than to curl up and go to sleep. The baseball coach had overnighted him the apartment keys and updated camp schedules, so he knew that he had tonight to move in and get settled, and then he'd be working every weekday after that. Even though he had a couple of hours of unpacking to do, the idea that he could potentially be asleep if he just let himself skip out on it made him that much more tired.

The university had provided him and another player with a furnished two bedroom apartment for the summer. Then he'd move into the Blanton Dormitory for the fall semester. The apartment was only minutes from campus and the baseball camp where he would work, so he planned to walk or buy a cheap bike instead of driving the car that his parents had surprised him with on graduation night.

Leaving home that morning had been exciting, terrifying and a relief all rolled together. His mother had been an emotional basket-case, while his father went over the route with him for the hundredth time and gave him some cash for the drive. Aeric thought his mother was going to chase after him because she'd followed the car to the end of the driveway. Thankfully, she'd saved both of them the embarrassment and just stood near the street to watch him drive away.

The trip through southwest Missouri and across a small corner of Oklahoma had been uneventful until he turned south on US Route 69. That's when he noticed the huge black smear across the morning skyline. As he drove closer, it became evident that something big was on fire and he was reminded of the industrial fires back home a few weeks ago. Those fires hadn't been the result of a terrorist attack, it turned out to be a disgruntled employee who'd started the fire and then set one of the hotels near the condiment factory on fire—not a second plant as originally reported.

Several thick columns of roiling black smoke drifted skyward to form a massive cloud that hung over southern Oklahoma like a dense blanket. When he got near the town of McAlester, the smoke was incredibly thick, causing traffic to slow down to ten miles an hour due to limited visibility. In town, he was diverted down back roads far to the east and then back south around the big army ammunition plant that was in McAlester.

The radio said that several of the massive underground ammunition storage facilities had exploded, but Aeric would have bet everything he owned that it was more than just a few of the bunkers. There was too much smoke for it to have been a small number of bunkers. The discussion of terrorists came up on the radio, but Army officials denied it, instead insisting that it was an explosion of improperly stored ammunition.

His mom called his cell phone when he was traveling wide around the site of the accident. She'd heard about what happened and wanted to make sure that he was okay. He assured her that he was fine and told her that he'd been diverted around the fire, not to worry about him. Of course, that sent her into a tailspin of worry since he'd been close enough to see the fires. After all, what if another bunker exploded?

When he crossed into Texas about fifty miles later, it was like a weight had been lifted off of his shoulders. He still had several hours to drive, including traveling through Dallas, but the fact that he'd arrived in the state that he'd call home for at least the next four years made him feel relieved. He was actually on his way to becoming a full-fledged adult.

Aeric looked up at his apartment building with a lopsided grin and turned off his car before sliding an arm through his backpack. *Might as well take a load when I go up*, he thought as he unfolded himself from the Pontiac. He wasn't overly large at six foot four, two hundred and thirty pounds, but he was pushing the manufacturer's recommended size limit for the small coupe.

He twisted around to pop his lower back and then walked up the sidewalk to the stairwell.

His apartment was on the second floor and he inserted the key in the deadbolt. He hadn't even turned the key completely around before the door knob twisted and a massive wall of a man opened the door. He looked like he was cut from rock, six seven, maybe six eight, big, broad shoulders, squared off chin and close-cropped blond hair.

"Hey, bro! Are you Aeric?" he asked.

"Uh, yeah. Are you Tyler Nordgren?"

His new roommate stuck out his hand, "Yup. I go by 'Ty' though."

Aeric shook it and stepped through the front door. The apartment was nice, not too large, but bigger than he'd been expecting. Ty had obviously already been there a day or two. Empty beer cans sat on the counter beside the sink and an open pizza box indicated what he'd eaten at some point. "Nice place," Aeric muttered.

"Yeah. Sorry about the mess, we don't have a trash can or recycling bin yet."

He breathed a sigh of relief. He'd wanted the full college experience, but that didn't include living like a slob in his mind—although the presence of beer was intriguing, Aeric wondered how his underage roommate had gotten it. "That's okay, I get it. So, which one's my room?"

Ty led the way through the living room down the hallway. The bathroom lay straight ahead with a bedroom on either side. "I slept in this one last night," he said indicating the room on the left. "You can have it if you want to be on the side with the parking lot, though. I don't really care which one I get."

"Oh, uh… I'll just take this other one. I don't care either."

Tyler helped him unload his car, which was a huge help and cut his trips in half. They cracked a beer and Tyler stood out in the hallway talking while Aeric unpacked his clothes in the closet.

"So, what position do you play?" Aeric asked as he shook out the t-shirts that his mother had wisely made him leave on their hangers.

"I'm a first baseman, but with Chase Hunter only in his second year, I may try to transition over to third so I can play this spring."

Even though Ty couldn't see him, he nodded his head. Hunter was a shoo-in for the big leagues. He batted .487 over the course of sixty-three games with 39 home runs as a freshman on the Longhorns run to their national championship last year. The kid was destined to be a star as long as he stayed healthy.

"What about you?"

"I play shortstop," Aeric replied. "Where are you from, man?"

"Lincoln, Nebraska. You?"

"Springfield, Missouri, but I really don't care if I ever go back, there's nothing there for me anymore. So, are your parents mad that you came all the way to Texas to play ball instead of going to Nebraska right there in town?"

"Nah. My dad realizes that my best opportunity to get scouted is at a College World Series winning school like UT.

Besides, Austin is a much better fit for me than Lincoln. People don't approve of me up there."

"Well if you got recruited to play for Texas behind Hunter, you must be pretty good," Aeric retorted, misunderstanding him.

"No, I mean they don't approve of me, of my lifestyle."

He popped his head out of the closet so he could see his giant roommate. "What do you mean?"

"I'm gay, man. They're not crazy backwards up there, but people give me a wide berth when I walk by. The LGBT community in Austin is huge and extremely supportive, so I think I'll fit in better down here."

Aeric nodded his head in understanding. There had been a lot of growing pains in his hometown over the years as the population there slowly accepted the fact that homosexuals were just people and not some abomination that they'd been made out to be by various religious organizations. There were problems every once in a while because some bigot would do something absolutely horrific, but for the most part, the issue had passed the test in the Springfield area. However, too far outside of the city limits and he expected that there were still a lot of problems with acceptance.

He hadn't ever considered living with a gay man before. It didn't matter to him though, who cared who the guy liked? Then, an epiphany struck him. "Have you met any cute girls that want to hang out with you that you could introduce me to yet?"

Ty smiled at him and flipped him off. "I'll keep my eye out, bro. I'm starving so I'm gonna order a pizza, what do you like?"

"Just about anything except anchovies or olives." And just like that, Tyler's sexuality wasn't a big deal. The dude liked beer and pizza, played baseball and looked like he could bench press a truck, what more could he ask for in a teammate?

TWO

Aeric dropped his backpack heavily on the floor by his dorm room door. It had been another long day of 100-level classes, information that he'd never use, but they were classes that the university mandated all students take. Tyler sat on the couch engrossed in the television while he ate a grilled chicken sandwich. The team trainers had put them both on high-protein, low-pizza diets after they each gained several pounds over the course of the summer. Ty's parents seemed content to fund his unlimited pizza and beer expense account and he always dragged Aeric along. Dieting sucked, but now that the fall semester had begun, they had to get back into baseball shape for the spring.

"You're not gonna believe what just happened," Aeric said.

"What?" Ty asked around a mouthful of sandwich. It came out sounding more like a cow's moo than a human's words and a large piece of bread fell out of his mouth onto the floor.

"Dude! For a gay guy, you're the messiest person I've ever met," Aeric teased. "Aren't you like, supposed to be super clean and smell like roses all the time?"

Tyler leaned to the side and farted with a laugh. "Man, you set that up perfectly!"

"Geez… Anyways, some homeless guy was talking on his cell phone and then began begging me for change so he could eat."

"Yeah, so?"

"The homeless guy had a cell phone…and was begging me for change," Aeric prompted.

The light went off in Tyler's head and he said, "Oh… You think that he shouldn't have been begging for money if he can afford a cell phone."

"Exactly. I told him that I wasn't giving him any money if he had enough to pay for a cell phone contract, and then he went on this crazy rant about how I was an over privileged, rich white kid who went to college while he spent his college years fighting in Afghanistan. Like, everybody stopped and stared at me and several people gave me the dirtiest looks—people we go to school with—and then they gave this dude money. Can you believe that? They made it seem like I was the bad guy for telling him that he had to prioritize whether he wanted a cell phone or food."

"Pretty typical stuff, man. We've talked about how people with money are demonized in my sociology class. You wouldn't believe how many of the people in our school actually believe that having money is evil."

"But they're at a university that charges a shit-ton of money for tuition," Aeric muttered. "They actually have money, or student loans, and they talk about how bad money is. Yeah, my freshman psych class has those debates too."

"It's just like all these riots," Tyler said as he gestured towards the television. "Some of them are about racism, some are about social equality, and others just want to bitch about something near and dear to them and a thousand of their closest friends."

Aeric glanced at the TV, "Shit, man. Is there another riot going on?"

"Yeah, this time it's in Cincinnati. They're rioting about the government response to the terrorism threat here in the states."

"Geez, what is that, four or five just this week?"

"Well, let's see," Ty held up his hand and counted off the massive riots that had swept the country during the last week. "Houston, New Orleans, Atlanta—"

Aeric interrupted him, "Did they find those news anchors yet?"

"Nope, the entire tower is just…gone. Fucking terrorists."

"Sucks."

"Anyways, there was Baltimore, Chicago and now Cincinnati. People are scared of this shit, man."

"Yeah, but by rioting about the government's lack of response to the terrorism, all they're doing is creating more problems," Aeric reasoned. "They think that they're telling our government to crack down on the extremists, but they create more propaganda for the terrorists to use and recruit even more people to their cause.

"And what about the police state?" he continued. "The government could easily end up with too harsh of a response and we'd end up being like Russia in the nineteen fifties. People were afraid to leave their homes, always wondering if they were gonna get snatched on the street or if the secret police were going to invade their homes. We can't live like they did."

"Whoa! This isn't your Psychology class," Ty responded with his hands up and accidentally knocked his plate off his lap. "You're in *la casa de Tyler*. I'm not some ditz who thinks that those people out there in the streets who say that they're protesting for social change are doing anything but causing more problems. I understand that the government's lack of response could swing quickly to too heavy of a response. It's the age-old debate about civil liberties versus security. Is there an acceptable middle ground there or do we always have to operate in the extremes?"

"You're right," Aeric admitted. "Sorry, Ty. I'm just really freaked out by all of this. I mean, it feels like we're unraveling at the seams and there's nothing that we can do about it."

"Relax, bro. It's only going on in the major cities, just like in the sixties and seventies. This is just another form of social change. It'll blow over after cooler heads prevail and everyone calms down."

"I don't know," Aeric said as he shook his head while he stared at the television. "This feels bigger. The extremists are attacking people who are different than them, *everywhere*. Paris is a war zone. London has an eight pm curfew… Hell, even Moscow is under siege. It seems like the only place that stuff isn't happening is in China."

Tyler snorted. "Don't let them fool you. They've got massive social problems, but their government just goes in and eliminates an entire village if something happens. We don't even hear about it, but I've read about things happening there that make Paris look just look like an out of control Christmas parade, man. China is an absolute nightmare."

Aeric considered his roommate's words. What the hell was happening all over the world? It was like the simmering pot of racism, social injustice and religious violence had suddenly overflowed and spewed out of the pot. He'd watched cautiously as it happened on other continents, but now it had erupted all across the United States and it scared the hell out of him.

"Are we, like, supposed to go to school or stay home?"

Tyler looked away from the television and shook his head. "Man, that's so far away, there's no way that the school is gonna close over this stuff."

"But this is a dangerous situation," Aeric countered.

"Weren't the sixties race riots dangerous? What about the war protests and domestic terrorism of the seventies, weren't those dangerous? The LA Riots, the recent race riots, sporting riots... All of those were dangerous and the country recovered— and I'm pretty sure that school wasn't canceled for any of those."

"I guess one of the coaches would give us a call if we were supposed to stay in the dorm, right?" Aeric asked.

"Yeah, they would. Besides, Austin is fine. We haven't had any incidents here."

"You're right. It's just—"

He was interrupted by the ringing of his cell phone. He looked at the screen, it was his father. "Hello?"

"Hey, Aeric, it's dad."

"I know. You come up in my caller ID."

"Well, it could have been your mother."

He sighed. "What's up, dad?"

"Your mother and I were worried about you and just wanted to check in to see if everything was okay."

"Yeah, we're fine. Everything that's happening is far away from us."

"I know, son. Things like this have the potential to get out of hand pretty quickly. I just want you to be safe and make smart decisions."

"I will. I won't get involved in anything dangerous. Our coaches are keeping an eye out for everything and will let us know if there's a problem."

"Your *coaches*? Listen, Aeric, it's right to trust your coaches and to listen to their advice, but if things go bad, they're gonna be looking out for themselves and their families, not you. Understand?"

"Dad, I'm not stupid, I know that they'll be more concerned with their own families, but nothing is happening down here. We're fine."

"You keep saying that. Promise me that if something seems like it isn't right, you'll just leave. Promise me that, okay?"

"Uh, okay, sure."

"Son, this is important to me. Just promise me, please."

"Sure. I promise to leave if the situation gets weird."

"Gaines don't break their promises, young man. I'm gonna hold you to that."

Aeric was starting to get irritated with his dad's overprotectiveness once again. It had settled down over the summer and he'd hoped that the distance away from home had possibly mellowed his parents' attitude towards him, but here it was again. He wasn't even halfway through the fall semester and they were treating him like a child again.

"Dad, I got it! I'll avoid any creepy guys in dark alleys. I've gotta go or I'm gonna be late for work."

"It's only four o'clock. I thought you didn't have to be at the camp until six."

Aeric muttered a curse under his breath. "Yeah, normally, but they changed the hours this week."

"Hmm, okay. One more thing before I let you go, don't use your credit card."

"What? That's the only way I can buy groceries, dad."

"Well, the damned hackers busted into our bank yesterday. They cleared out our accounts and ran up all of our credit cards. Yours is maxed out too. Just eat in the student cafeteria until we can get this sorted out, okay?"

Aeric cursed under his breath. Now the goddamned computer hackers were messing with his life. What the hell was wrong with those people, couldn't they just work like everyone else instead of stealing people's identities and stealing their money. "Yeah, sure, I'll have the lasagna in the cafeteria," he sneered.

"Look, son, I know it's not the absolute healthiest food that you need for baseball, but it's only a few days. The bank is aware of the charges, hell, their entire network was hacked and millions of dollars have been stolen. It took me three hours to get through to someone this morning, but everything should be okay in a few days. You'll probably have a new card mailed to you by the end of the week. I'll call you and let you know when things are back to normal.

"Shit—whoops, sorry, dad. I mean, *darn*. Okay, I'll make it work down here and see about cashing my check instead of depositing it."

"Good idea. You can't go wrong with cash."

"Yeah. Okay, I've really gotta go."

"Be safe, alright, son?"

"Yeah, sure thing, dad. Bye."

He stabbed the button to turn his phone off and Tyler looked over at him. "Your parents are freaking out a little bit, huh?"

"Yeah, my dad thinks that this is bigger than the news is letting on and now our damned bank got hacked, so I don't have any money."

"Now I know where you get your paranoid streak from," Ty stated.

Aeric considered throwing something at the big jock, but he figured that he'd just end up getting his ass kicked. "I'm not paranoid. As much as I hate to admit it, my dad's right. We need to be careful."

"No worries, bro. We will be. Man, I could totally go for a beer right now. All of your worrying is stressing me out."

"I'm down," Aeric said. "But I don't have any money and we're on that stupid diet."

"I've got you. Besides, one beer won't hurt anything. I'll take your ass to the gym and beat the hell out of you tomorrow."

"Yeah, one beer sounds good."

*****

They'd called him crazy, a sociopath, even a terrorist. What the fuck did any of those assholes know? He was a brilliant visionary, the mastermind behind the largest planned hack in the history of computing. He'd spent years cultivating his followers, assigning them menial tasks to test their loyalty and now he had a network of more than five hundred experienced hackers who followed his every command as gospel.

Justin Rustwood's life had been a series of setbacks and disappointments up until this point. He'd never been particularly good at sports and he became the target of many practical jokes when his parents forced him to try out for one of his high school teams each year. He developed a deep-seated hatred for the jocks that constantly made fun of him, beat him up and publicly humiliated the fat kid from Sonora, California.

After high school, he surprised his parents by joining the Army as a computer systems specialist. The only thing that he truly excelled at as a kid was computer programming and the Army trained him to be a computer hacker to defend against the invasive hacking of their computer systems. He became good, very good, and was quickly promoted in the newly formed Army Cyber Command, which promoted soldiers based on their computer skills, not how many stupid push-ups that a meathead could do.

Of course, he'd dropped the baby weight and the Army made sure that he built a lot of muscle, but he still hated the jocks that had ruined his childhood. Even in the CyberCom, the colonels and generals were all infantrymen, stupid, musclebound assholes who tried to attack cyber intrusions like they would an enemy on the battlefield by directing all of their forces to the point of attack. Justin knew better though, he'd begun hacking other networks on his own time, so he knew that for actual cyber-attacks meant to disrupt operations or steal information there were typically multiple points of entry. The main, easily recognizable, yet hard to defeat attack was meant to confuse defenders and pull all of their resources while the real attack was usually a subtle thrust from the side.

It was during one of these attacks that his shining Army career came to a crashing halt. Colonel Harris, the man in charge of his section, a Ranger who barely knew how to compose an email, let alone defend the nation's computer networks from a determined hacking effort, ordered him to focus his team's efforts on the main attack. Rustwood had argued against it, but ultimately conceded and had his subordinates defend against the attack while he searched for the real breach. He found it and stopped it, earning the appreciation of the Army, while also gaining an enemy in the colonel, who viewed his actions as a direct violation of his orders.

Things got worse for Justin as Colonel Harris made it his goal to punish him for disobeying his orders. One day, during a health and welfare inspection of the barracks, they found the Airsoft gun that Justin had purchased as a gift for his brother still in the package in his room. Everyone knew that it wasn't a deadly weapon, but the colonel pressed charges all the same and somehow was able to get the JAG to agree. He was busted down to private for having a 'gun' in his barracks room and then chaptered out of the Army without any benefits.

Over the years he continued to develop his computer skills and nurse his hatred for Colonel Harris, who'd retired and became an assistant coach for the University of Texas baseball team. Justin formed an online group of Hackers known worldwide as 'The Vultures', named after the marvelously adaptive bird of prey that could survive on the world's leftovers and then attack when enough of them were gathered.

Most of the members of the Vultures were like-minded. They were disillusioned with the world that rewarded people based solely on their looks, their personality, how fast they could run— all the things that a simple twist of the genetic Rubik's Cube had given them and not what they'd earned. Our society was based on the lies of the government, reality television programs and performance enhancing drug-addled superstars who pandered to every minority and blamed people of European descent for all the social ills. It was such a farce. The Founding Fathers would be shocked to see what their Great American Experiment had become. The world would be a better place if they could reset the clock and start over.

It was during a discussion with his disciples one day that the idea came to Justin. The Vultures *could* reset the clock. It was within their power to do so. All it would take would be to infiltrate the US Strategic Command's network and initiate an attack. Of course, they'd have to do the same for the Russian General Staff, which had access to their nuclear weapons. The Russians, predictably, would shoot back immediately. However, the primary reason for even bothering to hack their network would be to ensure that none of their missiles were targeted at places where the Vultures would be. They couldn't help to rebuild the world if they were obliterated in an attack.

He wasn't stupid or crazy. Justin knew that in order to achieve his goals, he would need to convince his followers to do unspeakable acts. As a student of history, he'd decided that the easiest way would be through religion. So he began to speak of the Reset in terms of a righteous crusade against evil and people ate it up. His followers grew, both online and off. The first time that he met a small group of Vultures in person he was regarded as a legend, possibly even a celebrity, which he thought was hilarious.

In order to prepare for the harsh life after the Reset, he worked out for hours a day to achieve peak physical condition and set up secret guarded warehouses full of shelf-stable food that were paid for through hacking the offshore accounts of the rich. He urged his followers to move to Austin, Texas where he'd set up shop so he could observe Colonel Harris. As time wore on and more of the Vultures relocated to Austin, they began to view him as a deity, the savior of mankind. And he'd begun to believe it himself. The females of the group freely gave themselves to him and the males offered their spouses or girlfriends for his use. Life was good, but the distractions couldn't keep him from moving forward with his plans.

"Brothers and sisters," Justin said to the assembled group in his luxurious home. "Tonight, we set in motion the beginning stages of the Reset."

He waited until the applause and murmuring died down before continuing. "It is imperative that you move to your safe location within the next few days," Justin said as the Vulture transcribing his words typed rapidly into their ultra-secure server so his followers around the world could hear his message.

"The world has digressed into hatred and villainy. Children idolize adulterous, murdering, drug-using football players who beat their wives. Our youth don't want to learn about mathematics or science, history or geography, all they want to do is play silly games with balls so they can have the chance to be a millionaire superstar and have paparazzi follow them to the restroom one day. Enough is enough.

"We have spent years preparing for the next several days. I applaud your secrecy, your ability to disguise our true intentions, and the advancement of your skills which have allowed us to gain access to the United States Air Force's nuclear network without their knowledge.

"We all know that the Reset will not be pretty and that millions of people will die. Be not afraid, for I have seen that the way is righteous. We are God's chosen. We will purge the earth of its evil. Even today, terrorism kills thousands of people a month, our police forces abuse the population, and minorities demand a greater piece of the pie. We are the chosen ones and we will cleanse the globe with fire.

"I have set in motion the first stage of the Reset. By the end of the tomorrow night, the world will know of the Vultures and the world will rejoice at the freedom from repression that we will give them."

Justin looked around the room, appraising his followers' reactions. Two of them were clearly shocked as if they thought all the work that the Vultures had done was just a game. He'd have to have those two removed before they ruined his plans. His eyes fell upon the trio of his favorite hackers. He stood, allowing his robe to open slightly and reveal the muscles that he'd worked hard to develop, and beckoned the three women to follow him to his bedchamber.

*****

"Alright! Who wants to do a shot?" Aeric yelled to the small group that had gathered in their fourth-floor room in Blanton Dormitory.

"Hey, I'll do one with you," Amber, a petite brunette from Katy, Texas, said as she slid her hand up his arm.

Aeric tried to blink away the fog in his mind. He knew that he'd met her earlier that evening, but wasn't sure if he'd been talking to her or one of the other girls that had seemed to magically appear in their room once they started drinking. They'd been discussing the merits of whether the government's response to the growing terrorist threat should be soft and only go after the cells in secret or if they should smash through the neighborhoods where the organizations were likely hiding. Then, the next thing he knew, the room was full of girls and a few of Tyler's guy friends.

"What do you want? We have SoCo, vodka or tequila," he slurred.

Her hand slid along the crease between his biceps and triceps, then up over the bottom of his deltoid. "Mmm...what kind of tequila?"

"Uh, we have Patrón Silver," Aeric replied.

Amber's fingernails dug into the back of his arm slightly as she pulled him down to her so she could kiss him. When she broke away, she said, "Let's do a shot of Patrón."

He walked into the kitchen and pulled two short juice glasses down from the cabinet. Even though their RA was really cool and didn't turn them in for having the alcohol, they couldn't take the risk of having shot glasses. It was stupid little things like shot glasses that you missed when you hid the booze that would get you in trouble for violating the dorm rules.

Amber slid up behind him and pressed herself up close while he poured the tequila into the two glasses that he'd selected. A shiver went up his spine as her fingernails trailed along his stomach. "So, you're a baseball player?" she asked.

"Uh, yeah," he answered with a nervous chuckle. Amber was extremely hot and she was totally interested in him. *This night is on track to end great*, he thought.

"I love baseball players," she purred.

It took him a little effort to spin around because she was so close, but he finally turned around and handed the pretty coed one of the glasses. "Cheers!" he said.

She raised the glass and replied, "Here's to an exciting evening."

He smiled back at her and downed the shot. The Patrón slid smoothly down his throat without the need for a chaser. "Mmm, that's good," he said.

Amber nodded and once again pulled him down to her. They were lost to their kiss when a nearby explosion rocked the building. The lights flickered and then went out completely. People in the living room screamed in terror while car alarms echoed through the night across campus.

"What the hell was that?" Amber asked.

"I don't know," Aeric replied. "It sounded like an explosion."

"Hey, guys!" someone yelled from the living room. "Come check it out, I think the Health Science Center just blew up!"

"The Health Science building?" Tyler asked as Aeric and Amber rushed towards the window where everyone was gathered.

"Yeah, I take classes there."

"Call 9-1-1!" a girl shouted.

"I'm trying," another answered. "The lines are all busy."

The partygoers were scared and confused, causing and Aeric's buzz quickly wore off. How had the chemistry building exploded? Was someone working on an experiment after hours that went awry and somehow caused a major accident or was it a planned explosion, an attack? Were the problems that plagued most of the country hitting Austin too?

"Come on, Aeric. We should go see if anyone needs help," Amber asserted as she slid her arm through his and pulled him towards the door.

"Uh, yeah. Okay. Ty, we're gonna go down and see if there's anything that we can do. Are you coming?"

Tyler turned from the scene at the window and said, "Yeah. I've got that big first aid kit in my bat bag, let's take that and see what we can do."

"Good idea," Aeric replied. Tyler always had his own collection of bandages in case he got injured when one of the trainers wasn't around. He returned carrying his entire baseball bag and led the way to the door. Aeric fell into step behind him and heard several others following behind him.

"This is so weird," Amber muttered.

"Yeah, I wonder what happened."

She shook her head and followed Tyler and Aeric down the stairs. The bigger man pulled out his cell phone and used the screen to illuminate the way. "Good idea," Aeric praised him and slid his own phone out of his pocket. He briefly checked the signal strength before turning it around. There weren't any bars on the screen.

"Huh, I don't have any signal."

"What? Let me see," Amber said and looked at his phone and then pulled hers out of her back pocket. "I don't have a signal either."

They stepped out of the stairwell into the dorm lobby. Fires burned at various points, but they hadn't generated enough smoke to set off the alarms yet. "What the fuck?" Tyler yelled.

"Hey, who's that guy?" a girl that Aeric didn't recognize as part of their initial group shouted. He followed her outstretched arm towards a man wearing a ski mask holding a large red can of gasoline.

His eyes locked with Aeric's for a moment and then he dropped the can, running from the lobby towards the street. "Hey! Get back here," he roared and took off after the arsonist.

When he exited the building, his senses were assailed by the turmoil. Everywhere he looked, it seemed like fires were burning while sirens screamed through the night. He gagged on the low-hanging acrid smoke and wondered how the fire at the Health Science building had spread so quickly. It must have been the masked man. Had he escaped?

"There he is!" Amber pointed over his shoulder.

He saw the man running towards downtown and ran into the street, directly into the path of a huge blacked-out truck barreling down University Avenue. Aeric froze like a deer in the headlights. His mind screamed at his body to react, but it wouldn't respond as he stared at his imminent death.

"Look out!" a girl's voice cut through the fog and he was hit hard in the back by her shove.

He felt her hands close around his waist and then suddenly pull him back towards the truck violently. An impossibly loud *thud* filled his ears as the truck impacted with the girl. Then he was spinning back around as he bounced off the side of the vehicle.

The truck slammed on its brakes, filling the night with yet another sound as the tires squealed against the pavement between the dorm and the Health Science Center. Aeric lay in a crumpled heap near the side of the road and his head pounded in rhythm with his rapidly beating heart. He tried to sit up, but couldn't get his body to respond.

His head rolled listlessly to the side and he locked eyes with Amber. Had she been the one to push him out of the way of the truck? His vision swam in and out as his body threatened to pass out, but a woman's screaming brought him back to the present. Only then did his sight clear up enough to realize Amber's beautiful face was close to his while her body stretched out grotesquely behind her. She'd been ground into the pavement by the heavy truck.

Her lifeless eyes stared at him in silent accusation of his betrayal. She'd tried to save his life and sacrificed her own instead. From the high point near the center of the road, a dark liquid reflected the fires of the burning buildings as it slowly seeped toward Aeric.

He squeezed his eyes shut to make the sight of the dead girl go away, to wake up from the nightmare that had descended upon his world. When he opened them, Amber's body was still there. He tried to move away from the blood that flowed towards him, but his body still refused to respond and he felt the first of it touch his cheek.

Aeric turned his head to pull his face away and noticed that it was snowing. The giant snowflakes falling from above seemed surreal to the baseball player. He thought that he'd left the early fall snowstorms behind in Missouri. The *snow* landed on his cheek, it wasn't cold like snow normally was.

It wasn't until the red and blue lights of the emergency vehicle illuminated the road that Aeric realized that it was ash blown up from the burning buildings all around him.

*****

The next few minutes were a mix of insane moments interspersed with surprising lucidity for Tyler. He was standing on the sidewalk when his best friend at UT and Amber, the girl from down the hall who'd asked him to introduce her to Aeric, got hit by a big police truck. The damn thing was painted all black speeding down the road with no lights on like it was going on some kind of SWAT raid. Hell, they may have been headed to arrest the arsonists, but there was no reason to be traveling with no lights on.

It took him less than a second to ascertain that there was nothing that he could do for Amber. She'd been mutilated by the huge tires, so he focused on Aeric. His friend's eyes were partially open and unresponsive. He instantly went into lifeguard mode. He'd worked as a lifeguard at outdoor pools in the summer and indoor pools during Nebraska's long winters every year since he was twelve. Having a little bit of a buzz didn't erase six years of constant training. The very first thing you did when you came across an injured person was to check for breathing.

Aeric didn't have a pulse. He rotated his body so that Aeric's back was flat on the ground and began CPR. He was cautious not to press too hard initially for fear of breaking the guy's ribs. If he didn't get something going soon, he'd go into the full chest compressions, which would probably end up fracturing the delicate rib bones.

It only took three rounds of compressions and breathing for his friend to begin breathing again. Frankly, he was shocked. He'd never heard of anyone responding to CPR as quickly as Aeric had. He kept breathing and Tyler moved to the next item on the checklist. Check for bleeding.

Fuck. He had a massive gash in the side of his head and he'd also been laying in the girl's blood, so Aeric was totally covered in it. He used the small first aid kit that he'd brought to try and bandage the cut as several hard-soled shoes came running up. A pair of EMTs took over bandaging his friend while a police officer took statements.

Tyler stumbled over to the officer in shock, while smoke began pouring from the Blanton Dormitory windows. The officer had everyone move to the far side of the street and one of the people from his party pointed at him, saying that he knew the victim. It wasn't true. He didn't really know her that well. Amber was just a girl on their floor who'd come to their impromptu party. He answered the officer's questions woodenly until it came time to the actual accident.

"Then that big fucking MRAP truck came barreling through here without any lights on and hit them both. It didn't even stop, just kept on going."

"That's under investigation, Mr. Nordgren. Just tell me the facts as you saw them."

"I just told you that the truck came through here without any lights on and hit my friends. Those are the facts as I saw them."

"Are you getting lippy with me, boy? Do you want to spend the night in jail for interfering with a police investigation?"

Tyler knew where this was going. The increasingly hostile police force wouldn't investigate their own shortcomings. They'd make a public statement about the tragedy of the events leading up to Amber's death, but they would never claim ownership of it or punish those responsible. It fucking sucked, but that was part of the price to pay for the increased security in America.

"No, sir. I'm just upset about my friend's death."

"Good, now, let's revisit your statement and tell me exactly what happened before I start asking you about why you're carrying around a bag with a giant baseball bat in it."

He sighed and began again, cautious to avoid anything that could be construed as blaming the police for the accident.

THREE

Aeric woke to the slow beeping of electronic equipment and dim lighting. He tried to sit up, but his body was too sore, so he used his hands to push himself up. A sharp pain in his wrist made him reconsider and he brought his hand up in front of his face. There was an IV line sticking out of the big vein on the back of his hand.

"What the hell?" he muttered and dropped his arm down to his forehead. Something soft touched his arm and he used his hand to feel around his skull. A bandage completely circled his head without obscuring his line of sight.

He turned slightly and noticed Tyler sleeping in a chair beside the bed with his mouth open. "Hey. Hey, Ty. Wake up!" he croaked through parched lips. His throat felt like it was on fire. "Hey!"

"Wha—"

"Wake up!" Aeric repeated.

Tyler rubbed the palm of his hand into his eye socket. "Oh, man, you're awake! Geez, I was really worried about you."

Aeric tried to grin, but his face hurt too much, so he gave up the effort. "I'm alright. Did I fall down the stairs at the party or something?"

Ty leaned forward and then stood up to look down on him. "You don't remember what happened?"

He searched his memory and nothing stood out. He remembered hanging out with some girls and drinking a lot, but not really too much after that except that he might have made out with someone. "Uh, it's all a little fuzzy after the party got going."

"You don't remember the Health Science building exploding or all the fires that the arsonists set on campus?"

The blurry memory of fires painting the night sky orange and red did ring a bell. He thought he'd dreamt that part though. "I... I'm not sure, man. I don't remember any explosions. The building blew up?"

"Yeah. It was after hours, so nobody was hurt in the explosion, but several hundred people died in the dorm fires."

Aeric choked. "Several *hundred*?" His throat was killing him. "Can you get me some water?"

"Yeah, hold on."

He heard a sink turn on and then Tyler came back into view and held the cup to his lips while he sipped the cool liquid. "They don't know how many people died yet. Multiple arsonists disabled the fire alarms in all the university dorms and then set fires on the bottom floors. If we hadn't gone downstairs to investigate the explosion, we'd probably be dead too."

"I'm sorry, Ty. I just don't remember any of that. Maybe I was more drunk than I thought."

"You did puke all over everything, but I thought that was because of the truck that hit you."

"Huh?"

"Do you remember Amber?" Tyler asked cautiously.

He smiled. It wasn't nearly as painful this time. "Yeah, that cute brunette from down the hall."

"She saved your life when we went outside. You were gonna get crushed by a big police truck—one of those big ones that the city bought from the military when we left the Middle East—but she pushed you out of the way."

"Oh wow! I— What is it?" he asked. His friend had tears running down his face.

"Amber was killed by the truck when she pushed you out of the way. It tore her to shreds."

He recoiled deeper into the hospital bed's mattress. "No! That… Oh, man, that sucks."

Tyler wiped his face with his hands and cleared his throat. "It gets worse."

"I don't know if I can take anything else, Tyler," he replied truthfully.

"You need to hear it. Some hacker group hacked into the computer systems of every plane that was airborne over the United States yesterday and turned off their flight control systems. Most of the planes crashed. There were some that were high enough that the pilots were able to recover and find a landing strip, but not many. We're talking thousands of planes that went down in an instant."

"Are you serious?"

"Yeah, bro. All those people are dead. The government is labeling it as a cyber-crime, not a terrorist act. There are massive riots in New York, Boston, LA… Well, you get the picture. All the places that have already had riots are having them again, except they've gotten out of control. I was watching the news until I got tired and turned it off. These aren't even disguised as peaceful protests anymore. They've gone to full-on mob violence. People are getting killed protesting the government's investigation into people getting killed. It's totally crazy."

"Is this really happening?" Aeric mumbled as he tried to clear his head and organize his thoughts.

"I'm afraid so. All of our stuff is gone, too. Blanton burned down. The university canceled classes indefinitely and the southeast side of town is a war zone. The police are fighting a losing battle with some of the Hispanic gangs out there."

Aeric tried to sit up again and Tyler placed one of his massive hands on him to hold him down. "We need to get out of town, Ty!"

"Don't get up. I'll go find a doctor or nurse and see what they say." He didn't wait for Aeric to answer and strode out of the room.

He turned his head and tried to see out of the window. It was hard to tell what time of day it was since the windows had a deep tint on them to keep the Texas sun at bay, but he thought it might be either late evening or early morning. Dark, angry clouds rolled by in the distance, some of which looked like they might have been from fires and not heavily laden with rain.

Amber was dead because of him. He'd been so drunk that he apparently couldn't even get out of the way of a giant truck. What a fucking waste of a life. She'd always seemed so vibrant and had a smile on her face every time that he saw her. Now she was gone—and so were a lot of other students. What kind of sick bastards would do something like that to innocent college students?

The tears flowed freely down his cheeks while he stared blankly out the windows. The world's sanity had been slowly eroding during the last twenty or thirty years, now it had gone completely mad. How had it gotten to this point? He understood the problems with the terrorists. They had been a constant threat since the mid-1970s, popping up when the population had once again settled into complacency and the organizations were relegated to obscurity. Unfortunately, those types of random attacks were things that Americans had come to expect. There was little that people could do to defend against them except to be vigilant.

The bullshit bucket had finally overflowed and was now lying on its side to fill the streets. The social inequality and difference between the haves and the have-nots wasn't any different than it had been for millennia. However, it seemed like everyone had developed a sense of entitlement and those who couldn't afford the same things as their more wealthy peers had struck out in every direction.

It started with the riots in the major cities and now it seemed like it had come home to roost in Austin. There was a clear disparity in Austin, an affluent city with a large, disillusioned youth population. He had a hard time believing that people would go so far as to commit arson and murder, but that's what was happening and there were certainly fires burning out in the city even now.

It suddenly occurred to him that he didn't even know what hospital he was in. Was he in the University Medical Center or Saint David, or even the one way out north of town on Research? It seemed like a silly thing to think about, but it filled his mind and he couldn't stop wondering where he was. The angle from his bed didn't allow him to see the UT Tower or any other distinctive buildings so he was at a loss.

He'd started to drift back to sleep by the time that Tyler returned with a nurse. "Hello, Mr. Gaines. Your friend said that you're awake. How do you feel?"

"Like crap," he admitted. "I got hit by a truck, people everywhere are dead and my throat is on fire."

"Well, that's probably because we had to perform a gastric suction on you—we had to pump your stomach," she amended when she noticed his confused look. "You had too much alcohol in your system for us to be able to properly administer medications. It's possible that your esophagus was accidentally scraped during the procedure."

"Hmm," he muttered.

"As to getting hit by the truck, well you bounced off of it really," she stated with a smile that made Aeric want to punch her in the face. A girl had died so that he could just "bounce off the truck." It was serious, not something to joke about. "You don't have any internal injuries, lots of bruising and a small contusion to the back of your head where it must have impacted with the truck, but there's no swelling in your brain or anything to worry about."

He forced himself to calm down. Her nonchalant attitude wasn't her fault. She worked with patients who died, or were dying, on a daily basis. Amber's death hadn't affected her the way it did him. "Okay, so am I free to leave then?" he asked.

"You've been in and out of consciousness for about thirty hours, Mr. Gaines. We'd like to keep you for at least a day of observation, but if you feel that you're healthy enough to leave, we can't make you stay."

He glanced at Tyler, who shrugged and said, "Where are you gonna go? Our dorm burnt down, remember?"

"Shit. Yeah, I guess I'll stay then."

"Ok, we'll notify the police department somehow. They want to get a statement from you about the events of the incident. With all the problems on the southeast, I'm not sure how long it will be until they can speak to you."

Aeric nodded, replying, "Well, they can always call my cell phone."

"Cell service is still out, man. Hell, even the regular phone lines are down," Ty stated.

"What do you mean? How are the cell phones down? They communicate over satellites."

"I don't know. The news is still able to broadcast, but other communications satellites don't seem to work. I guess the telephone lines must have been cut too. Austin is pretty isolated right now."

"What's causing all of this?" Aeric asked.

"Let me disconnect all of your wires," the nurse interjected. "I don't think you need to be hooked up to a heart rate monitor anymore. Then I'll leave you two alone and check back in on you in a couple of hours. Just buzz if you need anything." She unhooked all the wires and turned off the beeping equipment before she left. The IV stayed in his hand.

Tyler watched her go and then said, "I don't know what's causing all of this, Aeric. It seems like everything is happening all over the place. The internet has been a hotbed of activity for years with people all over the world calling for the overthrow of whatever government that they had, but it seems like some groups have actually begun to carry out their plans."

Once again, Aeric muttered, "Is this really happening? I mean are we really talking about the collapse of society because of disgruntled people banding together on the internet?"

Tyler gestured towards the television and shrugged. "That's what the news says."

"This…this sucks," Aeric mumbled at a loss for words. "Hey, do my parents know about what's going on?"

Tyler shrugged again and replied, "I don't know. I haven't talked to them, but the UT attack has been all over the news, so I'm sure that they know something is going on."

"Dammit! The phones don't work?"

"Nope, I've tried mine a bunch of times and the nurse said that the hospital's phones don't work either."

"What about the internet? If they're broadcasting the television over satellite, is the internet still up and running? I doubt that hackers, or whoever is doing this, would turn their primary means of communication off, right?"

"Good point. I hadn't thought of that since my cell phone internet connection didn't work. I just thought it was all down."

"Cell phone data flows over the cellular network, but I bet computers that have their modems hooked up to the cable company lines have internet access."

"Hold on, let me go find an internet lounge or something. Hospitals usually have them."

"Wait a minute," Aeric said. "Help me up, I want to go with you."

It took some maneuvering to get him out of bed, but they finally got him up and secured his open robe in the back. The IV drip pole had wheels, so they rolled that along beside Aeric and went looking for a computer.

"Where do you think you're going, Mr. Gaines?" the nurse who'd visited him earlier asked from her seat in the nurses' station.

"We're looking for an internet café or something like that so I can send my parents an email to let them know that I'm okay."

She raised an eyebrow and stated, "There's not an internet café in Saint David's."

"Is there anywhere we could go?" Aeric pleaded. "My parents don't know anything and I'm sure that they've seen the news saying my dorm was burned down."

She glanced at another nurse beside her, then stood up and said, "Come on around here. You can use my computer to send an email."

"Thanks," Aeric said as he slid around the counter.

He sat down in her vacated seat and grabbed the mouse, then opened up the internet and went to his email account. There were several emails from his mother. He didn't even bother to open them up. Instead he clicked on the New Email icon and began composing his message.

Hey Mom and Dad,

First off, I want to let you know that Tyler and I are okay. I was involved in a minor accident when our dorm burned down yesterday and was taken to Saint David's Hospital in downtown Austin. It's right near the university. I don't know how much longer I'll be in the hospital, but the nurses tell me that I'm medically cleared to leave the hospital. I guess we'll try and see what UT is doing for students who've been displaced.

My cell phone doesn't work and the landline phones are down also. The nurse was kind enough to let me use her hospital computer to send you this note. I'll send you another email once we get to a semi-permanent location or maybe I'll try to call and let you know where we are when the phones come back on.

I don't know if my car is alright. It was in the dorm parking lot, but I'm pretty sure that the keys were in the building when it burned down. Isn't all of this absolutely crazy? I haven't seen the news yet, but Ty told me about the planes.

Alright, guys. I love you. Don't worry about me, I'm fine, just need to get a place to stay for the next couple of nights until I can figure out what I'm going to do. Classes are cancelled for right now and everything is a mess down here.

Talk to you soon!

Love,

Aeric

He read the message and tweaked a few areas to make it sound more upbeat than he felt. There wasn't any sense in making his parents more upset than they likely already were. The nurse stood behind him, so he didn't bother opening any of the emails from his mother. He knew what the gist of what they'd say anyways.

Aeric closed out his email program. He didn't see the message from his mother telling him that his father had been on a plane to Austin to find him when his plane went down.

*****

Aeric signed the release forms and crammed the doctor's prescription for pain reliever into his pocket. "Thank you for taking such great care of me and for letting me use your computer yesterday," he said to the ever-present nurse.

"It was my pleasure, Mr. Gaines. You be safe out there."

He nodded and walked over to where his hulking friend stood off to the side for privacy. "Ready, buddy?" Tyler asked.

"Yeah. Are we gonna call a cab or walk?"

"Phones are still out."

"Crap, I forgot," Aeric admitted. "How far from the university are we?"

"I don't know," Tyler's big shoulders hunched up as he shrugged. "It's seven or eight blocks to the Athletic Department. I guess that's where we should start."

"It's as good a place as any. I mean, maybe Coach Harris will be there, or at least there'll be some type of notice for what we're supposed to do."

"I hope so. I don't know what else to do. Honestly, being able to stay with you in the hospital was the best thing that could have happened. Otherwise I wouldn't have had anywhere to go."

Aeric nodded his head noncommittally. It was time to figure out what they were going to do. It had been two days since the Health Science building explosion and the string of arsons on campus, which had burned all but one of the residence halls. Back at the hospital, the news had stated that the student death toll had grown to nearly ten of thousands as investigators searched through the wreckage.

The arsonist group had cut power to the fire alarms and blocked the stairwells before setting the fires in the lobbies of the buildings. Police didn't know if the desk attendants had been in on it or if they'd been victims too. Speculation was that the arsonists—correction, the *murderers*—had likely killed the attendants before they started their fires. They knew what they were doing and the school's students paid the price.

Even the street war in the southeast had escalated to include most of the city to the east of Interstate 35 and parts of the downtown area as well. Austin's emergency response services were literally overwhelmed as the injured inundated the hospitals and clinics, while the dead lay stacked like cordwood near the curbs for the garbage trucks to pick up.

The first body that Aeric and Tyler saw freaked them out. It had multiple gunshot wounds to the body. The white button-down shirt that the man had worn when he died was stained maroon with dried blood. They saw several more bodies in the short trip from the hospital to the athletic department. It got easier for them with each one.

They finally reached the athletic offices building, nestled in the shadows of the giant UT football stadium where they'd reported after class every day. The power was out and even in the full light of the early afternoon, the place looked sinister and haunting. "You think anyone's in there?" Aeric asked.

"I don't know, man. Looks abandoned. We won't know unless we go in, though."

"Shit. This is the part in the movies where everyone in the audience is screaming at the people to not go into the building," he muttered.

"Well, neither of us are virgins, so we should be safe." Tyler's comment brought a smirk to his face.

"Yeah, I guess I'm just being stupid." He took a deep breath to steady himself and then started walking towards the building behind the bigger man.

Tyler pushed his way through the building's front door and called out, "Hello? Anyone in here?"

There wasn't an answer, so they went deeper into the building and their nostrils were assaulted by a strange, yet familiar smell. It was metallic, and reminded Aeric of the way that his hands smelled after handling old change. "What's that smell?" he asked.

"I don't know. It smells like when you open up the hood of a car after a long drive or something."

"I don't like it. This place hasn't ever smelled like that before," Aeric said. Then, he took a turn and called out, "Hello?" The darkened hallway yawned back at them in silence.

"I don't know, Aeric. It's pitch black further down this hallway. I doubt anyone is just sitting back there in the dark."

He nodded his head in agreement. "Yeah, I guess nobody's in here."

When they turned to leave, a voice called out from somewhere in the darkness, "*Aww, the poor football players can't find anyone to cuddle up with.*"

"We aren't football players," Aeric responded to the creepy voice without even thinking. "We play baseball for the school. Where are you?"

"You're still jocks. Your time ruling the world with your stupid over-sexed, beer- and testosterone-fueled attitudes is over. The bible says, 'The meek shall inherit the earth.' That time is now!"

Aeric felt his friend's body tense beside him and he placed a restraining hand on Tyler's arm. "Not worth it, Ty," he whispered. "We can't see shit in here and that dude might have some type of trap set. You saw all of those dead bodies outside, things have changed, man. He sounds crazy, so there's no telling what he's capable of."

The big man pulled against Aeric's hand for a moment and then relented. Tyler yelled into the darkness, "You don't know us. We could be the nicest people in the world."

"You sure showed him," Aeric whispered sarcastically.

"We know your kind. That is why your world must die and a new one will be reborn. We will Reset the world, make it a place of true equality where it doesn't matter what you look like or how much money you have. We will choose what values and attributes are important, not some stupid ability to catch a ball and lift heavy weights or looking pretty in a bikini."

"What the hell are you talking about? Come out here so we can see you," Aeric demanded.

"I am not as stupid as you two, blindly rushing into somewhere that you have no business being."

Indeed, Aeric *did* sense that they were walking a very fine edge between stupidity and outright danger. He tugged gently on Tyler's arm and they slowly backed away towards the entrance. The voice seemed to get nearer as it teased, *"Run along home to mommy, boys. Say hello to Colonel Harris for me if you see him. Tell him that the Vultures are looking for him. We'll find where he weaseled off to eventually."*

Aeric resisted the urge to laugh at the stupid name that the guy in the darkness called himself—or were the Vultures some sort of street gang that he'd never heard of before? Admittedly, he'd been self-absorbed with his classes and partying in between the mandatory team workouts, so he didn't know anything about the various local Austin gangs. The Vultures sounded like something that a minor league hockey team would call themselves, not a street gang.

Vultures feast off the remains of dead animals, was that what this guy meant? Were they preparing to feast off the remnants of a dead society? His initial reaction to laugh died on his lips when he thought of dead things. Was that what the metallic smell in the air was from? Were there dead *people* down that hallway? He quickened his pace to leave the athletic department offices as fast as he could.

Society wasn't dead as the voice in the darkness alluded to. It *was* on life support, though. Just a few more pushes towards the edge of the cliff and they'd be spinning headlong into an irreversible future. They reached the doors and Tyler pushed his way through them onto the sidewalk. From the darkness of the building came the laughter of a madman…and the sound of a pump shotgun racking a round into the chamber.

They'd both grown up hunting and being around guns, so they knew what the sound was. They dived away from the doorway as the glass doors shattered and the boom of a shotgun exploded from the darkness. They didn't wait for the second round before they scrambled to their feet and took off sprinting towards the center of campus. After two blocks, they slowed to a walk to catch their breath.

"What the fuck was that?" Tyler asked, looking back towards the athletic offices.

"I don't know," Aeric answered. "Have you heard of the Vultures before?"

"No. I don't know what he's talking about."

"Me either. Something about that place wasn't right. I didn't like that he could see us, but we couldn't see him. Then, the mother fucker shot at us!"

"Why would that guy be sitting in the dark like that?"

"Because he's a fucking psychopath," Aeric replied. "I think I know what that smell was."

"What's that?"

"Have you ever helped your mom in the kitchen and opened a package of meat?"

Tyler nodded and said, "I don't like where this is going. Let's head over towards Blanton Dormitory and see if there's anything left."

"Good idea," Aeric agreed and began walking towards their old dorm. Once they'd crossed the street and after several glances over his shoulder, he continued, "So, you know that blood smell that comes from a package of raw meat? That's what it smelled like to me."

"So you think that there's some dude sitting in there with a bunch of dead bodies?"

"I don't know, man. But with all the shit we've seen, just in the walk from the hospital to campus, I wouldn't put it past someone who was off in the head to do that. He already tried to kill us."

"Not really," Tyler countered. "If he'd wanted to kill us, he probably would have shot us in the darkness. What does he want us to talk to Coach Harris about?"

"Does it matter? The guy's a loony. I wonder if his Vulture group, or whatever, is behind any of this."

"Behind it, like you mean the arsonists?"

Aeric shrugged. "The arsonists, the hackers, the gunmen who've shot some of the people that we've seen, I don't know. That guy in there was definitely a whack-job though."

"We should call the cops."

He looked over at his big friend who slapped his forehead. "Oh yeah, I forgot. Maybe there will be police or firefighters at the dorm that we could talk to."

"Yeah, maybe," Aeric replied without conviction. He doubted that there'd be much of anything left for them in Austin.

*****

24th Street was silent as they walked the few blocks towards their old dorm building. The campus was mostly empty, giving it the feel of an old, abandoned town and the few people that they did pass scurried quickly away from their view. The charred hulk of the Mallet Chemical Library to their left reminded them that they weren't walking through some Old West ghost town. They were witnessing the first stages of a war.

They turned up University Avenue towards Blanton. All along the bottom row of windows, dark burn marks seared the light brown brick. It became more random as the flames licked alternating windows on the higher floors. Their room had been on the fourth floor and Aeric allowed himself a moment of hope that their things had escaped the devastation that the lower floors had suffered.

A dark stain of dried blood near the center of the road caused Aeric to stop. The stain stretched over ten feet, ending in a large splotch where it had pooled on the side. Amber died on the first night of the problems in Austin so they'd collected her body, but small chunks of meat littered the pavement and they hadn't taken the time to wash away the blood. It reminded him of how the highway department handled dead deer back in Missouri.

"At least they had the decency to pick her up," Aeric said as he gestured towards the grizzly scene at their feet.

"I'm sorry, man. I know that you two liked each other."

He looked up with red-rimmed eyes, the tears threatening to overflow. "It's not even that, Ty. I barely knew Amber. It's just that this whole thing is so messed up. There are bodies all over the place, burned out buildings, weird dudes threatening people from inside powerless buildings. When is it gonna stop? This is the twenty-first century for fuck's sake. We were supposed to have moved past all of this bullshit."

Tyler nodded his head, but didn't say anything.

"Alright," Aeric sighed. "Let's see if any of our stuff is around."

His roommate peered up towards the fourth floor. "It doesn't look like the flames made it that high. Maybe our room is okay."

"I hope so," he replied without commitment.

The fire department hadn't even bothered to block off the entrances to the burned out building with tape. They'd been too busy trying to stop the fires that burned unchecked around the rest of the city. It was like all the social rejects and degenerates had teamed up to ruin the small, beautiful city and the residents suffered because of it.

They stepped through the shattered glass doors into the lobby. The acrid stench of burnt, stained wood singed their nostrils and Tyler scrunched up his nose. "This place reeks."

"Yeah, I'm not so sure that it's safe to be in here," Aeric replied as he looked around and then up at where the ceiling should have been. Instead he saw the sky above. The fire had burned the hottest here at the center of the building and destroyed all four floors and the roof in this section.

Tyler glanced around, "It should be alright. Looks like the outside structure is fine. The walls and stairwells are made of concrete, so we should be okay."

"Yeah, but is it going to collapse while we're inside?"

"It's been safe for two days," Tyler reasoned. "What's it gonna hurt for us to go up the stairs real quick? I've got some irreplaceable things that I want to keep."

"Fine, let's make this quick." Tyler was much more of a risk-taker than he was. He just wanted to get the hell out of the dorm before it collapsed on them.

They made their way around the charred remains of the front desk to the stairwell. Aeric's mind replayed blurred segments of that night. He thought that this was where they'd come down the stairs and found the arsonist at work, but they may have come down the other set of stairs. The stairwell seemed to be intact, so they eased their way up, taking their time before they placed their full weight on each step. Aeric trailed his hand across the wall as they went for support. It came away covered in deep, black soot.

Peeled paint covered the back of the steel fire door that led from the stairwell to the fourth floor. There had clearly been a massive amount of heat on the other side and Aeric doubted even more that anything was left of their possessions. Tyler pushed the twisted metal handle down and pulled the door into the stairwell.

"Well, I guess that's that," he stated and stepped out of the way so Aeric could see. The floor was missing, it had been burned away.

"There's no way we can get around this. It doesn't look like anything survived the fire."

Tyler looked over his roommate's shoulder and asked, "You think we could make it over to the room somehow? I mean, there's those metal bars that we could walk across." He pointed towards the floor joists that had once supported the floor, but were now twisted from the heat.

"I don't think so, man. Besides, there's nothing left down there."

"How do you know? The walls of the rooms are cinder block, so maybe they insulated our stuff."

Aeric turned around to face his friend. "It's over. Our shit is gone, man. Even if our stuff didn't actually burn, it was so hot that everything would have just melted."

Tyler stared down into his eyes for a moment and then looked back at their old hallway. "You're right. I don't know what I was thinking... So what are we gonna do?"

"Let's get out of here first. We need to find someplace safe to sleep for the night. Then maybe tomorrow we can rent a car to leave town or something."

"You've got to be twenty-five to rent a car, Aeric."

He frowned. "You think they'd still follow those rules?"

"Yeah. It's probably worse now. What about buying bus tickets?"

Aeric hadn't considered purchasing bus tickets to go back to Missouri. It was a foregone conclusion in his mind that he'd go back home to be with his parents until this all blew over. He didn't know what the hell he was doing. He was only eighteen and this past summer was the first time that he'd ever made an entire day's worth of meals for himself. It made sense to him to return home.

"Bus tickets? That's a good idea," he admitted as he walked carefully back down the stairs. "I don't have any identification— or money. My wallet was in the dorm along with the keys to my car when everything happened. I can't get a new driver's license down here, so first thing tomorrow morning I'm going to the student identification center to see about getting a new student ID. Then I'm going to the bank with my new ID and getting cash. Then I can see about a bus ticket out of here."

He'd come to the part in the conversation that he dreaded to hear the answer. "What are your plans?"

Tyler considered it for a moment and then said, "Missouri is north of here, kind of on the way back to Lincoln. I can go with you to your parents' house and then continue towards home on my own."

Aeric let out the breath that he hadn't realized that he'd been holding. Having the big man at his side was a huge advantage that would help to keep some of the thugs away. Aeric wasn't a small guy at six-four, but he was dwarfed by Tyler's size. "That'd be great, man. Thank you."

"No worries, bro. Do you want to try and find some food? I'm starving."

"Yeah. Most of the restaurants that we've passed have been closed. Maybe one of the convenience stores is open."

They exited the building that they'd called home for two months and went north on University to Dean Keaton Street. Two blocks to the west was a row of campus-friendly restaurants. If none of those were open, then there was a gas station a block north of there that was sure to be open.

As they neared the larger street, cars whizzed by in both directions. Were they running away or was it simply people coming and going from work, regardless of the dangers that faced them in the city? "I guess people are still going about their lives, huh?" Aeric said with a weak gesture towards the cars progressing through the powerless intersection.

"Guess so. They've still gotta pay the bills, right?"

He grunted in agreement but chose not to say anything else. Tyler was right, people still had to buy food and pay their mortgages. This was just a crazy confluence of events that would blow over in time. Those who did the right thing and continued to contribute to society would be fine, it was the ones who took part in all of the chaos and acted like this was the end of times that would face justice.

When they got to the small shopping center, it was just as Aeric had feared. The storefronts were darkened and several windows had been broken out leaving glass littered along the sidewalk. His mind wandered back to his thoughts of justice that he'd had only minutes before. Would the police ever be able to bring everyone to justice? Had they gone too far down the path towards anarchy?

It was an insane thought. Only days had passed since the problems came to Austin. Other cities had been dealing with some of these issues for weeks—although, not as bad as the arsonists murdering thousands of college students in their sleep. Would the US Army be sent in? He knew that there was a big army base somewhere nearby to the north, he'd passed the signs on the highway when he drove down several months ago. In fact, why wasn't the Army already on site? It wasn't that far away, they should have been here by now.

He didn't have the answers, but his stomach grumbled in protest at not being fed since he left the hospital. They'd eaten at the row of restaurants several times since they were so close to campus and the sight of them made him even more aware of his hunger.

"Looks like other people had the same idea," he stated, pointing towards the smashed windows.

"Yeah, and then they got pissed off when the taco shop wasn't open because it didn't have any power," Tyler replied. "Fucking assholes. We're not moving past this until the average citizen steps in to help out."

"What do you mean?" Aeric asked. "Like becoming a vigilante or something?"

Tyler's eyes sparkled as the retreating sun's reflection off the windows of the city's taller buildings hit him in the face. "I meant that we all had to just hunker down and not take part in the violence and looting. I hadn't thought about people becoming vigilantes and striking out against the people doing this. That's a good idea."

Aeric reached out and wrapped his fingers around Tyler's elbow. He gave his friend a good shake and said, "Snap out of it, buddy. We're not trained to fight crime or whatever crazy thing that you're thinking about. This is real life, not a video game. We get killed and there's no respawn. What we need to do is get some food and then hole up somewhere close to campus for the night."

Tyler grinned at him. "No respawn, that's good! I wasn't planning on becoming a vigilante, man. We just need to think about self-protection." He hefted his bag to his shoulder and continued, "The only weapon that we have is my baseball bat. Well, maybe my cleats too, but those would be pretty useless except as an absolute last resort."

"If we're trying to use your shoes to defend ourselves, the odor will probably knock them out before the cleats touch them."

"We'll use everything we have to our advantage," Tyler deadpanned. "Let's see if that gas station is open."

They turned north on Guadalupe and walked up the block towards the gas station. As they neared it, gunshots rang out from somewhere close. They dove behind a set of two trash cans that sat on the corner across from the gas station. "What the hell was that?" Tyler asked.

"Gunfire!" Aeric replied and unzipped the bag on Tyler's shoulder. He pulled out the bat and one of the shoes then zipped it back up.

Two men ran out of the store with a garbage bag and hopped into a car sitting in front of the building. The tires squealed as they fled the scene of the robbery. "Oh, geez," Ty said. "You think they killed somebody in there?"

"I don't know—maybe?" Aeric responded. "Let's go and see if anyone needs our help."

They ran across the street to the store and Aeric yelled through the open door. "Anybody hurt in there? We're here to help!"

No one answered, so they rushed inside and stumbled upon a scene that would soon become commonplace to both of them. The store's single employee lay slumped over the counter. It looked like they'd gone around the counter and shot him behind the ear. The small bullet hole belied the damage to his face when the round exited. Blood dripped slowly towards the floor and pooled where customers usually stood in front of the counter. The cash register drawer was open and empty. The man had been killed for a couple hundred bucks.

Tyler turned his head from the grisly scene while Aeric went up to feel for a pulse. As he pressed his fingers against the employee's throat, the body slid backwards into the employee area and the man's brown eyes, surrounded by some slightly yellowed whites, stared lifelessly at Aeric.

He considered what they should do for a moment. The phones didn't work and they hadn't seen any police officers since the truck that killed Amber that first night. Suddenly everything clicked in Aeric's mind. They were on their own, with no place to live and Austin was now a dangerous city with no police presence. They needed food and shelter—and possibly weapons.

He reached across the bloody counter and yanked several plastic bags away. "Ty, start grabbing the canned food and bottled water."

His roommate looked at him like he was crazy. "You want to rob this place, too?"

"Everything in here will be gone by morning. We're just the first ones on the scene."

"That's not how I was raised, man. That dude died in here, we need to find the cops."

Aeric slammed his hand down on the counter and blood splattered outwards in all directions. "Shit," he muttered and used the magazines to wipe away the blood. "Ty, this is a really bad situation that we're in. Austin isn't safe and we need to leave. Hell, for all we know, the entire country is falling apart, what with the riots, the hackers and the gangs. There are dead bodies in the street, piled up and forgotten. No one gives a *fuck* about anyone but anyone else right now. We need to take care of ourselves. That means food, water and shelter, the three basic necessities of life. Either get that through your head or we're done and I'm taking off without you."

Tyler continued to stare at him for several seconds as the wheels turned in his head. "Fuck it. Alright, what are you getting?"

"Cigarettes," Aeric replied and hurried around the counter.

"What?"

Aeric reached overhead and began pulling cartons down. "These things are going to be like currency soon, man. Just fill your bags with all the canned food and water that you can hold. Maybe we'll be able to use the cigarettes to pay for a ride out of the city."

Tyler nodded and began grabbing canned food off the shelf and putting it into his bag. "Hey, grab toothbrushes and toothpaste too!" Aeric recommended while he continued to pull down cigarettes from the sales rack above the counter.

The clink of cans going into Tyler's bat bag was almost drowned out by several other people rushing through the doorway. Aeric searched the counter for some type of weapon and only found the large plastic spatula that had the bathroom key attached to it. He sighed and hefted the cleat above his head. Tyler was more prepared and placed the bat on his shoulder so he could level one of the men if it came to it.

"Hey, we don't want any trouble!" one of them said as he glanced at all of the blood and then back at Tyler's massive figure. "We just want some food, too, man."

Tyler glanced over at Aeric for instructions. He shrugged and continued grabbing the cigarettes while keeping an eye on the newcomers, who'd gone to the chip and cracker aisle. The bat slowly lowered and Tyler started shoving more food into the bag. Once he'd gotten about sixty cans of the gas station fare— mostly variations of pasta and meat sauce—he went to the refrigerated section and opened up the glass door to get water.

Aeric came around the corner once again and grabbed two cheap drawstring backpacks from a display. He pushed the plastic bags into the packs and crammed the rest of it full with packaged beef jerky and some cookies. "Ready?" he asked Tyler.

"Yeah. Let's get out of here."

They walked confidently, but quickly, out of the store and hooked around the building towards the west on 26th Street. At the next intersection, they took Nueces Street north. "Holy shit!" Aeric finally said. "Can you believe that just happened?"

"I thought that we were going to get in a fight for sure."

"If things stay like this, it will probably get to that pretty soon. Right now, people are just concerned about staying safe while they wait for the cops to show up." He lifted the shoe and stated, "We need better weapons."

"Wait, we're not leaving town?" Tyler asked in misunderstanding.

"Yeah, we're getting out of here, but we have a long trip ahead of us. Austin is a big town and we've got a long drive back to Missouri. That's about twelve hours in the best conditions. Right now, I'm not sure how clear those roads are."

They had only gone north two blocks when the street lights at the corner of 28th and Nueces flickered and then died, plunging the intersection into darkness. Aeric peered as far down both sets of streets as far as he could see and was met with total darkness. Far to the southeast, the clouds that hung low over the city glowed orange with the many fires that burned freely in the conflict zone.

"Shit," Tyler muttered. "Looks like we just lost power."

"What the hell does that mean?" Aeric asked.

"It means that we need to get off the street and find someplace to hole up for the night. I don't want to be out here in the dark without any real weapons."

"Uh, so where are we supposed to go?"

They looked around but it was too dark to see much of anything. Aeric thought he saw the dim outline of buildings and said, "I think there's as set of apartments to the northeast, along Guadalupe."

"Fine by me. How are we gonna get inside though?"

"Knock? I don't know. We'll figure it out when we get there." Aeric was beginning to wonder if Tyler was up to the task of traveling across the country. His size alone was extremely intimidating and that was a huge advantage, but he didn't seem to want to make any decisions on his own. He seemed content to follow Aeric's directions. Aeric didn't know if that was a good or bad thing.

As they jogged down 28th Street, the apartments that Aeric had vaguely seen loomed into view. Another set was just off to the north, it was slightly taller with a total of seven floors instead of the five floors of the building that stood directly in front of them.

Gunshots rang out nearby, followed by several more. "We should probably try the taller building right there," Aeric said as he gestured towards the northern building. "There are more floors, so at the very least we could probably sleep in a stairwell."

Tyler nodded and said, "God, this sucks."

The apartment complex that they'd chosen had retail stores on the bottom floor and apartments above them. It took some work to find the door leading into the building due to the near total darkness of the cloudy night, but they finally found a glass door that opened.

"I don't know how secure this is," Aeric admitted. Now that they were on their way into the building, he was already beginning to second-guess his decision.

"Hold on," his roommate's voice floated from the darkness. The sound of a lock twisting into place behind him announced that Tyler had locked the deadbolt on the door. "I don't know if that will help much, but it might stop someone who's just checking quickly."

"Good idea."

They stumbled deeper into the hallway that presumably led to a set of stairs, trailing their hands along the wall to find an opening. Aeric bumped into a small table and something glass fell to the floor, shattering and filling the small space with the *boom* of the initial explosion and then the tinkling of glass as the pieces skidded across the tile.

"We need to find weapons and a damned flashlight," Aeric hissed. He was so mad at his clumsiness that he could have punched the wall—an unfortunate habit that he used to have in high school. A broken hand and loss of an entire summer of training had cured him of it, though.

"Hey, I've got something over here," Tyler said excitedly.

Aeric pushed away from the wall that he'd been following and felt his way blindly across the open space as glass crunched underneath his shoes. "What is it?"

"A door. I don't know if it goes to the stairwell though."

There was a locked handle that snapped off after three solid hits from Tyler's aluminum baseball bat. Through feel and trial and error, they were able to push out the handle on the other side and open the latch. More blind groping confirmed that they'd found the stairwell.

"I think we need to secure this door behind us," Tyler whispered.

"Yeah, but how?"

"There was an upholstered chair on my side. We could put that up against the door."

It wasn't much, but they were able to maneuver the chair through the doorway and used the heavy chair as a weight to keep the door closed. Again, the only thing that they could do was to hope that a cursory inspection was all that anyone trying to get into the building would do.

They crept up the stairs and were slightly out of breath by the time they made it all the way to the seventh floor. Thankfully, the door leading from the stairwell wasn't locked and they slid into the hallway without making any more noise.

"I guess we go as far away from the stairs as possible, that way, in case someone tries to break in, we'll have some warning."

"Aren't *we* breaking in?" Tyler asked. Aeric couldn't see his face, but he knew the look that was likely on his friend's face. He probably wore a smirk and the eye on the side where his mouth turned up would be squinted.

"Yeah, okay. But we're the good guys."

"How do you figure? We just stole a shitload of food and cigarettes, broke through a locked stairwell door and now the apartments are vulnerable to someone else coming in here and robbing them…or worse."

He hadn't thought of it in those terms before. He'd only been concerned with finding a place to rest for the night, not how his actions would affect the residents of the building after they left. "Shit, you're right, Ty. I just wanted to get off the street, y'know?"

"Yeah, man. We can't always go around only thinking about ourselves. That door wouldn't have stopped a determined thief, but it might have stopped some random dude walking by the apartments."

Down the hallway, a door creaked open and Aeric tapped Tyler on the shoulder to make him stop talking. "You hear that?" he whispered.

"Yeah."

"Come on."

The darkness of the hallway was complete and total. There was absolutely no light coming in through the window on the far end. They made it about fifty feet along the hallway and a door slammed shut. Aeric rushed forward and felt the slight reverberations in the next door down.

"This is where that door was open," he whispered to Tyler.

"Well, are you going to knock?"

He shrugged, and reached out to the door's contoured metal. He pulled his hand back and used his knuckle to knock three times. The sound echoed down the hallway.

"I'm sure this was the door," he muttered and knocked again.

"Go away!" a woman's voice called from the other side of the door.

"Please, let us in. We're just looking for a place to sleep for the night. We won't hurt you."

"I have a gun! It's pointed right at the door."

*****

Veronica Delgado searched her apartment for a weapon. There were knives in the kitchen, but the men outside would probably hear her move away from the door and use that opportunity to break in. The remote for the television was on the arm of the sofa, so she grabbed that and crammed it into the pocket on the front of her long sleeved shirt.

The man on the other side of the door said, "Please, ma'am. We're not looking for any trouble, we just want someplace safe to stay the night and then we'll be on our way tomorrow morning."

"Well, find someplace else!" Veronica said loudly, hoping her neighbors would hear the commotion. She was so pissed at herself for opening the door to see what was happening in the hallway. That was stupid. Her father always told her to stay put when the power was out. Darkness hides all sorts of deviants, just like the weirdo out in the hallway who was trying to get into her apartment.

"You're the only person we've seen since the power went out," he said.

"You haven't seen me," she countered. "Get out of here before I shoot you!"

Her voice had wavered slightly and she hoped that the door hid the sound. "We're students at UT. Our dorm burned down a couple of days ago. Please, we don't have anywhere else to go."

"You're students?" she asked. That was something different. There *had* been a string of arsons on campus that seemed to target the dorms and some of the more well-known locations like the LBJ Library.

"Yeah." The guy sounded like he was offended that she'd ask.

Veronica decided to test them. "If you go to Texas, give me the name of one of the Natural Science professors."

"Do you know?" the one she'd been talking to asked someone else in the hallway.

"No, man. I didn't have science this semester," another voice answered.

"We're both freshmen, ma'am," the first man said. "I had Sociology, Introduction to College Life, Intramural Athletics, Biology and Creative Writing. I don't know who any of the science teachers are."

She peeked through the peephole and could see the shadows of two large men. On a whim, she asked, "What sport do you play?"

"Baseball," he answered automatically.

Veronica smiled. She followed Texas baseball and could use this line of questioning to determine the legitimacy of the men's claim to be students who were essentially homeless. "Who's your first game against next spring?"

"Texas Christian. Look, we really are students. Can we just come in?"

"Don't rush me, asshole. You're lucky that I haven't shot you yet," she said. "What dorm do you live in?"

"Blanton. But it burned down two nights ago," he replied.

"Where did you stay last night, then?"

"The hospital. Saint David's."

"Did you get burned?"

"No, I got hit by a truck when we were chasing the arsonist."

"You got hit by a truck?" she asked incredulously. "Wait, did you say that you were *chasing* the arsonist? Did you tell the police?"

"Yeah. We were having a small party in our suite when the Health Science building exploded and we went down to see if anyone needed any help. That's when we saw the guy in the lobby setting fires and chased after him."

Veronica decided that the guy was either an outstanding liar or he was telling the truth. She turned the deadbolt, leaving the chain engaged and pulled the door open slightly. The candle burning inside her apartment illuminated the hallway, revealing two big men standing on either side of her door. "How many of you are out there?"

"Just us two."

"You, big guy. Come here so I can see you," she ordered and held up her cell phone camera's light to shine additional light into the hallway.

The second man walked into the light from her cell phone. She looked him over and then said, "Okay, I've seen you on campus before."

"Thanks… I think," he answered.

"Alright, at least one of you is a student." She glanced back at the smaller of the two and continued, "I'm not sure about you yet, but you've got a kind face so I'm willing to give you a shot."

She pushed the door closed once again and lifted the chain out of the way. As she held the door open, she reminded them, "Don't forget, I have a gun."

The cute one—actually, they were *both* cute— looked at her hand underneath her shirt and she knew that he doubted that she actually had a gun. "We really don't mean any harm. We just need a place to stay tonight and then I promise we'll be out of your hair." He tentatively stuck out his hand and said, "My name's Aeric. This is Ty."

She grasped his hand with the one that she'd had under her shirt. "Veronica... Oh, dammit! Okay, I don't have a gun, but I do know taekwondo."

He released her hand and held both of his up. "I surrender! We're going to leave the city tomorrow and just want a good night's rest."

She stepped completely out of the way of the door to let them in. "Come in. My name is Veronica. I go to UT also. Pre-Med."

They squeezed through the half-open doorway and she quickly closed and locked the door behind them. Aeric's gaze wandered quickly over her apartment, appraising everything in the room. One thick candle burned on the coffee table in the living room in front of a large, oversized chair that matched her blue couch. She had a modest television set and a few movies sitting on top of a DVD player underneath it. She'd been cooped up in the room since the night of the dorm fires and she hoped the place looked clean, given the circumstances.

"Nice place," he commented.

"Thanks. It's close to campus and affordable, so...yeah. You said that you were going to leave town tomorrow?"

"Yeah, we're going to go to Missouri where my parents live."

"Why didn't you just drive through the night?" she asked.

"Yeah, fearless leader," Tyler deadpanned. "Why didn't we just drive through the night?"

He gave his roommate the finger and said, "We don't have a car. My keys were burned in the fire, but we're going to find a bus that will take us."

Veronica gestured towards the television with her chin. "Before the power went out, the television said that Austin was pretty isolated. The few main roads that are still open are being used by the military."

She could tell by the way he seemed to deflate that he didn't know about the roads only being open for the military. "Maybe we can find a car then," he replied. "We'll have to take the back roads and avoid the highways all together. It'll take a little longer, but we'll get there."

"You haven't really thought this through, have you?" Veronica asked.

"I was in the hospital until this morning!" he answered in a high voice. "We need to leave town. There are murderers out there and dead people all over the street. Hell, we almost got jumped by some weird creepy dude calling himself a vulture when we tried to go into the university athletic department."

"Wait, you know about the Vultures?" she asked.

Aeric looked over to Tyler and shrugged. "Other than some voice coming from the darkness down the hallway, no. He did make it clear that he doesn't like jocks and threatened us, but we couldn't see anything and decided against trying to fight someone in the dark. Then he shot at us with a shotgun and we took off."

"The Vultures are a group of hackers," she stated, ignoring the obvious question about whether they'd been hit. If they'd been shot, they probably would have already been asking about bandages or something, especially when she'd told them that she was Pre-Med. "They're behind the navigational control glitch that crashed all of those planes and the news said that they've been actively seeking ways to hack into the Air Force nuclear missile program. So far the government has stopped their targeted attacks, but all the guests on the news said that it's probably only a matter of time before they infiltrate the system and gain control of the nukes."

"What the hell do they want the nukes for?" Tyler asked.

"Who knows? Besides their digital calling card that they leave behind every time they hack, no one knows much about them. The authorities don't even know if the Vultures are a domestic group or an international one. You guys really haven't heard about them?"

Again, Aeric glanced at his friend for confirmation. There was a strange dynamic between the two. Aeric seemed to be marginally in charge, or at least the one doing most of the talking, but Ty was the person whom he looked to for information. The bigger man shook his head indicating that he didn't know about them either.

"I guess we missed that episode of CNN," Aeric replied.

"It's been all over the news, but it's easy to get one story lost between all the riots and the terrorist acts that were actually happening versus stuff that was just planned to happen."

"Well, with the power off, they're probably shut down, right?" Aeric remarked.

Veronica stared hard at him for a moment. She hadn't thought about them being shut down along with the power. "I don't know. Maybe? Do you think that's why the power went out?"

"It seems like an easy way to stop a cyber-attack if you're at a loss for what to do, and fighting for your life on multiple fronts, like the government is right now. If they purposefully turned off the power, it seems like they're throwing the baby out with the bathwater to me."

"Huh?"

"Yeah, Aeric. What the hell do you mean by that backwoods bullshit?" Tyler asked.

"Sorry, it's a Missouri thing. It means to throw away something valuable—the electricity—to get rid of something you don't want. In this case, it was the hackers."

"Hmm, now I understand the saying," she replied. "There are a lot of very important systems on the network and shutting it down would be more harmful than good if they did it on purpose."

"Wait a minute," Tyler interjected. "What if they understood that the lack of heat and air conditioning, loss of refrigeration, lack of communication—basically everything associated with electricity—was the lesser of two evils? I mean, it's only October, so the weather is pretty mild everywhere. If they chose to shut everything down to keep these hackers out of the nukes until they could find them or until they developed better defenses, then maybe it's a good thing."

Veronica and Aeric looked at Tyler and then back at each other. "You might be right, buddy," Aeric conceded. "I mean, it makes sense. There are tons of backups and fail-safes to keep the power from going out without some major work, right?"

"All it would take is a few downed power lines, like in the northeast during winter storms," Veronica said.

"I don't think so," Aeric countered. He gestured towards her darkened window and continued, "Think about it. The entire city is out of power, not just a few blocks or sections of the city. I think this was definitely caused by a deliberate act and if you think about it like Ty just said, it makes sense that the government shut the power down to stop those hackers from getting into their network."

"So, then we should just sit tight and let the government work out the kinks, then," she concluded.

Aeric held up his hands. "Well, I don't know about sitting it out. At least not here in Austin. Have you been outside since all of this started?"

"No. Once they cancelled classes and the phone service went out, I just came home and started studying for mid-terms and watching the news. Then the power turned off about an hour ago and I was sitting here listening to music on my phone while I studied, it's not good for much else right now. When I heard the stairwell door open up, I peeked out to see who was out there."

"I'm glad that you did, but promise me that once we leave, you won't open the door for anyone else," Aeric said as Tyler nodded his head in approval.

"Why are you guys being so weird about things? I don't just open my door to anyone. You were students in need of help."

Tyler stood and walked to the window. "That could be a cover for some very bad people, Veronica. We actually are students who needed a place to stay, but it's not a nice world out there right now."

"You mean all the fighting down in Southeast? Isn't that crazy?"

Aeric carried on Tyler's line of thought, "It's not just that. On the way here, we witnessed the murder of a convenience store clerk. It looked like the only thing that they took was the cash from the register and then they took off."

"Oh my God!"

"On the walk from the hospital to campus, we passed probably twenty bodies that were just left like garbage on the curb, waiting for the sanitation crews to come take them away. I don't know what's going on, but everyone is crazy."

Veronica found herself staring into Aeric's deep brown eyes and only the sound of the curtains being drawn pulled her away from them. "What are you doing?" she asked.

Tyler continued messing with the curtains for a moment and then replied, "I think it's best if people don't see that there's someone living up here. You can see candles and some camping lanterns shining in a few of the windows across the way and it's a dead giveaway that someone's there. I just don't think it's a good idea to advertise that there are people here."

"Wait, what do you mean?" she asked with a quiver in her voice. "This is all gonna blow over, right? If the government is behind the power outages, they'll beef up their security and have the power back on soon."

Aeric nodded and said, "I hope so, but I'm not sure. It makes sense that the government shut down the power grid to keep the hackers out, it really does. But there was a lot of crazy stuff going on even before the electricity went out. Murders, riots, plane crashes. What if all that was only the beginning of a total collapse?"

"You mean like the end of the world or something?"

"Something like that," Aeric agreed. "Not like fire and brimstone Armageddon or anything, just the total collapse of the world as we know it. Everyone always talks about how technology has made the world a smaller place, but in reality it's just created more problems. People settled at various places on earth because they wanted to be separated. Now all that pent up anger and forced interaction has come back to bite us in the ass."

"Is he always like this?" she asked Tyler.

"You mean all doom and gloom?"

"Yeah, it seems so negative. Things are bad out there right now, but it can't be the end of everything." A nearby scream pierced the night in contrast to her statement.

Tyler slid aside the curtain and then looked back at his partner. "Shit, Aeric. It looks like a gang is beating someone right down there in the parking lot." He watched for a moment and then said, "Are we gonna stand by and let that happen or do we go out there and stop them?"

More screams emphasized his point. Aeric and Veronica went to the window to see for themselves. In the parking lot below, a group of men had surrounded someone who knelt on the ground. They took turns stabbing him every time he stood to escape while two men holding rifles stood back from the group, watching to make sure that no one snuck up on them. Harsh laughter drifted up the seven stories to their window and grated on Aeric's nerves like nails on a chalkboard.

Oh, God. She knew the guy that they were torturing. He was her neighbor from across the hall. They'd messed around a little bit before she decided that they were too different to be in a relationship. She put her small hand through the crook in Aeric's elbow and squeezed his forearm. "I think I know that guy. It's hard to tell, but I think he lives across the hall from me," Veronica muttered. "Are we going to go down there and stop them?"

Aeric looked back and forth between her and Tyler. Both of them had asked that he do something about what was happening downstairs. Veronica wondered what type of man he was. Would he stand by and allow the murder of an innocent man or would he get involved and try to stop it?

*****

Aeric couldn't believe his ears, had Veronica just suggested that they go down to the parking lot and get involved in the violence? He'd never even been in a real fight before. His size had always been intimidating enough to keep him safe. He'd been slapped by his ex-girlfriend Kate and even that had brought tears to his eyes. He had no idea how he'd handle a real punch. The men in the parking lot had knives. They would probably skip the fistfight and slash at him with their weapons.

He didn't know what the future held or how long Austin would be lawless, but this was the first time that he had a real life-and-death decision to make. If they stood by and did nothing, then the man would surely be killed. On the other hand if they went down to stop the men, they'd likely get killed. All Aeric and Tyler had were a baseball bat and a pair of cleats. They wouldn't be able to stand up to anyone with just those things.

Was it even their place to protect people that they didn't know? In his mind, Aeric thought that was the right thing to do. From the sidelines, it was easy to say what the correct choice was. But when he was actually faced with the possibility of torture or death because of a choice between right and wrong, that distinction became a whole lot murkier.

The decision was taken away from him before he could make it. One of the thugs stepped forward and grasped the man's head from behind. Blood fountained into the night as he slid his knife across the victim's throat. Veronica gasped and turned away from the window and Aeric stepped back in shock. He couldn't believe that they'd just witnessed a murder. In truth he was relieved because they didn't have to go down to the street and face their own death. Did that make him a coward?

He stared in silence at the small opening in the curtains where they hadn't fallen completely shut. He didn't feel like a coward and had always considered himself a risk-taker, but then again, he'd never been faced with such a momentous challenge before. He tried to reason with himself that even if he and Tyler had charged headlong down the apartment's stairs, they never would have made it in time to save Veronica's neighbor. It was easy looking back on it now to determine that waiting had been the smart thing to do.

Aeric's sense of moral justice and self-preservation warred within him. He'd done the right thing to assess the situation before acting, but his lack of action had allowed that man's death to occur. He argued that it wasn't his place to go around rescuing people who've gotten themselves into trouble. Then, his thoughts reversed and he told himself that both he and Tyler should have responsibilities to the residents of the city. They were both physically stronger and more intimidating than most people, so they should use those gifts for good.

What was good? What was evil? How did he know that Veronica's neighbor hadn't been evil himself and the men below had simply reacted and carried out vigilante justice because of the lack of police? They could have found him raping or murdering someone and stopped him. What if they were simply doing the same thing that he and Tyler discussed doing?

Of course, he'd likely never know, but he did know that justice didn't entail torturing a man. His mind took those thoughts and carried them further. Those men had tortured him for fun. Their cruel laughter was evidence of that. *They* were the evil ones. *They* must be stopped. *He* was the one who had the strength and ability to stop them.

Something in his mind snapped and his resolve hardened. The police were fighting a losing battle with the gangs in southeast Austin. It was his responsibility to ensure that bastards like the men below would never do anything like that to helpless people again. Aeric Gaines vowed to himself that from here on out, he'd do whatever he could to put an end to the evil of this world. He would never again question himself about whether he was considered a coward.

"Veronica, can I have your knife? I'm going hunting."

FOUR

"What do you mean?" Veronica asked.

"We can't allow those men to do the same thing to someone else. I'm going to make sure they never leave this place... and let others know that it won't be tolerated."

Aeric felt her take a small step backwards in the darkness. "My friend is already dead. We needed to stop them from hurting him. It's not your place to go out there and exact some type of revenge for what they've done. We have police, the FBI, heck, even the Army for that sort of thing. I wanted you to go scare them off, not get into a fight with them."

Everything seemed so clear to him now. "None of those things matter anymore. Those organizations are gone, a thing of the past. We need to stand up for ourselves and stop those types of people. If we don't stop them and let others know that we won't let it happen, then it will just get worse."

A wall of muscle stepped silently over to him. "I'm with you, bro. Those men are just like the bullies that I've dealt with my entire life. They won't stop until you make them stop."

"Thanks, Tyler," Aeric responded. "Veronica, please. The only other weapon that I have is a stupid shoe with metal cleats on it. Can I have your knife?"

"Are you two crazy?" she questioned. "A few of them have guns. It doesn't matter how big and tough you are, if those guys shoot you, you'll die."

Aeric couldn't figure out why she'd wanted them to charge into battle a few moments earlier, but was backpedaling now that it was time for action. Maybe he never would truly understand the way a woman's mind worked. "We know that they have weapons. But we can't let those people survive. What if they come up here to your apartment after we're gone? You saw what they did to your friend. They'd probably gang rape you until you bled to death. People like that don't deserve to live."

"You realize that you're talking about murder right now, don't you?" she asked, sidestepping his comment about them coming into her apartment.

"It's not murder, it's *justice*," he replied. *God, I sound like a fucking Hollywood action hero cliché*, he thought.

The girl paced back and forth for a moment and then surprised Aeric by wrapping her arms around his waist and hugging him tightly. "Okay. Here, take it," she said as she pressed the kitchen knife into his hand.

"Thank you," he slid the knife down along his pant leg to avoid accidentally cutting her and squeezed her in another embrace. "Lock the door behind us and don't open it for anyone else, okay?"

"Aeric, I'm scared."

"I am too, Veronica. But we can't allow people like that to keep doing those sorts of things."

The flickering candlelight played off her silky black hair as she nodded her head into his chest. "You ready, buddy?" Aeric asked his friend.

Tyler grunted and replied, "As ready as I can be."

They moved the chair that they'd placed in front of the door enough to squeeze through and waited until they heard the locks engage before heading towards the stairwell.

"What's the plan?" Tyler asked.

"Let's go down the stairs and see if we can sneak out. There were two men with rifles, but we don't know if there were pistols in the group. We have to assume that there were."

"Okay, so there are two rifles and..." Tyler trailed off as he thought. "There are five guys with knives, maybe pistols. Are we going to kill them or beat them up?"

"I can't believe that I'm saying this, but we're going to kill them," Aeric replied. "If we beat them up they'll just come back and search the apartment complex for us. That means they'd beat up people for information. We need to make sure that they never threaten anyone again."

"What the hell has happened to the world?"

"It's gone mad. Maybe even thinking about killing those men means that we've gone mad, too, but we can't afford to think like the old days or else we'll end up dead."

"I'm with you, man. I've lived in fear of bullies my whole life. Afraid of what they'd say about my orientation, afraid that they would call me names or do something to my family's home because I'm gay. Even with my size, I couldn't escape living in fear that something would happen. I'm done with that. It's no way to live."

Aeric stopped and placed a hand on his friend's arm. "Well, that world is gone, too. Let's survive this night and then we'll face tomorrow."

"Okay. So, do we take out the riflemen first or the others?"

He considered it for a moment. It made sense to take out the guys with rifles first, but it really came down to opportunity. If he'd relied on what he learned from the movies, he would have assumed that the pistols were more dangerous in a close fight. But he'd been around guns his entire life and knew how easy it was to miss with a hand gun, especially when adrenaline and nerves played into it. Rifles forced the user to add an extra level of stability with their second hand and at close range. The extra stability was usually enough of an advantage to hit the target.

"I don't know," he admitted. "I've obviously never been in a gun fight, but I think that the rifles are the biggest threat. Plus, we know that they have rifles and only assume that they have pistols, so we have to take out the riflemen first, right?"

Tyler pushed past him without saying anything. Aeric assumed that he'd nodded, but couldn't confirm it and trailed after his friend.

They reached the bottom floor and pulled the upholstered chair away from the door that they'd blocked. The small atrium that opened to the street was still silent so they crept out into the darkness.

"You ready?" Aeric asked.

It was too dark in the tiny hallway to see more than shadows, but he saw the baseball bat rise up and then slap down on Tyler's open palm with an audible thump. "Yeah, let's do this."

Aeric moved down the foyer to the glass doors and peered out. The body sat by itself in the middle of the parking lot while three of the men stood close together, less than twenty feet from the doorway where Aeric and Tyler watched. None of the other thugs seemed to be present.

"What are they doing?" Tyler asked.

"It looks like those guys are on lookout. No idea about the other four. Maybe they're in one of the stores stealing shit."

"Probably the best opportunity that we're gonna get," Tyler said quietly.

"So, are we just going to kill them?"

Tyler didn't answer his question directly, instead he replied, "I'll get the two on the left, you take care of the one on the far right."

Just as the big man didn't answer Aeric's question, he didn't say that he was going. Once again, he pushed past Aeric and went through the door. He had to rush out to keep pace with him. For a large man, Tyler moved with incredible silence. Then everything happened in slow motion.

He watched as the aluminum baseball bat glinted slightly in the light coming from apartment windows and then impacted into the back of a man's head with a distinct crunch of skull bones. The bat reversed and Tyler hit his second target in the face. Then, Aeric's own feet carried him to the man that he was supposed to kill.

The molded plastic of the kitchen knife felt strange in his hand as he stepped in close behind the man and wrapped an arm around the thug's neck. Aeric pulled him in tight to his chest, locking his strong muscles in an unbreakable grip. He thrust the blade forward into the man's right kidney and he let out a gurgled scream. The knife resisted for a moment as he pulled it out, caught on some type of tissue or clothing. It came free and he wrapped his knife arm completely around the front of the man to his left side and stabbed towards himself into the man's stomach. The soft tissue there was no match for the sharp point and the knife sliced open muscle and intestines. He stabbed several times and then slid the blade between the thug's ribs, hitting something hard. The man's body relented to Aeric's powerful thrust and the knife continued up over the bone into the lungs. He pulled it out again and stabbed into the lower back once again.

The man began to spasm and Aeric had a difficult time holding him, so he slid him to the ground and stepped heavily onto the side of his head. He almost lost his balance as the oblong object under his shoe rolled slightly and the man's cheek was pressed into the pavement. The thug beat weakly against Aeric's calf muscle as he bent down and pushed the knife through the side of his throat with the serrated edge facing outwards.

Aeric pushed hard against the handle and pulled up viciously like he was slitting the throat of a deer to put it out of its misery and then stepped quickly away. Another thump behind him announced that Tyler was still dispatching his man. He'd taken the life of another human being in less time than it took the big man to beat the other.

"Grab their weapons," Tyler ordered. "We'll shoot those mother fuckers when they come out."

"Got it," Aeric answered in a daze. Had he really just stabbed a man to death?

He picked the rifle up from the ground where it had fallen. It was a simple lever action 30-30. He held it up into the tiny bit of light from the apartments and cocked the lever slightly. The bright brass of a round in the chamber contrasted against the black metal and wood of the rifle. There was at least one round and he prayed for more.

"Here," Tyler said as he handed a pistol to Aeric. "Both of my guys had a pistol and each of 'em has a pretty full magazine."

"Thanks. How are you feeling?"

"Let's just finish this and then we can talk about our feelings."

Aeric stopped talking and followed Tyler back towards the building. It was clear to him after the events of the day—and especially after the last few minutes—that their relationship had evolved. The big man didn't want to make decisions and was totally fine following Aeric's directions, but once those decisions had been made, he would carry them out and Aeric would be the follower.

Flashlights inside the small smoke shop gave away the location of the other thugs. As Aeric and Tyler walked quietly towards the doors, they could see the men stuffing fine cigars and packages of the e-cigarettes that were so popular on campus into plastic bags. Aeric grimaced at what they were stealing. Just over an hour ago, he'd done the exact same thing at the convenience store when he'd taken all of the cigarettes for currency. Was he just like the murderers in the smoke shop?

Then the thought that he might be worse crossed his mind. Only one of the men had actually killed Veronica's neighbor while he and Tyler had both killed people now. It was a sobering thought that he may be considered the bad guy. They weren't the bad guys, were they?

"Same as last time," Ty's voice interrupted his thoughts. "I'll take the two on the left. You take the two on the right."

He nodded and pulled the hammer back on the rifle. The 30-30 was a simple design that he'd used before. It would only fire with the hammer cocked when he pulled the trigger.

"Are we going inside or shooting through the glass?" Aeric asked.

"Does it matter?"

"No, I guess not."

"Then fuck it. We can just stand outside and shoot them on the inside before they notice us."

"Got it."

They stopped less than five feet from the shop's glass windows, completely draped in the shadow of the awning above the door. He pulled the rifle hard against the pocket of his shoulder where his chest muscles connected with his deltoid. It was a practiced motion that years of going to the rifle range, and hunting with his father, had instilled in him.

He heard the rustle of fabric as Tyler raised his arm and said, "One… Two… Three!"

They both fired through the glass simultaneously and then Aeric worked the lever action to eject the spent cartridge and chamber another. The things that his mind noticed were strange to him. He noticed the glass flying inwards towards the lighter case and he heard the brass casing tinkle as it hit the concrete, but then he couldn't hear the screams of the men inside as they dove for cover.

He brought his gun up and squeezed the trigger once again at his second target. The man's momentum carried him behind a counter. Aeric was certain that he clipped the man in the shoulder, but he hadn't killed him.

"You get yours?" Tyler asked casually as he slid over behind the decorative concrete pillar on his side of the door.

Aeric followed suit and moved behind the pillar on his side. "Head shot on the first one, I think I hit the second dude in the shoulder, but pretty sure that he's still alive. What about you?"

"Both of mine are down."

A heavily accented voice yelled out from inside the store, "I'll kill you, motherfuckers!" Gunfire erupted and chips of concrete flew in all directions as the man inside the smoke shop began firing his pistol towards Aeric.

He felt a cold, empty certainty in the pit of his stomach that the man inside was going to kill him. He'd been a fool playing the part of a vigilante and now that he'd encountered an actual criminal, the man would murder him like Aeric had murdered his companions. The teenager wondered about his mom and dad in Missouri. Would things ever settle down enough so that they'd eventually find out what happened to their idiot son?

A loud curse drifted from the store and over the ringing in his ears, he heard the clicking of the pistol's hammer falling on an empty chamber. Aeric started to ask Tyler what he wanted to do, but the big man was already moving. He charged through the shattered glass with a quickness that belied his size and fired two rounds over the counter into the man behind it.

Aeric risked a glance around and saw Tyler bend over to pick up one of the flashlights. Before he could question his friend, the man was walking around shining the flashlight in the faces of their enemies. "Making sure that they're dead. Grab their bags and weapons. We need to get back up to Veronica's apartment. We made a lot of noise and people are probably going to start looking out their windows soon."

Aeric accepted Tyler's directions and grabbed the men's backpacks and scooped up pistols while his friend rifled through the pockets of the dead. The world around them had changed so much in only a few days. He wondered for the hundredth time if Austin was alone in the madness or if it had spread across the entire United States. Surely what Veronica had said about the Army coming soon was the truth. He wanted to believe that, he *had* to believe that.

They went back into the building through the vestibule and into the stairwell. The chair slid easily back into place behind the door and they took the stairs quickly to the seventh floor. Veronica called out to them as the door from the stairwell opened, "Aeric, Tyler… Is that you?"

"Yes!" Aeric replied as they rushed down the hallway. "I thought we told you not to open the door until we asked you to!"

"I was worried that you got hurt. After all the shooting stopped, I didn't know what happened."

"Let's get inside," Tyler said.

"Oh, okay," she said and led them back to her apartment.

Once the door was locked, Aeric allowed the backpacks and the rifle to fall to the floor and then rushed past Veronica to the bathroom. He hunched over quickly and vomited into the toilet. The memories of the blood flowing freely from his victims almost overwhelmed him. He'd killed two men tonight, one of them like a dog. His clothing was covered in the blood of his first victim and the white porcelain of Veronica's toilet was smeared with it where he'd grasped the sides.

He gagged a few more times, choking out the remaining contents of his stomach and then sat back against the wall. His mind kept replaying the screams of his victim as he stabbed him repeatedly and then slit his throat like he would if he were field dressing an animal on a hunting trip. The way the man's body had been so tense against his, and then gone slack against him as his life began to flee, made Aeric's skin crawl.

Then, he thought of his second victim. It didn't impact him nearly as bad as the first since he'd shot him from a distance, but it was still a horrible feeling to know that he'd ended the man's life. The men had been part of an earlier evil, but he had no way of knowing who'd done what. For all he knew, both of them could have been volunteers at a children's hospital and were just in the wrong place at the wrong time. Who was he to decide who was allowed to live and who would die?

The questioning and second guessing of his actions was maddening and he didn't hear the soft knocks on the bathroom door. The flickering candle on the counter threw wild and crazy shadows across the walls, adding more boogeymen to those that his mind already struggled to deal with. He stared blankly at the drying blood that coated both of his hands and gathered in dark lines along the crevasses of his palms and around the edges of his fingernails. He was dimly aware of someone walking into the room and the soft scent of lilac as Veronica slid down the wall beside him.

"Ty went to the apartment across the hall to see if that guy is there or if…or if it was him in the parking lot," she opened.

He heard her, but wasn't interested in what she said. "He was about the same size as you. Played high school football or lacrosse, I can't remember which. Ty's going to get you some new clothes."

The idea of cleaning away that poor man's body fluids sounded appealing, but Aeric couldn't bring himself to say anything. "There's still hot water in the apartment's hot water heater and the water pressure is still holding up in the building. You should shower."

She sighed and slapped her hand on her knees. "Aeric, you're probably thinking about what you did. You need to stop. Those men were evil and you did the right thing. I know that you're a good person. Otherwise, this wouldn't be affecting you so much. It had to be done."

She shifted and he saw her look directly at the side of his face. "Fine. You're getting in that shower. You stink and you've got blood all over you. You're ruining my stuff. If you're not going to do it yourself, then I'm putting your ass in there."

Veronica didn't wait for him to not answer her once again. Instead, she stood up and bent over him. He saw her darkened form untie his shoe and pull it off, then the other. It felt strange to have someone taking off his shoes. He felt totally removed from the situation and was simply a casual observer of the actions occurring to his own body.

Her fingernails scraped lightly against the skin above his beltline as she grasped the hem of his shirt on both sides and slid it up over his torso. The collar got stuck around his chin as she tugged it gently up over his head, and then pulled the shirt the rest of the way off of him and down his arms. He was starting to come around and let out a little yelp when her fingers plunged inside his pants.

"Oh knock it off, you big baby. I have to unbutton your jeans."

Finally, he spoke. "I… I can do it."

"Then stand up."

"I just need a minute."

"Well, I gave that to you," she countered. "Now the minute's up and you're ruining my bathroom. Stand up."

"Please. I just feel… I don't know. I feel terrible."

Her fingers dove back inside his waistband on either side of the button and then twisted as she unbuttoned them. "A shower will make you feel better," she said and unzipped the zipper and spread open the fly to widen the waist.

She reached around and grasped the top of his jeans and jerked them downward as he breathed in her scent. It reminded him of walking through his mom's flower garden after it rained.

"Lift your ass," Veronica ordered.

"You smell nice," he mumbled while he followed her directions.

"You don't." She worked the jeans back and forth over his thighs, past his calves and then down around his ankles. She wadded up his pants and threw them into the corner and then stood up.

Veronica turned away from him and the splash of the water in the bathtub filled the small room. Aeric allowed himself a moment to imagine that none of this was happening, that it was all a crazy dream and that he heard his roommate in the bathroom turning the shower on.

Then the sound of the toilet flushing away the contents of his stomach reminded him that the events of the past few days had really happened. He was homeless, didn't own anything and had killed two men. The city was rapidly descending into chaos and thousands of people were dead.

"Either you stand up and get in the bath or I'm gonna force you up."

"Yeah, okay. Fine. I'm getting up. Can I have some privacy, please?"

"No."

He quickly glanced at her and said, "Huh?"

"I'm not leaving until you're up and actually in the shower. Now come on, I want to be able to have a hot shower, too. It might be the last one I ever get and my hot water heater isn't very large. Get in there before all of its gone."

Aeric felt bad enough about everything that had happened, he didn't want to ruin what could potentially be her last hot shower, but she wasn't going to get in until he'd cleaned himself up. He shifted his weight and then used the counter to help pull himself up. "Okay, I'm up, Veronica. I'll get in the shower."

"I'm not leaving until you get in."

Now he was beginning to get irritated. "Oh, come on! I'm a grown man, I can get in the shower myself."

"You're wasting my hot water."

"Please, give me some privacy."

"You don't have anything that I haven't seen a million times—wait, I don't mean a *million*. Less than a hundred times, with only a couple of guys." She grinned at him, "That sounded bad. I'll turn around while you take off your underwear, but I'm not leaving until you actually get into the shower."

He sighed and then rolled his finger in a circle to indicate that she should turn around. Once she'd turned her back on him, he pulled his underwear off and stepped into the shower and closed the curtain.

Veronica had been right, the shower made him feel much better. By the time he was finished washing the blood away, he felt a million times better. He smiled that his mind had chosen to use the word million because of Veronica's embarrassment at her own use of the word only minutes before.

While he was in the shower, she'd laid out a towel for him on the counter and cleaned the blood away from the toilet and floor where he'd been sitting. Nothing could be done about the smear on the drywall where his back had rested against it, though.

While he was toweling off, another soft knock announced her return. He wrapped the towel around his waist and said, "Come in."

The door opened slightly and Veronica's head poked through the opening. "He wasn't there, so Tyler picked out a few sets of clothes for you. They look like they'll fit you pretty well."

"You think your friend was the man down in the parking lot?"

She stepped into the bathroom and put a small armload of clothes on the counter. "I don't know," she answered and leaned back against the sink. "Just because he wasn't home doesn't mean that he's dead. I thought I recognized his face down there, but it was difficult to see with the lighting and the people all around him...."

Veronica trailed off and Aeric felt like he should hug her or something, but he barely knew the woman and didn't want her to be offended. "Did you know him well?"

She looked up at him and frowned. "Not really. We actually went on one awkward date last year and both of us decided that we were way too different to make anything work. Besides saying hello in the hallway or elevator, we didn't really talk much. It's just sad, y'know?"

"Yeah. I'm sorry."

She nodded and then patted the clothes. "Well, here you go," she said. "I hope something fits."

Veronica started to go and he stepped quickly across the bath mat. "Hey," he said as he grabbed her wrist lightly.

She turned back to him. "What?"

"Thank you… Thanks for making me get up. I was just in a weird place after what happened."

"I know," she answered and placed her own hand on his upper arm. "We all need a little help sometimes."

Aeric watched the candle light flicker in her eyes and wondered if he was supposed to kiss her or something. The last girl that he'd made out with ended up as hamburger underneath a giant police SWAT vehicle and besides Kate, his long-term high school girlfriend who'd tried her best to ruin him at Central High, he didn't have much experience with girls.

She stared back at him, her face dangerously close to his with her hand on his arm. Then the moment passed and Veronica stepped back. "Okay, get dressed so I can come in here and shower. I think Tyler wants to shower, too."

And then, just like that, she was gone and Aeric cursed his stupidity. The girl had *wanted* to kiss him and he'd been too stupid to act on it. He had a lot of growing up to do if he was going to survive in this new world.

FIVE

Aeric woke to find himself lying in the front seat of an abandoned sedan while Tyler snored softly beside him. His lower back ached from the way the seat rose up at a strange angle when it was fully reclined. What was the point of the damn seat reclining if it was going to twist you into the shape of a pretzel?

He sat up and pulled the lever to bring the seatback up while he rubbed at the stubble on his chin. They'd made it as far north as Mexia down side roads until their stolen vehicle had run out of gas and they'd been forced to walk until nightfall. They came across the car that they'd slept in just before the full darkness had set in. The previous owner of the car was nowhere to be found, but the empty fuel gauge told them all that they needed to know, so they broke out one of the back windows and unlocked the car for a secure place to sleep overnight.

He'd tried unsuccessfully to convince Veronica to leave Austin and come with him to his parent's house in Springfield. She was holding out for her own parents to come and find her in the city, and didn't want to be gone when they arrived. Aeric promised her that he would be back in only a few days after he checked on his parents and they'd given her one of their pistols with enough ammunition to defend herself if things went bad.

It was all he could do. They weren't together and she didn't owe him anything, so they'd bid a sad farewell to her the morning after he and Tyler had killed the men in the parking lot. She'd surprised him by giving him her parent's address in San Angelo, and kissing him deeply on the lips, before closing the door to her apartment and locking it. They waited until they heard the chair push back in place against the door and trudged out of the apartment complex headed north.

Their first stop was at a car dealership in town. They discovered the body of a well-dressed man at the key box. It looked like he'd been ordered to open the safe and then he was killed once he did. There weren't any other employees present so they selected a couple sets of keys at random and used the keyless remote to find which ones they had. Then it was a simple matter of determining which one had the most fuel and driving out of the city.

Just as Veronica had reported, the interstate was blocked off to traffic. Military vehicles diverted them away from the exit, going so far as to fire into the air to ensure that they complied. The crashed vehicle with bullet holes through the windshield that they passed was convincing enough for them, so they diverted back into the city and traveled under the highway to the east, and then north along one of the many back roads out of the city.

Tyler seemed content to be with Aeric and follow him through the dangerous mission that he'd assigned to himself. When Aeric asked him what his plans were, his answers were always non-committal and he'd change the topic. Aeric wondered if the big man wanted to go to Nebraska after they went to Missouri or if he'd written off his family altogether. Either way, he was grateful for the company while it lasted.

His partner snorted and then choked on drool that had been in his mouth. "Ah, fuck," Tyler muttered when he finally stopped coughing.

"Morning, dear," Aeric quipped. "How'd you sleep?"

"Like shit, man. My back is killing me!"

"Mine too. We should probably try to find some sleeping bags and just sleep out in the open from now on."

"Yeah, I can't spend another night like that. What's the plan for today, boss?"

Aeric grimaced. He hated when Tyler called him that. "Where are we?"

Tyler pulled the map out of his pocket and handed it to him. "We're somewhere in here," he said as he jabbed a finger along Texas State Highway 14. The area that he indicated was north of the town of Wortham which they'd passed through yesterday morning, and south of Interstate 45.

The residents of Wortham had been less than receptive to the two out-of-towners who walked through and they'd been turned away at every door that they tried. It was a shame that the town, once probably a nice community with friendly people, had been turned into such a dreary place. Signs had been placed at both of the town's gas stations, telling travelers that they weren't welcome and that they were out of fuel. Small town America had deteriorated just as quickly as the cities and it made them wonder what had happened to cause it all the way out in the middle of Nowhere, Texas.

"We probably walked, what? Six or seven miles after we left town yesterday?" Aeric asked.

"Something like that. We must be getting close to the interstate. I wonder if the Army is set up there, too."

"Only way to find out is to go," Aeric responded as he opened the door and unfolded himself from the sedan. He walked across the road and pissed into the ditch before returning to his friend.

He absently rubbed his stomach as it rumbled. "What have we got for breakfast?"

Tyler held up a can of spaghetti rings and meatballs before tossing it to him. "Enjoy, sweetheart!"

"Aw, you get me the nicest things!"

He pulled the plastic spoon that he'd been using for three days from his backpack and peeled back the lid of the pop-top can. The cold meatballs tasted terrible, but after taking an hour to build a fire and heat the canned goods on their first night out from Austin, they'd discovered that the wax lining of the cheap gas station cans would melt and cover the food. Since then, they'd just eaten whatever they had cold, although it was high on Aeric's priority list to pick up a cooking pot when they found the sleeping bags.

They finished their meal in silence, and then checked through the car for anything useful, before putting their backpacks on and continuing north along the highway. They'd had to get inventive with the bags that they'd taken from the thugs in the smoke shop. Veronica didn't have any zip ties—which would have made it much easier—so they had used tape to secure the shoulder straps of two extra bags onto each of their backpacks. The result was that they each carried three backpacks worth of canned food, bottled water, beef jerky, cigarettes and a few changes of her neighbor's clothing. The contraptions were, surprisingly, not too bulky, but they hadn't had to do more than simply walk with them, so far. Neither of them were confident that they'd hold up well if they had to run with them.

Aeric and Tyler were still within sight of the car that they'd camped in during the night when the world changed irrevocably. A brilliant white light appeared high in the sky above them and Tyler glanced up at it.

"Ahh, my eyes!" he screamed and fell to the ground with the palms of his hands digging into his eye sockets.

Aeric, who'd been looking behind them at the car when the high-altitude explosion occurred, didn't see what had happened to Tyler. He turned around in time to see the tail end of the massive fireball in the sky that had faded from the brightness of a thousand suns into an orange, smoke-filled mass spreading outward in every direction.

"What the hell?" he shouted just as the reverberations of the explosion reached him. The noise became a gale-force wind that scared him badly enough that he had to dive to the ground beside Tyler's writhing form.

"Ty! Are you okay?" he screamed above the noise.

He saw Tyler's lips move, but couldn't hear anything, then the sound and wind stopped. "My eyes are fucked up!" his friend answered.

"Did you see what happened?"

"There was a bright light in the sky and then an explosion," Tyler replied. "Shit, I can't see anything but a big, white blur in the middle of my vision and dark splotches around the edges."

"I think we need to get back to the car!" Aeric shouted.

"You might be—"

Tyler was cut off by the sound of another explosion, this one to the south, followed rapidly by a third further north and then another to the southeast. They huddled close to the ground against the wind, but it didn't return as strongly as it had with the first explosion. Aeric helped his friend to his feet and they stumbled back to the car as the sound of thunder rumbled across the morning sky.

As they headed back towards the car, a huge column of smoke could be seen far to the south. "Shit," he muttered and doubled his efforts to get Tyler back to the car.

When they got there, he opened the back door and threw the two backpacks into the seat. Something seemed different about the car, but he couldn't put his finger on what it was, so he slammed the door and opened Tyler's door for him. Again, something seemed odd, but he eased his friend down inside.

"There you go, buddy," he said and then closed the door gently before running around to the driver's side of the car. Off to the northwest, another massive cloud of smoke and ash drifted skyward where the original burst had been. *Dallas.*

He turned almost due north along their original line of march where more smoke billowed angrily towards the heavens. *Oklahoma City.* To the south and then southeast even more smoke poured from the earth. *San Antonio and Houston.*

Aeric opened the door and sat down heavily into the seat. "What's happening?" Tyler asked.

"I think we were just bombed," he answered. "Shit! That's what it is!"

"What?"

Aeric ignored him and opened the car door. Then he shut it and opened it again. "What the hell are you doing?" Tyler asked in confusion.

"The dome lights in the car don't work anymore," he replied distractedly and then turned around into the back seat to dig the flashlight from his pack.

"What the hell does that mean?" Tyler asked in confusion.

Aeric pressed the button on the side of the flashlight several times and then banged it against the steering wheel. "Goddammit!"

"What is it?" the big man demanded.

"Everything electronic is down, man."

Tyler grunted, "EMP."

"What's that?"

"I saw a show on the History channel about it. It's an electromagnetic pulse. Nuclear weapons give them off and the military is developing weapons that can just give off EMPs without bombing. It kills everything with circuitry and almost everything electronic that's been built in the last seventy or eighty years would be toast."

"Was that what those explosions were?"

Tyler shrugged and looked blindly around the car, "Maybe?"

"Does that mean our guns won't work?"

"No, those are mechanical. Well, hell I don't know."

"Hold on," Aeric said and stepped out of the car. He pulled the 30-30 from the back seat and cocked the hammer. He fired the rifle into a large cedar tree beside the road.

"Okay, our weapons work fine. What does that mean for our trip?" Aeric asked.

"It means that we're walking, riding a bike, or finding a horse to get around from now on," Tyler replied bitterly.

"That sucks."

The conversation trailed off for a moment before Tyler asked, "How far do you think it went?"

It took him a moment to respond. "Sorry, I forgot that you didn't see them. There were explosions all around us, but at different distances. If I was to guess, I'd say it was Dallas, San Antonio, Houston… Maybe Oklahoma City."

His friend shook his head. "I can't believe that someone would shoot a nuclear missile—four missiles—at us."

"The crazies were out in force down in Austin, maybe—" he stopped in fear of what his mouth would say.

"What?"

"Do you think Austin got hit?" Aeric asked.

Tyler tapped the side of his head and replied, "I can't see. Did it look like it?"

He turned in the seat once again and looked southward through the back window at the darkening sky. "I don't know. I assumed it was San Antonio, but it's possible that it was Austin. I mean, San Antonio is a bigger city, but Austin is a capital city. Who knows what was actually targeted."

Tyler nodded his head in agreement. "Maybe it was San Antonio."

Aeric wondered if they should go back to Austin to find Veronica, but doubted if it would do any good. If they returned to the city and found it destroyed, then they'd have nothing to show for traveling as far as they had. But if they got down there and it was intact, why would Veronica change her mind and decide to go with them? It was better to stick to the original plan and find out if his parents were okay, then return to Austin, or even San Angelo where she was going.

"Maybe," Aeric agreed.

"I assume we're not walking today."

"It's probably best if we keep out of the open today. If there is some type of automatic response to the bombs, then there may be a counterstrike. I wish we had a house or something that we could hole up in instead of this car."

"Anything's better than nothing though, right?"

"Yeah. Get some rest, man. Maybe your eyes will be better after a couple of hours with them closed."

He fingered the folded up paper with Veronica's address on it that was stuffed in his pocket. When Tyler reclined the seat, he pulled it out and began memorizing the words on the paper.

*****

"Okay, big guy, how are your eyes this morning?" Aeric asked his friend the next morning. The dark sky had lightened up enough to see the surrounding area through the car's side windows. A thick layer of ash covered the windshield and the sloped back window that made it impossible to see out of either of them.

"Better," Tyler replied as he looked around. "Most of my vision is okay except I have these little white dots right in the middle." He held his hand in front of his face and then far away. "It's a little disorienting, but I can live with it for a few days. If it goes on too long, though, I'll have to go see a doctor."

Aeric tapped his friend and pointed at the dark clouds looming overhead that continued to drop ash across the hood of the car. "I don't know if doctors will be able to do much for you. Looks like it may be a while before we'll be using microscopic lasers again."

Tyler chuckled, "Yeah. Guess I forgot about that part. I was worried about not being able to see that ninety-eight mile per hour fastball coming at my head, but there's probably some higher priority things going on, huh?"

Aeric yawned and stretched his hands above his head. "I still can't believe that you were able to sleep through all of that last night. Seemed like there were explosions coming from everywhere at once. There were times when it was bright enough that if you didn't know that it was supposed to be nighttime, then you'd have thought it was morning."

Tyler grunted and opened the door. "Gotta pee."

Ash drifted in the open door and landed on the seat. The simple piece of ash made Aeric wonder what the future held. He wondered what it had come from. Was it from a burning forest or from the city? Had it been a part of someone's home, their work or from a supermarket that they frequented? Or, more sinister, was that piece of ash the last remnant of a person's body as it burned in the superheated columns of fire that had taken everything?

How much of the United States was effected by the explosions? How much of the *world* had just been thrown back to the Dark Ages? From the size of the fireballs that he'd seen and the giant columns of smoke lifting skyward, he had to assume that they were nuclear missiles and not some type of asteroid strikes, or EMP bomb. Outside of the big airburst that had temporarily blinded Tyler and released the electromagnetic pulse that killed their electronics, every other detonation could have been a conventional weapon of some kind or another. *Yeah, right.*

It was highly unlikely that the US had suffered its fate alone. The more likely scenario was that there'd been a global nuclear war. He didn't have any basis for his theory other than what he'd seen in movies and read in action novels, but it made sense that the missiles were pre-programmed with targets and would automatically launch once the authority was given. If the Vultures or some other hacker group had gotten into the network and begun the first strike, then others would retaliate and the US would legitimately counterattack the nation that retaliated against them. It would be a vicious cycle until either all of the missiles had been launched or the computers that controlled them were shut down.

The door to the car opened and the piece of ash that had caused his contemplation flew into the air and then spiraled out the door. Tyler sat down heavily and Aeric started laughing. "What?"

"It looks like you're covered in dirty snow, or *really* bad dandruff."

Tyler pulled the visor down and looked in the mirror. He had a thick layer of ash in his hair and on his shoulders. "Hmpf," he grunted and ran his fingers rapidly back and forth over his hair to get the ash out of it. When he was done, his hand came away covered in a mixture of dark soot and white ash.

Aeric looked out the window at the falling ash. From inside the car, it actually looked pretty as it covered the road and lay in soft, fluffy layers on the thick needles of the cedar trees that lined the highway. He could almost imagine that it was snow, falling on a peaceful winter day. But that flight of fancy was far from the truth. The crap falling from the sky was the remnants of his nation.

"We need to get moving," he said.

"Yeah, I don't know how much longer I can stay cooped up in this little car," Tyler agreed and twisted his back to emphasize his point.

They ate a quick meal and tossed the cans on the floorboard before getting out of the car. Aeric stretched for a moment and then went to relieve himself. By the time that he'd come back, Tyler was already digging through the backpacks for something.

"Whatcha looking for?"

The sound of ripping fabric answered him and then Tyler's big, meaty fist thrust backwards at him. There was a ripped t-shirt dangling between his fingers. "We should probably cover our mouths so we don't breathe in all that soot and get cancer or some other stupid fucking illness."

"Good idea," Aeric agreed. "I guess we need to add gas masks—or at least those little paper masks—to our shopping list, huh?"

"Along with better backpacks and some light jackets," Tyler stated.

"How the hell are we gonna pay for all that stuff?"

"Credit card?"

Aeric punched his friend on the shoulder. "Are you dense, bro? Remember, electronics don't work anymore."

"We'll figure something out. Maybe we can barter with all those cigarettes," Tyler replied. He started walking north and then called over his shoulder, "Oh yeah, we'll need good walking boots too."

"Sounds like we need to raid an REI or something," Aeric muttered while he tied the cloth around his face. Then he fell into step behind Tyler, following the path through the ashes that he'd made.

*****

It turned out that they were much closer to the interstate than they'd anticipated and must have walked more than six miles the day that they left Wortham. They entered the small community of Richland after walking for less than thirty minutes.

The small, red-roofed convenience station allowed them in, but the owner told them that the Army troops had cleaned out most of the supplies that she had. They scoured the bare shelves, not finding much of use besides several lighters and some Texas flag bandanas that they could use to cover their faces and help with the ash. Aeric offered two packs of cigarettes for the meager haul and the woman accepted them as payment for the goods.

They thanked the owner and then, on a whim, Aeric asked about the soldiers that the woman had mentioned. "Oh, they're an okay bunch," she replied. "Paid with cash and haven't bothered anyone. I was actually a little bit afraid of them at first when they pulled up with all those guns, but everything was fine. They're situated just up the road near the highway. Folks aren't allowed to travel on the interstate right now, that's only for military traffic, so their job is to keep everyone off of it."

"Our car ran out of gas a few miles back and we haven't seen anyone driving in since then. Have you seen much traffic?" Aeric hadn't outright lied to her since it had been more than a few miles, but generalities were okay.

"You know, it's funny," she said. "This mess with the Army keeping people off the roads has only been going on for two weeks and people are already rationing gas like you wouldn't believe. I sold out a week ago and haven't been able to get a new truck yet."

"Two weeks? The power went out in Austin four days ago."

"Well, the soldiers were on the highway before then. They didn't shut it down to traffic until about the same time that you're talking about, but they've been around for a while."

Tyler tapped him roughly with an elbow and asked, "Why were the soldiers already pre-positioned? Did they know something was gonna happen?"

He shrugged, how the hell should he know? A week ago he was worried about midterms, now here he was on foot in the middle of Texas after a global nuclear war. "No clue. Hey, thank you very much, ma'am. You've been really helpful."

"I'm sorry I couldn't offer you fellas any food or anything, but like I said, those soldiers cleaned me out!"

"No worries," Aeric replied with a wave and pushed the door open. The bell ringing on the handle sounded too normal to him, reminding him of better days and was in stark contrast to the dark gray clouds of low-hanging smoke that seemed to loom over the countryside.

"Shouldn't those damn clouds be clearing off soon," he grumbled as he adjusted the packs on his back and started to walk to the road.

"Depends on how many fires there are," Tyler said. "Remember a few years ago when those volcanoes blew in Iceland? They said the ash cloud would get blown all over

Europe for weeks. What if fires like the ones that we saw last night are burning all over the world? They may stick around for a while because the wind currents will continually lift up the ash, keeping most of it aloft for a long time."

Aeric stopped and stared at his friend. Sometimes the things that came from his mouth were profoundly thought-provoking, other times, they were profoundly stupid. In this instance, it was the former. "How do you know so much about ash clouds?"

"I watched a Discovery Channel special on it."

"So, how long are we talking about here?"

"I don't know, man. There have been cases where it was like three weeks, the winds way up in the atmosphere just kept shifting everything around. But volcanoes throw millions of tons of ash into the air, surely this isn't as bad."

Aeric glanced at the sky and replied, "I don't know. There were a lot of massive explosions. All combined, they probably put more dirt and ash into the air than any volcano ever did."

"Maybe," Tyler replied and continued walking towards the Interstate 45 on-ramp. "Hey, are we gonna try to get some bicycles or what?"

"Where are we going to get them from? We'd have to steal them and I'm not really interested in becoming a thief."

"It's not stealing if the owner isn't around. Maybe they're dead."

"Well, that's certainly a morbid way of looking at things."

"Is it morbid or just realistic?" Tyler asked. "Look, if those really were nukes and we've just erased a hundred years of electrical engineering across the globe, then things are gonna get bad. Like, real bad. You think those murders and settling of scores that happened in Austin were bad? All of that happened before we were on the losing end of a nuclear war. Think about what the next few weeks are gonna be like."

"Fuck! That's another smart comment from you in less than two minutes," Aeric moaned. "Any more and you'll be elected mayor of some weird survivalist commune or something."

"Nah, they don't want gay dudes in a survivalist camp, they want people who're gonna reproduce. Nope, I'm better out here on the road watching out for you."

He had another good point, this time inadvertently. The future of mankind would hinge on being able to reproduce and those who didn't might end up as outcasts. Aeric shook his head. He wouldn't let that happen to his friend. He already had enough issues with his family's lack of acceptance that he'd been able to put behind him for a while down in Austin. There was no way that Aeric would let anyone be like that with him from here on out.

"Well, I need all the help I can get, so you're welcome to stay with me as long as you want to, bro. We'll see about *acquiring* a couple of bikes soon, too."

"I just want to ride in style."

As they walked, the tan outline of military vehicles took shape on the overpass and another was parked sideways across the on-ramp. Rolls of coiled barbed wire stretched across the road and about one hundred feet into the fields on either side to keep people from driving around the blocked road. Signs on the side of the road told travelers that it was closed and directed people to either turn around or proceed along the service road without attempting to enter the interstate.

"Looks like they're serious about keeping people off the road," Tyler said.

"Yeah, I don't like this. Looks almost like they knew something was gonna happen," Aeric said as he adjusted his grip on the rifle and then put his arm through the sling to rest it on his shoulder. He didn't want the soldiers to think that he was walking up to them in a threatening manner with the gun.

"There's that conspiracy theory streak again. What point would the government have for starting a nuclear war?"

"Maybe that wasn't their intention. Maybe they were planning to raid Austin to get the Vultures, I don't know why, but just like that gas station owner said, they were here before the shit got bad."

"I wonder how much of the interstate system is blocked off," Tyler said idly as he raised his hands above his head and kept walking forward. "I mean, there's no way that they blocked off every interstate and every on-ramp. We don't have that many soldiers."

Aeric followed his friend's lead and raised his hands too. "You're right. Maybe just the ones that lead between really important points are being secured."

"COME FORWARD SLOWLY," a soldier ordered through what looked like a cheerleader's megaphone. It was another indication to Aeric that they'd known something was going to happen. He couldn't imagine that a non-electrical method of making your voice louder would be standard equipment for the Army.

They walked slowly forward as they'd been directed, continuing to keep their hands in the air as far from their weapons as possible. When they neared the vehicle, a soldier wearing a full chemical protective suit and mask stepped out from behind the door. He had his weapon pointed at them, not towards the ground or off to the side, but directly at them.

"What's your business?" he asked. His voice sounded distorted and muffled through the mask that he wore.

"We're trying to go to Missouri. My family lives in Springfield and I'm going home," Aeric answered truthfully.

"Missouri got slagged. There's nothing left."

Aeric dropped his hands and demanded, "What do you mean?"

"Put your hands back up!" the soldier ordered with a threatening step forward.

He lifted his hands once again and said, "I'm an American citizen. I'm just trying to move past your checkpoint to go home."

"How do we know you're telling the truth? You could be trying to get a read on our position and troop strength so you can attack us." The soldier in the turret of the Humvee slewed the large machine gun left to right slightly as if to emphasize the man on the ground's point.

"What?" Tyler asked. "You know this is all crazy, right?"

The soldier shifted the barrel of his weapon towards the bigger man and a small cascade of ash fell from his helmet. "Crazy? What's crazy is that we were put out here two weeks ago with no explanation of what was happening. The only thing we were told was that under no circumstances was anyone allowed on Interstate 45. Then the fucking missiles started hitting yesterday.

"Like I said, man, Missouri is gone. We had our big Stealth Bomber airbase near Kansas City and St. Louis on the east side of the state. We heard on the radio that they were both wiped off the face of the earth."

Aeric took half a step forward and then backed up quickly when the rifle aimed back at him. "But Springfield wasn't hit, right?"

The soldier lowered his weapon slightly and looked over his shoulder to another masked individual in the passenger seat of the Humvee. The soldier inside looked down at their lap and then back up, shaking their head. "No, Springfield wasn't hit the last time that they gave us updates about what's left."

"So let us through. We don't want any trouble and we're not getting on the interstate. All we want to do is go to my family's house in Springfield."

"You plan on walking?"

"If we have to," Tyler answered. "Look, I know that you're just doing your job, but we aren't a problem. We'll travel up the side road here until we get to Corsicana and then shoot down Highway 31 to the northeast. You guys will never see us again."

"That must be hundreds of miles," the soldier answered and lowered his weapon to the low ready position.

"Yeah, it's a long way, but we're going to try and find some bicycles that are for sale or something. Then we'll make it the rest of the way there."

He relaxed even more and allowed the rifle to hang freely on the strap from his shoulder. "You'll want to try and avoid Little Rock. We got word that it was wiped out before our radios went down. Cheap pieces of shit were supposed to be shielded against

EMP, but I guess all of the detonations so close were just too much for the circuitry."

"Was it Austin or San Antonio that got it to the south yesterday?" Aeric asked.

The door to the Humvee opened and the soldier from the passenger seat stepped out. "Last we heard, it was San Antonio that got hit, not Austin," she stated.

Aeric was a little surprised to hear a woman's voice coming from behind the mask, but he didn't let it show. "Oh, good," he replied. "We have friends back in Austin. I don't want them to be dead."

"Things are going to get very bad pretty soon. Food and resources are going to dry up without the large distribution centers in the cities sending food out every day," the woman said. "New England is… It's just gone and most of the big cities were hit too. I don't know what happened with our higher headquarters, but we stopped getting updates from them a few hours before the radios went out."

"Wait, isn't your equipment protected against things like EMPs?" Tyler asked. He shrugged at Aeric's questioning look and said, "More Discovery channel stuff I guess."

"Our radios still work. The lights are on and all that, but there's nobody on the other end. I don't know if that's because the relays were knocked out or if our base is just gone. After the first couple of big explosions, we lost comms with Fort Hood and we were getting generic updates from a substation, but now I… I just don't know what the situation is."

"Lieutenant, are you sure you should be giving that information to these people?"

She swiped her hands across the air and made a path through the drifting ash. It swirled away from her on the miniature wind current that she'd created. "Look around you, Sergeant Cantrell. Everything is burning. Maybe not right here, but the world is falling apart. These two men aren't any threat to us or the nation. They're just trying to get home. We're doing our job to keep them off the interstate, but we don't need to keep making them feel like criminals—put your damn hands down, you two."

Aeric lowered his hands slowly. "If your headquarters are gone, what are you going to do?"

"We're going to do our job, sir," she answered. "We'll stay here until we're released or run out of food. Then? I don't know."

"After we go to Springfield to get my family, we're coming back to Austin and then maybe a little town called San Angelo if things in Austin are bad. We have a friend who lives out there."

"Okay, why are you telling me? I don't care where you go. You're free to move past our checkpoint, sir."

He sighed in frustration. "I mean, if you guys find yourself with no place to go, that's where we're headed when everything is said and done. Our friend told us all about the nice little city on the banks of a couple of lakes. There's a small Air Force base there, but I'm sure they could use your firepower to help defend them if things get as bad as we all think they might."

The lieutenant's eyes wrinkled at the corners and he could tell that she was smiling behind the mask. "We might take you up on that. My home was in Boston and Sergeant Cantrell is from Maryland. Those don't exist anymore. If things are as bad as I fear and we haven't heard from Higher, then we'll have to move in a couple of days. We'll head back to our base at Fort Hood first, but depending on what we find there, we may try to make the trip. The Air Force base that's there, Goodfellow, is the next closest active duty installation, so that's where we would be required to go anyways."

"I don't know if that's what I want to do, ma'am," the sergeant replied. "We haven't had any contact with anyone in more than twelve hours. We could just disband and I'll try to make it back home."

"We're still a part of the First Cavalry Division, Sergeant Cantrell, and you'll follow orders. If we get back to Fort Hood and nothing is left, then you're free to go off and do whatever you want to do. Until then, we stay here. Once we only have twenty-four hours of rations left, then we RTB," she said using the military slang for Return to Base.

"Yes, ma'am," Sergeant Cantrell nodded inside his mask and hood. "Part of our orders also stated that we weren't supposed to interact with the local population, but you're basically telling this guy—who we have no clue who he is—your life story and our mission in the area."

She turned on him and closed the short distance between the two of them in three quick steps. "You are relieved of this watch, sergeant. Go get Corporal Samuels to come relieve you and then turn in. The situation has obviously messed with your mental state and you need some rest."

The man started to protest, but thought better of it. He shot the two newcomers a cold, hard glare and then headed towards one of the Humvee's parked on the bridge overlooking all of the approaches. "I'm sorry about him, he's been really on edge since we got here and the nuclear war sure as hell hasn't helped. He's gotten on my last nerve. I mean, you heard him, he wants to cut and run instead of following our orders."

"Well, I'm not in the military, but he kinda has a point," Aeric said. "The US Government probably doesn't exist anymore, what are you guys a part of now?"

"America, sir. I know that sounds stupid. Hell, it sounds stupid to me when I say it, but even if the government is gone, we still volunteered to defend America and her people. That's what I'll keep doing and I hope my men will too."

Aeric held his hands in front of him to placate the lieutenant. "I'm sorry. I didn't mean to upset you. I was just asking what you planned to do if the government has totally collapsed."

"It was on the verge of collapse before the war and we were out here to defend people, so what's changed if it did collapse or got blown to oblivion?"

Aeric had to admit that she had a point. The military was a tool that the government used, but ultimately they were there to protect the people. If the street war in Austin was any indication, they'd be invaluable in the coming days. "You're right and I'm sorry. I didn't mean to offend you. I'm glad that you're out here protecting us."

Her eyes softened once again behind the thick plastic eyepieces of her mask. "It's okay. What was your name? I don't think that we ever exchanged names."

Aeric briefly considered giving her a fake name, but he had no idea why he would be thinking like that, it didn't matter. "My name is Aeric Gaines and this is Tyler Nordgren. What's your first name, Lieutenant Griffith?"

"Lorelei," she replied. "We're all hopeful that Fort Hood is still there, but I don't know. You said you came up from Austin, was anything wrong when you drove by the exit for the installation?"

Aeric shrugged and replied, "I don't know. We left a few days before the— Are we calling this a war?"

She nodded and replied "Might as well be. Regardless of who in our government initiated it, we got word that the United States shot the first missile before things went crazy and whoever we shot *at* retaliated."

It made sense that this one little Army unit on the ground wouldn't have many details about what happened. Aeric was still positive that it had something to do with the Vultures, though. They'd been actively trying to hack into the network that controlled the nuclear weapons before the war started.

He lifted his chin slightly. "So when we left Austin, the Army was there to keep us off the highway, but we made it north to Mexia down the back roads before our car ran out of gas and we couldn't find any more."

"Hmm, fuel is going to be a problem. We have some jerry cans of diesel fuel, but if you're saying you couldn't find gas before the nuclear detonations, what's left will probably be scooped up quickly."

"I don't know, Lorelei," Tyler said. "People were grabbing all the fuel they could for their cars, but if those don't work anymore, then wouldn't there be a lot of gas just sitting abandoned in their fuel tanks?"

She nodded and used a gloved hand to scratch at the back of her head through the hood. "You're probably right. Those television shows have paid off for you."

Aeric focused on her hand and then looked her up and down to take in the protective suit that she wore. The suit resembled a pair of heavy-duty coveralls and she wore rubber gloves and overshoes over her boots. Every time she moved, the fabric made a strange swishing sound like it was nylon, but also some other type of material. "Should we be worried about radiation?" he asked.

"Yeah, you should. You guys need to cover up. All of this ash that's floating around is probably contaminated. You'll need more than the long sleeve t-shirts that you're wearing, maybe like a rain poncho or something, and definitely a hat of some kind to keep it off your head and away from your eyes. If you could find a gas mask, that would be the best thing, but these are hard to come by if you're not around a military base."

She'd tapped the mask that she wore when she said that last part. "There's a Walmart on the western side of Corsicana, which is just a little bit out of your way since you said you were going there first before shooting off towards Arkansas. They probably have most of the things that you'd want."

"Good idea," Aeric agreed. "I think that's a good place to start. Thanks, Lorelei."

A short soldier came waddling up to the group and Aeric had a hard time deciding if he was fat or if he just had too many layers of protective gear on. "Ma'am, Sergeant Cantrell sent me out here. He said you told me to relieve him."

"That's right, corporal. These gentlemen are moving along now, but you'll be switching shifts with Sergeant Cantrell full time. Got it?"

"Yes, ma'am. Should I move my gear from my truck to yours?"

"Yeah, that's fine. And have Cantrell come get his shit out of my truck," she called after the corporal who'd already started back towards the other vehicle to retrieve his gear.

"Okay, fellas, you should get moving. I think my troops are probably getting a little freaked out that you've been here so long. Normally, everyone comes and goes quickly without stopping to talk. They were already jumpy today because of what happened, I don't want one of them accidentally shooting you."

Aeric blanched and he couldn't help looking over at the giant machine gun on top of the Humvee. The thing looked like it would maul an elephant. "Yeah, I don't want them shooting us either. Thank you for passing along the information, Lorelei. You've been a huge help."

"It was nice to talk to you guys too. It gets kind of lonely when you're in charge."

He stuck out his hand. "Well, I hope we see you in San Angelo."

"Actually, Aeric, I really hope that we never see each other again." She laughed at his obvious surprise, even behind the bandana. "What I mean is that I hope Fort Hood is still there and we don't need to meet up in San Angelo."

"Oh," he grinned. "Makes sense. Stay safe, Lorelei."

She thumbed over her shoulder to the .50 caliber machine gun on the Humvee's roof and said, "I think I'll be okay. Watch each other's backs and don't trust anyone."

"That's certainly not a very nice way to live," Tyler replied.

"It may not be nice, but it'll keep you alive. Safe travels, my friends."

SIX

It was twelve miles from Richland to Corsicana. By the time they trudged into the parking lot of the Walmart where Lorelei had suggested they go, both of them were dog tired. A lifetime of playing baseball had conditioned them to short periods of intense bursts of speed. It hadn't prepared them for the extended periods of walking that they'd subjected their bodies to on this trip. Spending almost twenty-four hours inside a cramped sedan hadn't helped either.

As Aeric walked, he was also beginning to develop a slight hot spot on the sole of his left foot and he definitely had a blister on his little toe. He still wore the shoes that he'd been wearing the night of the party, they'd been fine for walking around for short distances, but he needed to upgrade to either a pair of running shoes or a good pair of hiking boots that would offer ankle support once they started going through the Ozark Mountains to get to Missouri. Tyler had mentioned it before, but footwear had now become one of the highest priority items on his shopping list, second only to food and ammunition.

They trudged wearily towards the outline of the giant building that likely held everything that they needed. Streams of people moved in and out of the darkened front door carrying bags or pushing carts. Aeric glanced in some of the carts as people rushed by. Most of the carts held food and perishable products, but there was the occasional disillusioned individual who ran by with a large screen television or some other worthless electronic gadget. He knew that those things would never function again. Apparently the ones who looted the electronics section thought that it was just a power outage. They'd learn quickly enough that all their new possessions were just large pieces of junk.

The sounds of Corsicana's panicked residents echoed out of the building in a dull buzz, interspersed with the occasional gunshot from inside or somewhere in the neighborhoods surrounding the store where thugs murdered people for their supplies. It was becoming dangerous on the streets and this was only the second day after the nuclear war. *What would it be like in a week?* Aeric wondered.

"I think we should walk over to the pharmacy entrance and avoid the food side of the store," Aeric announced when they were halfway across the parking lot. "Everything that we need, except food, is on the opposite side anyways."

"Yeah, I was thinking the same thing," Tyler responded, eyeing the grocery entrance warily. "We'll need more soon, but I don't want to get mixed up in that mess."

When they went inside the building it took Aeric's eyes a moment to adjust to the total darkness of the interior of the store. Over the past few days, he'd gotten much better at seeing in the dark, what with the lack of power and the constant clouds of ash that kept the sun from shining through and made every moment of the day seem like it was dusk. Tyler's eyesight was still iffy, though.

"Are you ready?" he asked as he held the rifle against his shoulder with the barrel facing the ground like his father had taught him when they went quail hunting. Besides walking with the gun pointed outward, having the barrel aimed towards the ground was the fastest way to be prepared to shoot if he needed to. It was a simple movement to lift his hand that grasped the wooden forestock, bringing the weapon into a firing position. The low-ready, as it was called, also helped to prevent unintentionally killing someone if he had an accidental discharge.

"Yeah, I think this is as good as my eyesight's gonna get," Tyler answered his question about whether he was ready to enter the store. "I still have those annoying spots right in the center of my vision and the darkness makes it worse. Where are we going first?"

They'd discussed their list several times during the trip from Lieutenant Griffith's checkpoint. Both of them agreed that they would likely encounter problems in the store, so it was best to have what they needed in a prioritized list before entering and getting sidetracked trying to find things.

"Sporting goods," Aeric answered. "We need ammunition for our weapons and then sleeping bags. The camping section will have those as well as some rubberized jackets to help keep the ash off of our skin. Then we'll go for boots and foot care stuff."

Another boom rose above the cacophony of voices in the grocery section as someone shot their gun. A few panicked screams pierced the darkness, but most of the people in the store had grown accustomed to the violence and continued to gather their supplies, heedless that someone had likely just been shot. Society had deteriorated rapidly into chaos and would likely continue down the path towards total anarchy.

Aeric and Tyler walked rapidly past the pharmacy towards the back of the store where the sporting goods section was typically located. The soft orange glow of a fire near their intended location drew them like moths. Aeric stepped into a dark liquid and started to warn Tyler to be careful, but the big man's feet had already slipped out from underneath him. He landed hard in the sticky substance.

"Aww, shit, man!" Tyler yelled out. "I'm covered in cough syrup."

"Cough syrup? I thought it was blood!"

Tyler gripped Aeric's offered hand and pulled himself up off of the floor. "That might have been better. Now I'm all sticky and smell like sugary, cherry-flavored medicine."

Gun shots rang out in rapid succession and they both dove to the floor, there was no telling where the bullets would go. There were several weapons that answered the first and then everything went silent. After a few seconds, people began to move around once again.

"We need to hurry up and get the fuck out of here," Tyler said.

"Yeah," Aeric agreed. Now they were both covered in cough syrup. He wrinkled his nose at the smell, Tyler had been right, this stuff *did* stink.

They gave up trying to walk and rushed to the sporting goods section. A fire burned in a small metal wastebasket and illuminated the ammunition area. It looked like someone had used a fire starter log so they could see what caliber was written on the side of the boxes. The heavy plastic case that normally held a few rifles and shotguns was smashed against the floor. It reminded Aeric of an empty egg shell after the chicks had hatched. He wondered what kind of mayhem those weapons would cause.

"Dammit! I was hoping for another gun," he moaned.

"Forget it. Let's get the stuff on our list and go," Tyler said.

The boxes of ammunition were in total disarray and it looked like people had just shoved them out of the way to find what they needed. Nothing was in order anymore, so Aeric ran his fingers along the shelf until he found the label for the 30-30 ammunition. After moving the boxes of 30.06 and .310 cartridges, he finally found the ones that he'd been looking for. He raked six or seven boxes into his backpack and then sidestepped to the 9-millimeter ammo.

"We're almost done, just give us a second," Tyler's voice boomed behind him.

"We're taking that ammo. Get out of the way."

Aeric turned to see three men standing at the end of the aisle. All of them held rifles menacingly. He held the stock of his rifle with one hand and lifted up the other to try and placate the men. "Look, there's plenty of ammo available. We don't even need rifle ammo, just 9-mil."

"Back up until we get our shit," the leader of the group said.

"We don't want any trouble, we're just getting some ammunition for our pistols," Tyler replied.

"I don't give a shit what you want," the man challenged. "I'll kill you if you don't step aside."

"Sir, we need the ammo for our weapons just as much as you need it for yours." Tyler stated. He wasn't going to back down.

"Kill them, Red!" one of the other two said gleefully.

The man elevated the barrel of his rifle towards Aeric's midsection while his mind played over the next several seconds and what would happen if he didn't stop them. It wasn't a pretty picture. If they let these assholes boss them around, they'd likely hound them until they ended up shooting both of them in the back. They had to be dealt with.

He shifted slightly, using Tyler's bulk to hide his movements. The 9-millimeter Glock that he'd taken from the second man that he'd killed felt like it weighed a ton as it slid out from under his shirt. His finger slid into the characteristic square trigger guard and he depressed the little switch in the middle of the trigger that acted as the Glock's safety mechanism.

Aeric stepped out from behind his roommate to shoot, but the big man fired his own weapon from inside his pocket first. The bullet went directly into the chest of Red, the man who'd done most of the talking. His mouth formed an almost comical "O" shape that was clear in the strange orange glow of the trash can fire. Aeric's ears rang from the gun's explosion, but he didn't allow that to stop him. He pivoted on his lead leg and squeezed the trigger on his own pistol, this time crumpling the second man's face inward as blood sprayed into the aisle behind him.

By the time he'd turned towards the third man, he was already running away. Tyler yelled something to him, but the blood pounding though his body didn't allow him to think. The only thing he knew was that he had to stop these three before they tried to kill him and his companion. He opened his stance like his father had taught him when they fired at aluminum cans in the field and brought the sights up to his eye level. The coward was running away, one more second and he'd be toast as well.

He eased the trigger back. The bullet would strike the man right between the shoulder blades and put the thug out of commission. It was a good thing that he did for the city of Corsicana. If he didn't take them out, they would have robbed any number of people. Tyler slapped his hand at the last moment and the bullet veered slightly, catching the man in the shoulder and sent him tumbling to the ground around the corner.

Aeric glared at his friend, "What the hell did you do that for?"

"Leave it, man!" Tyler shouted over the ringing in his own ears. "That guy was running away. We need to get out of here!"

"Bullshit. He would have ambushed us on the way out. We're not leaving without getting what we came for." He turned and took two quick steps towards the 9-millimeter ammunition, then shoved every box of ammo that he saw into the pack. It sagged noticeably in his grasp with the added weight. Then, for good measure, he grabbed two more boxes of the 30-30.

"Sleeping bags," he ordered as he walked down the aisle scanning for products that would be useful. Into his backpack went chemical lights, two large hunting knives, two multi-tool pliers, a collapsible shovel, a small hatchet and some heavy-duty wool socks.

"Got 'em," Tyler breathed as he came around the corner carrying three boxes. "I also got a tent that we should be able to sleep in."

Aeric started to chastise him about being stupid because they could always just stay in a vacant house or car, but he stopped himself. The man—who was just a teenager like himself—was trying to help. "Good job. Let's get jackets and boots. Then we can leave."

As he started to exit the aisle on the back side, he had a quick thought and turned back into the camping section. It was extremely hard to see, but then he found it, a water purifying system with water bottles. They still had several full bottles of water from the convenience store, but the purifier would take away the stress of potentially running out of drinking water.

He grabbed the box and shoved it under his arm. They'd get everything situated when they got someplace relatively safe and defensible. A woman's shriek pierced the store from somewhere near the front and a baby began to cry. What kind of asshole would bring a baby out into the radiation to loot a Walmart?

Tyler led the way towards the footwear section as the store began to get darker the further away from the more frequented areas that they went. When they arrived at the shoe section, they were completely alone in the darkness. They worked their way along the back wall to the small work boot display. The store stocked eight different boot brands, so he went for a steel-toed model that didn't seem to be too heavy and would likely be able to withstand the rigors of constant movement. He found his size thirteen and quickly slipped his shoe off to try it on. The boot wasn't the most comfortable shoe that he'd ever worn, but it would work so he put the other one on while Tyler looked for boots to replace his own poor footwear selection.

"Hey, I need help finding fifteens," Ty staid. "I can't read the numbers on the boxes in the darkness."

After scanning the shelf for a moment, he pulled the box off and handed it to his partner. Tyler made the boot switch as well and Aeric grabbed some gel inserts from the rack on the end of the aisle before they ventured out from the quiet shoe section back to the main part of the store. Just as before, people seemed to be fighting over everything.

The men's clothing department was on the way to the front door, so they weaved in and out of clothing racks, headed towards a large display which held coats and scarves for the coming winter months. The closely-packed racks threatened to dislodge the boxes that each of them held precariously under their arms, but they made it to the coat section without too much of a problem.

Aeric and Tyler both needed extra-large or possibly even a double-XL, which severely limited their options. They were able to find coats with a hood, but where Tyler's was black and blended into the darkness well, Aeric's was bright yellow and dark blue. He'd have to fix that—good thing that there was plenty of ash and dirt available to help him tone the color down.

"Anything else?"

"The cooking pan," Tyler replied. "But that can wait. We need to get out of here. This place is dangerous."

He agreed. The men who'd confronted them at the ammunition display were evidence of that fact. "Okay, you're right. Let's get out of here, get this stuff stored away and then find someplace to sleep for the night."

As they moved towards the front, the baby's cries got louder. They passed a group of women and children huddled around the prone form of a man off to the side of the entry area near the shopping carts. They were the ones with the baby. He made eye contact with one of the kids as they passed through the entry. Tears streaked down her cheeks, tracing lines through the darkened ash on her dirty face. For such a small child, she looked so sad. *Her life wouldn't change,* Aeric thought. *Happiness is a thing of the past.*

Then he noticed the clothing of the man on the ground and the dark stain on his shoulder. It was the man that he'd shot. These people must be the families of the men who'd confronted them in the back of the store. Guilt threatened to overwhelm him. Had he killed that little girl's father? He had to grip Tyler's shirt for support.

"What is it?" the big man asked.

"We just need… We need to get out of here," Aeric replied.

They left the group behind and went out to the parking lot. He cursed himself silently for not thinking about the effects of his actions. He'd dealt with the threat immediately before him, but those men also had families who relied on them. Had he doomed those people to death or some fate even potentially worse than death? What would they have to do in order to survive without the protection that the men they'd killed provided for them?

He didn't want to think about it, but his mind wouldn't stop, regardless of how much he begged it to. Would they be alright or would the women turn to murder or prostitution to provide for their children? What about the baby? Did they have enough food for the winter and had just been trying to get the ammunition for defense? He would never know the answers to those questions.

They were shocked to see an older truck driving through the parking lot when they got outside. It slowed down at the stop sign near the exit, but the brake lights didn't work. "Hmm, look at that," Tyler said. "I guess the old vehicles that don't have a lot of electronics in them still work."

"Makes sense," Aeric answered, thankful for the distraction from thinking about the fate that he'd doomed those people to. "If most of the parts were simply mechanical and not electrical, then everything should still be working."

"Hmm, maybe we should get motorcycles instead of bicycles."

Tyler's comment made Aeric stop in mid step. "Shit! We were in Walmart. We could have gotten bikes there."

"Yeah, I guess so. Want to head back in?"

The thought of going back into the store and passing by those families again terrified him. What if the man that he'd shot in the shoulder recognized him and the women attacked? Or worse, what if the kids came after him? He didn't know if he could shoot a woman, but he *knew* that he couldn't shoot a child. Surely, there'd be another store with bikes not too far down the road. It was a Walmart for Christ's sake, they were almost as prolific as Starbucks.

"Uh, no. I don't think so, man. Let's just walk for a few miles, maybe there will be something later on."

The big man shrugged and said, "Okay. Doesn't make any difference to me. Where are we staying for the night? I'm exhausted."

Behind them, more gunfire erupted inside the store, answering the chorus of weapons that seemed to be firing everywhere in the small city of Corsicana, Texas. "Someplace safe, but close. I don't want to be out walking around in the night, there's no telling what people are going to do out here. They're panicking."

"What about that house right there?" Tyler asked while he pointed at a darkened home a half of a block from the parking lot where they stood.

"Don't you think that's too close?" Aeric asked.

"I wouldn't have suggested it if I did."

He deliberated with himself for a few seconds and then finally agreed. They needed to get inside somewhere during the night, and that place was just as good as any other. The only thing that they had to worry about was the house's owners.

That was the tricky thing. It wasn't like the people had just vanished into thin air out in the rural parts of the country, they were still present. It wasn't a far stretch to imagine millions of people running around in the darkness, all looking to increase their odds of survival by taking from the weak. Or was that a stupid line of thought? Yes, there was some gunfire as old scores were settled, but ultimately, the human race would band together as a community and overcome this, right?

"Fine, let's go knock and see if anyone is home."

They trudged doggedly up to the front door of the house and Aeric pushed the doorbell. Nothing happened. He sighed at his stupidity and then knocked. The lack of any type of electricity would take some getting used to since it had been around for his entire life. Seriously, who thought of a doorbell as electric? It was just a doorbell.

He was surprised when the barrel of a pistol pressed against the glass of the side windows and then the locks on the door turned. It creaked inwards to the end of the safety chain and a man asked, "What do you want?"

Aeric cleared his throat and replied, "We're looking for a place to stay for the night out of the ash, can I—"

"Go away, we don't have any food."

"We're not asking for food, just a place to stay."

"Ain't got that either. Get out of here!"

"Can we stay in your carport?" Tyler asked from further down the driveway where he could see the vacant structure.

"Well… What can you give me for my trouble?"

"We don't have anything to give—" Aeric stopped himself. "Do you smoke?"

"Yeah, why?"

"I can trade you an unopened pack of cigarettes for one night in the shed. We just want to have someplace semi-secure out of the ashes to sleep."

"You really think that you can bribe me with cigarettes?" the man asked.

"We're not trying to bribe you, sir. The fact is that before too long, there won't be any cigarettes left. The companies that were manufacturing them are either gone in a nuclear blast or don't have any power to run their machinery. These could be the only ones you see for a long time."

"Give me three packs and you can stay."

"We don't have that many. I can offer you one pack. All we're gonna do is sleep in your carport. It looks like it's empty except for some boxes and stuff, so it won't harm you at all."

The man considered it for a moment and then stuck his hand through the door. "Fine, give me the cigarettes, but you need to leave by morning."

Aeric smiled and answered, "Of course. Thank you!" Then he stepped back to the edge of the porch and slowly took his backpack off. He unzipped the top pouch and made a show of digging through the pack like he was searching for the cigarettes instead of moving all of them around.

When he thought that he'd spent enough time searching, he brought out a random pack and zipped the backpack closed. "Here you go," he said.

The man grasped the cigarettes and pulled them through his door. "Okay, I don't want to shoot you, so don't come back to the door tonight. Like I said, you need to be gone by morning."

"Thank you!" Aeric said again as the door slammed shut in his face and locks were twisted into place.

He shrugged at Tyler and then the big man led the way towards the carport. Tyler dropped the sleeping bags on the gravel floor and began stacking things up at the entrance. "What are you doing?"

"I'm trying to make this place as secure as possible," Tyler answered. "We're out of the ash, but if anyone else gets the idea to find shelter, then we may have a fight on our hands."

"Shit, Ty. You're right. God, I can't believe how messed up things are right now."

"Yup," he replied and then worked in silence stacking boxes. When he'd finally made it look like the shed was full from a distance he turned to Aeric and asked, "Mind telling me what the fuck that was back there in Walmart?"

"They were going to shoot us. I heard them egging on the guy who had the rifle. If I didn't take matters into our hands, then they would have blasted you."

"No, I'm talking about the guy you were gonna shoot in the back," he grunted. "I had it. Those two were the antagonists. The third guy was just a lackey. We can't go shooting people in the back, man."

"Sorry, I was just caught up in the moment and didn't want the guy ambushing us on the way out."

"I get it, it's just… Now that family has to take care of him and he's probably gonna die anyways." He stared at the pile of boxes that he'd built and then turned back to Aeric. "Are you alright? I mean, you took those first two kills really hard and you seem to be fine with what happened today."

"Yeah, I'm alright, thanks. I don't want to say that I've hardened up or something stupid like that, but I knew without a doubt that those men were going to kill us, but we still don't know about the group at Veronica's place. Yeah, sure, they killed that guy, but there's no telling what he'd done to them—or to their family—prior to what we saw. We didn't even give them a chance to see what they were going to do. We just killed them before they knew what the hell was happening."

Tyler accepted his explanation with a slight nod that he could barely see in the growing darkness. "Good, I just wanted to make sure. Things are going to get much worse, Walmart proves that. I can't have you flaking out on me."

"No worries. I'm good."

"Alright, I'm exhausted, let's roll out these sleeping bags and get some sleep."

"I'd kill for a toothbrush," Aeric muttered.

"Yeah, you probably would," his friend chuckled.

*****

Tyler couldn't sleep. He was irritated that those men had made him shoot them, and if he was being honest with himself, he was a little worried that he was losing his humanity. He hadn't hesitated in Austin to kill the men who'd taken part in the torturing of Veronica's neighbor and hadn't even felt any remorse afterwards. The men at Walmart did appear to be threatening, but there was no way of knowing what their intentions really were. He'd told Aeric that they were going to kill him. Was that the truth or was it simply easier to kill them and continue on with their plan to load up on supplies?

Was that it? Had he allowed the situation to dictate his actions? There had been multiple murders and gun battles from the food side of the store, had he let the emotions of the moment escalate his own response?

Whatever the reason, he still didn't feel any actual remorse for taking those men's lives. It was more of a feeling of letting himself down, not that he was sorry for getting the drop on them. They certainly had acted threatening towards Aeric when there was no need to act that way.

Tyler tossed and turned for what seemed like hours. He didn't have any way to tell time since both his watch and cell phone had stopped working when the big EMP knocked out all of the electronics. As he lay there, Tyler really began to think about the journey. If what Lieutenant Griffith had said was true, everyone that he'd ever known in the world was dead.

His entire extended family lived in Lincoln. They'd expected him to go play baseball, and then return to the family homestead, just like his father and grandfather had. They'd both left to fight in Vietnam and Korea, respectively, and then returned to Lincoln to work on the farm.

The homestead was what ended up killing them all. Nebraska was littered with nuclear launch facilities. Besides Washington, DC and the missile command center in Colorado, the launch sites would have been the very first targets as the adversary tried to knock out the United States' capability for launch. If the Vultures had hacked into the system and simply fired pre-arranged targets without changing any of the target data, then his entire family was dead.

That left Aeric. He was the only person that Tyler knew from before the war who was still alive. The guy had become like a brother to him over the course of the summer and fall semester together, and had proven several times already that he needed Tyler's help to survive. He'd make sure that he got back home, but didn't know what else that would entail. He glanced over at Aeric, who was snoring softly. He hadn't snored before that Tyler had heard. He must have been as exhausted as Tyler felt.

One thing was for sure, Tyler wasn't built for walking over four hundred miles. They were both fooling themselves if they thought that they'd be able to walk that far with only a couple backpacks full of food and cigarettes for trade. They'd constantly have to go into situations like what had happened at Walmart and be in real danger every three or four days trying to get food. They needed bikes. Bikes would cut their travel time by at least half, maybe more.

Tyler looked out the shed's window at the lightening sky. Somehow, he'd tossed and turned all night long and morning was approaching. The gunfire had ceased hours ago, which meant that either everyone was dead or that people had gone home, too exhausted to carry on for the night. The timing was as good as it was going to get and he could go back to the store without putting Aeric in danger also.

That made up his mind. He'd go back to the store and get the bikes on his own. Aeric was his only remaining friend, he couldn't stand the thought of the guy getting hurt, or worse. This way, he would be able to sneak in, get the wheels and sneak back out before anyone knew anything was different.

He unzipped his sleeping bag as quietly as he could and pulled his legs out of the noisy material. Then he slipped on his boots and grabbed the pistol and baseball bat. He really needed some other way to carry the bat besides in his hand all the time. *Maybe some type of belt sling would work to hook the end of the bat into,* he thought as he quietly moved boxes out of the way.

The trip back to Walmart was uneventful and the inside of the store was mostly quiet, like he thought it would be. He went in the same side that they'd gone through earlier that night and noticed the man that Aeric had shot in the back was still laying there, dead, in a large puddle of blood. He must have been hit in the lung and then bled out. *So much for a hardship on the family,* Tyler thought.

He weaved his way back to the sporting goods section and as he went, he could hear voices talking from the food section. They must have set up down on that end and were now guarding their stash. It didn't' matter, he wasn't about to go down there. He found two bikes that looked big enough for them and picked them up. It would be easier to carry them on his shoulder than to try and wheel them both along.

As he was leaving the sporting goods section, he noticed the bow and arrows. The thought of using a bow was appealing, but not practical if they were going to be on a bike, but the arrow quiver, *that* had a practical use that he could apply. He grabbed a packaged quiver and stuffed it under his arm.

*****

Aeric woke to the sound of the boxes being moved aside. He frantically searched inside his sleeping bag until his fingers wrapped around the pistol that he'd slept with. He pulled it out and pointed the weapon towards the entrance. His hand shook in the cold of the early morning, but it was steady enough to shoot if it came to that.

"There are people in here," he shouted. "And I have a gun pointed right at you!"

He heard gravel fly as whoever was outside dove off of the driveway. "Hey, it's me!" Tyler said from outside. "Don't shoot!"

"Ty?" he asked in confusion. The man's sleeping bag still lay a few feet from him, but it was obvious that he was no longer inside it. "What the hell are you doing?"

"Put that shit away, man!"

Aeric obliged and set his pistol down. "Okay, it's safe."

"Geez, man! What the hell?" Tyler asked as he moved the boxes and stumbled inside the carport.

"What are you doing outside?"

"I went back to Walmart."

"What?" Aeric asked in alarm. "You shouldn't be going places by yourself, man. If you'd gotten yourself killed, I would have no clue where the hell you were."

It was difficult to see, but Aeric thought that Tyler looked remorseful. "You're right. Sorry."

"It's okay, just don't do it again, man. We stick together from here on out." His friend had been properly rebuked, so he asked, "What'd you get?"

His friend looked up at him and smiled. "I got two bikes, both big mountain bikes with twenty-one inch wheels. We should be okay to ride with that size."

"Alright, I forgive you, big guy. This is freakin' awesome, man!"

"I'm glad that you approve. There weren't very many people out when I woke up, so I snuck down there. Got a frying pan and some multivitamins too," he said as he held up his haul. "I wanted to get some more food, but the grocery section still had people in it. I could hear them down there, they're guarding the food."

"Corsicana is fucked. The sooner we get out of here, the better."

"It ain't gonna be any better anywhere else, man."

"I know, but it just makes me feel better to say it. Okay, let's eat and get out of here on those bikes."

They didn't make a fire in the shed to try out their new cooking pan because the homeowner kept moving aside the curtains in the house to see if they were still in the carport. They ate a hasty meal of canned food and then began packing everything up. Thankfully, Aeric had packed away the ammunition in the various pockets of his three-backpack amalgamation the night before, so all they really needed to do was secure their sleeping bags and the few things that they'd pulled out. The unopened tent took some work and scavenged rope from the carport to get secured to the back of Tyler's seat, but with a little bit of effort, they were able to get it balanced fairly well.

"We really are going to need more food and water soon," Tyler said forlornly. "We've got about three or four more days' worth of food, maybe less for water, just depends on how much we eat and drink."

"Aw, man, I could go for a beer," Aeric replied mistaking Tyler's comment. The stress of the last few days had built up inside of him, it didn't matter that it was early morning, a drink really did sound good to him right then.

"Yeah, right? Maybe we can find something after we get started and have a couple of beers when we set up camp tonight."

They finished packing in silence and Aeric waved to the shadow of the homeowner as they pushed their bikes past the window. The curtains dropped quickly as if he'd thought that they wouldn't see him spying on them.

"Alright, so we're headed east on Highway Thirty-One to Tyler, is that right?" Aeric asked.

"Yeah, in Tyler, we'll go northeast," Tyler responded with a chuckle because the town shared his name. "It's about sixty miles from here. I think that we can make it there by nightfall now that we have the bikes."

They'd planned on taking three days to reach Tyler, Texas on foot, but the addition of the bikes was a huge help that would eat up the miles to Missouri rapidly. "Wow, you think so?" Aeric asked. "That's gonna speed this trip up dramatically!"

The morning flew by with little difficulty besides the thick layer of ash on the ground. Aeric estimated that it was a little over half an inch thick and continuing to fall. That small amount wouldn't have been an issue for them if the damn stuff wasn't so slick. Twice during turns the bike's tires had lost traction and slipped out from underneath him. He was able to look at it in a positive light though, since his bright yellow jacket was now a dirty, muted mustard color from the ash that ground into the fibers when he fell.

The temperature was a little cooler than they'd experienced further south as well. Tyler guessed that it was because the warmth from the sun wasn't able to penetrate the thick clouds of ash that still swirled overhead. He mentioned another show that he'd seen that had stated a nuclear winter would occur after a global nuclear weapons exchange, but the program had also been quick to point out that it was only speculation since there had obviously never been a global nuclear war. Well, it was time to test the hypothesis.

If the weather did turn, then the remaining population would take a major hit as people froze in their homes. Aeric had no way of knowing how many people actually survived the nuclear exchange part of the war and how many would die in the coming weeks from radiation, but he had to assume that given the spread of America's population there were tens of millions of survivors living in rural areas. If that were the case, the food supply would probably dwindle quickly—hell, the convenience store back in Richland hadn't even been able to survive ten or fifteen soldiers for less than a week without a resupply. For most of the survivors, other people were going to become a problem soon because they weren't able to produce their own food and fought each other for it, like had already happened with devastating effects in the town they'd just left.

As they rode down the highway, they passed a few of those very same survivors traveling on foot in both directions. Neither Aeric nor Tyler bothered to ask the people where they were coming from or where they were headed, instead they just held their weapons across the handlebars and pedaled as fast as they could to get away from them.

He had a lot of time to think as they rode and marveled at the absurdity of it all. Before the collapse and the war, people had lamented that the increased connectivity of the world had actually created a more isolated society which communicated more over the internet than in person. Now, that people were forced to communicate in person, they were scared to death of every interaction and even more nervous of strangers than they were before everything went to shit.

Aeric hoped that his father, who was known to be both headstrong and over-protective, just kept his head down and didn't do anything dumb trying to keep his mother safe. If they just stayed in their home until he made it there, then they would be fine. He could get food for them and assist in whatever way that they needed.

After hours upon hours of riding, they reached the outskirts of the city of Tyler. Cars had been pushed across the road and large hand-painted signs announced that outsiders weren't welcome. A group of heavily armed men leaning on the vehicles seemed to emphasize the point that anyone not from the city would be turned away.

Aeric eased his aching rear end off of the bicycle seat and used the kickstand to keep it upright before walking towards the men with his hands in the air. He winced at the cramps that had formed in his ass cheeks and legs from the constant pedaling on the mountain bike. "Hello," he started tentatively.

"That's close enough," one of the men said. "We have guys with deer rifles just a few houses away, so you and your friend have scopes on you right now."

Involuntarily, he glanced beyond the speaker at the buildings on either side of the road about two hundred yards further down the highway. "We don't mean any harm and don't want to take anything from here. Hell, we don't even want to sleep here."

"Then turn around and go back the way you came from, stranger."

"We're trying to get to Missouri where my family lives."

The man threw up his hands in an exaggerated shrug before saying, "I really don't care, mister. Go around Tyler then. You ain't welcome here."

"There's not any easy way around," Tyler stated. "We have a map and there are no back roads that wouldn't add twenty or thirty miles to our trip. Come on, man. Just let us use the ring road around the city, we won't even go anywhere near the downtown."

The guard seemed to consider it for a moment and then said, "Hold on. Don't make any sudden movements or you'll end up like those fellers." He pointed to the ditch beside the road and began to walk back towards the barricade.

Aeric followed along the line that he'd indicated. When they'd walked up to the checkpoint, they had been focused on the obstacles and the men guarding them, they hadn't seen what rested in the ditch. Several bodies lay on top of each other with bullet holes drilled neatly in their heads. After seeing them, he snapped his attention back towards the buildings where the snipers were probably located.

"Holy shit, you see that?" he asked Tyler.

"Yeah, man. Just do like he says and don't make any sudden movements."

"There's not a chance in hell. You think that they're gonna let us through?"

"Well, they didn't just outright shoot us, so we have that going for us," Tyler replied. "Maybe those people threatened them or something. They probably know this area as well as anyone, they know that besides the ring road around the city, there's no easy way to continue northeast from here."

"Maybe we should have just gone north and then into Oklahoma."

"There's only Little Rock to deal with as a potential nuclear target in Arkansas," Tyler stated. "Going due north would put us in the fallout zone for Dallas. Maybe Oklahoma City and Tulsa, too. It's easier to go northeast and then due north through western Arkansas."

"What about all the mountains there?" Aeric asked.

Tyler looked over at him with questioning eyes. "What do you mean by mountains? I didn't think Arkansas had mountains."

"Yeah, they do. Not huge like the Rockies or anything, but they're pretty big. We used to drive through them every year to a baseball tournament that was held in Harrison."

"Wait, do you mean hills like we have in Austin or actual mountains?"

"They're pretty big. Riding a bike will be tricky."

"When the hell were you going to share that with me, fearless leader?"

"It slipped my mind, okay? I wasn't thinking, I was just happy to get moving, even happier that we had bikes and could cut the length of the trip in third."

"Shit. Shit, man!" Tyler said and dropped his hands. He slapped them against his pant leg in frustration.

A chunk of pavement flew up beside them, followed by the report of a single shot from somewhere behind the barricade. Tyler stopped and immediately raised his hands once more.

"Hey! What did I tell you about not making any sudden movements?" the man who'd spoken to them earlier called out from where he was huddled with three other men.

"I'm sorry!" Tyler yelled. "We were having a discussion about our route."

"Well, stay patient and quiet or it ain't gonna matter!" Tyler nodded his head and stared off towards the side of the road away from his roommate.

Aeric felt bad. "I'm sorry, man. I totally forgot about the mountains. Look, I told you about how McAlester was a flaming wreck when I drove through back in June, right? There's no telling what it's like now, so it's better that we didn't go that way. It might have been the target of a nuke, probably most military sites were."

He looked back at his friend. "Yeah. We just need to spend a long, hard time looking at a map."

Aeric couldn't resist himself and said, "You said, 'long and hard' what a pervert!"

"God knows I could go for some of that too," Tyler answered with a sad smile.

He'd expected Tyler to reply with something sarcastic, not the dejected answer that his big friend had given. "Hey, what's wrong? Besides the fact that our heads are in the crosshairs of a sniper right now."

"I don't know, man. If we survive this—and that looks less likely every time we have any type of interaction with other people—then where does that leave me? Let's say we join some type of community, we'll say San Angelo for the fun of it. Those people are going to want someone who can help add to the gene pool, not a gay man who can't even cook. I mean, besides being strong, I don't really have any skills that would be useful to some type of post-apocalyptic society."

"You're pretty good at killing people," Aeric reminded him. It was another example of how much their lives had already changed. They stood ten feet from a pile of dead bodies and talked openly about murdering people in cold blood.

Tyler chuckled and said, "Yeah, but by the time we make it back to Texas—if that's even what we decide to do—then everyone who's left alive will be pretty good at killing people too. I'm just bummed, that's all."

"Oh great, now you're talking about bums. First it was long and hard, now bums. When is it *ever* going to end with you?"

Tyler smiled, "Look who's talking about ends now."

Once again, Aeric was grateful for his friend's lack of sensitivity about his sexual orientation. For now, it seemed like

Tyler's melancholy had passed. He was right though, he'd have to determine what he could give to a potential community in order to be useful to them. That made Aeric wonder what *he* had to offer that was useful. Like Tyler, he was strong and could swing a baseball bat very well, but those were about the only skills that he had.

"Alright, you two. Come here," their host ordered.

They walked stiffly forward. Was this where they got shot or stabbed to save bullets? "We talked about it. You're right, there ain't no easy way around and to turn you fellers back when you ain't done nothing wrong wouldn't be the Christian thing to do. Lord knows we're trying to do some good deeds before the Rapture happens. We'll guide you around the city on the Three Twenty-Three over to Highway Two Seventy-One, that will take you northeast towards Arkansas."

Aeric breathed a sigh of relief and said, "Oh wow, thank you!"

"We talked about it," the man said as he indicated the other three men. "If you're just passing through, there's no reason not to take you around. But you've gotta get past the barricade on that road before you camp for the night. Deal?"

"Deal," both Tyler and Aeric replied in unison.

"Okay then, let's get started. It's about six miles from here to Two Seventy-One and then another half a mile or so until you reach the barricade."

"You're going with us?" Aeric asked.

"Yep. I'm Tim. Jacob and me will be riding our bikes behind you two and will shoot you both dead as doornails if you try to escape into Tyler. You hear me?"

"Of course," Aeric replied. "We'd never try anything like that. I'm Aeric and this is Tyler."

"Huh," Tim grunted. "Tyler. Maybe we shoulda given you a warmer welcome. Alright, go grab your bikes and we'll move the cars so you can get through."

They returned to their bikes and walked them through the opening that the guards had made by putting one of the vehicles along the side of the road in neutral and pushing it a little ways into the ditch. As they passed through, Aeric thought about how this type of barricade would stand up to a determined group trying to overrun the city. It wouldn't. It was useful for stopping individuals and small groups, but anything larger than twenty or thirty men would be able to absorb the damage that the defenders could inflict on them and continue on.

They hopped on their bikes and rode slowly down the highway with Tim and his companion following behind on their own bicycles. As they rode, he thought about the ways to defend this place. For one, they were much too spread out. He didn't know if there were certain key locations away from the downtown area that they needed to secure or if the city's leaders had just thought that the roads made a convenient place to defend from. If it were him, he would have pulled back well within the ring road, which still gave them a twelve-mile square area to defend. He didn't know how many people that the city of Tyler boasted, but even that reduced coverage area was just too much space.

It was strange to think about the defense of an American town. What would they defend against? The thought hit him hard in the stomach because he already knew the answer, but he hadn't wanted to think about it. As the food became more and more scarce, people would leave wherever they were and begin searching for more. Human nature was to join together in groups—for defense and for attacking. Every little town would become a target. The bigger cities that remained would probably destroy themselves from the inside first, and then the smaller towns would be hit by the survivors from the city.

It wasn't a pretty line of thought. Smaller towns in the Midwest and American South likely had residents who farmed small gardens and had greater access to locally-canned goods, but the cities would quickly run out of food. All those people in apartment buildings in the downtown areas, probably with only about a week's worth of supplies, would soon be searching for ways to provide for themselves and their families. It seemed like he was lumping everyone into a general category and knew that some would have much more food than what he'd thought, so as a general guide, he set ten days as the point when they would begin to see real problems with food.

That timeframe, about five days from now, put them on the road still. Would his parents be alright? He thought that they were probably a little better off than their neighbors, but wasn't sure. They had a lot of deer meat and frozen food in the chest freezer in the garage, but that wouldn't have lasted long once the power went out. They would have had to eat a lot of it right away or it would have spoiled.

Aeric grinned at the thought of his mom and dad having the neighbors over, grilling all that meat and giving it away. His parents loved to host parties and his dad always had a pile of hickory wood for grilling and smoking meat, so even without power, they'd have been fine for cooking. He could imagine them trying to make the best of the situation and playing lawn games with everyone while the meat cooked.

Finally, he admitted it to himself that he missed his parents. When he lived with them—and to a lesser extent when he was in Austin—he'd despised how they constantly looked after him and took care of him. Now he realized that he was a fool and wished that he was with them. They'd always had his best interests in mind and had never said or done anything negative to him. Why had he thought that they were suffocating him? All they wanted was for him to succeed in life and he'd acted like a spoiled brat. He vowed that he'd make it up to them. He would make sure that they were safe and that they knew how much that he actually appreciated them.

But what did being safe actually mean? Did that mean staying with them in Springfield or did he plan on making good on his promise to Veronica, a girl he really didn't even know? His father's words snuck into his mind that Gaines's always kept their promises. Did that saying have any real meaning in the new world that they faced?

Of course it did. Men of honor kept their word. He could convince his parents of the safety that Veronica had promised him in San Angelo and they'd come with him. What did Springfield have to offer them now that the world was ending? The weather was already noticeably colder after only a few days of the ash clouds, what would happen when the earth rotated farther around the sun and the northern hemisphere was in its natural winter cycle? It would become bitter cold, that's what.

Texas was a much better option than Missouri for the coming winter.

His thoughts made him question if his parents would even be willing to leave their home. He'd convinced himself that Texas was a better option, but could he convince them? They'd lived in that house for over twenty years and their entire adult lives had been spent there. Would they be willing to leave based on what their eighteen year old son said? He'd been out in this world and had already done terrible things to survive. They'd probably been sheltered behind their home's walls and hadn't seen the evil in the world. Why would they listen to him?

Because they had to. He'd make them listen. They didn't know the dangers of this new world like he did. It would be up to him to impress upon them the dangers of living in the bigger city, and it would only be a matter of time before their home became the target of some type of marauding band looking for food. He'd seen science fiction movies about the dismal future before and knew what was in store for people if they didn't properly prepare for disaster.

The real problem was that the dismal future in those movies was now.

SEVEN

Ash. It drifted from the skies, blanketing the world in a thick layer like freshly fallen snow. Each tree bough along the road had its own pillow of ash, slowly choking the life from the plant. In places, the wind had whipped the layers of ash away from the road and it lay in piles along the sides, filling the drainage ditches. There wasn't a surface as far as the men could see that wasn't covered in the remains of their civilization.

They'd camped just outside of Tyler after Tim and his partner had left them on the north side of town and then started the morning as fresh as could be expected. It took Aeric several miles of riding to get the stiffness out of his aching body and every push down on the pedals had been agony as his muscles protested their overuse.

That was two days ago. Yesterday, they'd turned up Interstate 30 expecting another confrontation with the military. Except for the abandoned vehicles that had lost power when the EMP hit, the interchange was empty. Several wrecked cars forever entombed the remains of their drivers. Thankfully, they didn't find anyone alive. What would they have done if they had?

They took advantage of the wide, relatively flat interstate and made great time, despite their soreness. By the end of the second day, they'd traveled more than a hundred miles from Tyler, Texas and were nearing their turn north into Arkansas just west of the town Texarkana.

Last night, they made camp in eerie silence along the interstate. In fact, they hadn't seen anyone alive since they turned onto the interstate earlier the day before. Aeric was worried that they were drifting into a radiation zone—which they likely were—but Tyler assured him that they would find massive devastation before they entered an area that had been hit with a nuke. He'd seen all the television programs about nuclear war, so Aeric had to trust him for now, but he planned on going into the first intact bookstore that they found and picking up books on nuclear war and survival so he could read up on the topic himself.

After a couple miles of riding today, they were going to take the exit for New Boston, which according to their map was the town right outside the Red River Army Depot. Aeric remembered the last army depot that he'd seen in McAlester, Oklahoma and it wasn't a pleasant memory. The plant had been burned to the ground by terrorists last summer while he was driving through on his way from Missouri to Austin. The dark, smoke-filled sky immediately surrounding the plant had looked a lot like the entire sky did now.

At Exit 201, they turned their bicycles onto the ramp from the interstate down to the intersection with Texas State Highway 8. They passed more cars filled with the dead and had to weave in and out of traffic that had been stopped at the light when everyone died. "What the hell happened here, man?" Aeric muttered as he looked at the long line of vehicles.

The cars all held the bodies of their drivers and many had passengers as well. It looked like they'd died suddenly, no doors were opened, no accidents after the vehicles lost power while driving at highway speeds, nothing. The people were simply sitting in their useless vehicles, dead.

"I think everyone in this town is dead," Tyler answered with a shrug. "Look at them. They're all in their cars, like everyone died at the same time."

"I've got a bad feeling about this place," Aeric said as he looked around at the buildings and mostly unharmed vehicles. There was very little damage to the surrounding area except for where the cars had continued rolling after their drivers died and they'd ran into something. The buildings were intact. Most of their windows weren't even broken out. Even the little flower cart on the corner was still upright with its previous owner laid out on the grass like he'd simply died of a heart attack and fallen over.

"We should be fine. Since everyone's dead, we should get some supplies from that Walmart over there," Tyler said, gesturing towards the large store on the opposite corner.

"Aren't you worried about the radiation? This looks like everybody died from radiation to me."

"Look, man. Yeah, I'm worried about it, but there's nothing we can do about it since we're already here." He looked around and stated, "Besides, I think I know what happened."

Aeric regarded him skeptically. "You do? What do you think happened here, then?"

"Remember that first airburst that we saw to the northeast, the one that temporarily blinded me?"

"Of course. You think this was where it happened?"

Tyler looked around and nodded. "It makes sense. If the nukes were preprogrammed and they were fired at targets that were in the computer, they may have hit this ammunition depot with a high-altitude burst. They're used when the enemy wants to kill everyone, but leave the infrastructure in place, minus the electricity of course. The military targeted cities or ports that they want to use later with high altitude bursts."

"Okay, man. You're freaking me out with how much you know about this shit. How many Discovery Channel shows did you watch?"

Tyler ignored his question and continued, "The burst way up in the sky does a few things. First, it sends out a massive EMP burst over a wide area—the higher the burst, the larger the area that's affected. Which is why everything lost power over a hundred and fifty miles away."

"It could have been from the nuke that wiped out Dallas, only fifty miles away from us."

Tyler nodded, "Sure, you're right. It all happened so close together that they probably both caused it. Anyways, a high altitude burst also sends out the same massive amount of radiation that other warheads do, which kills everyone nearby almost instantly, but then most of the radiation dissipates quickly. That's how an army is able to travel through a city that they've hit with a high altitude bomb."

"And you think they hit this place that way so they could re-use the ammunition stored here?" Aeric asked.

"Yup. It makes sense. We're a few hundred miles from the coast, so if an invading army had been using their ammo all along the way, they'd need a resupply."

"Don't they use different caliber weapons than us?"

"Maybe they'd make it work. Shit, I don't know. But I do know that there's an empty Walmart right there and we're almost out of food."

"Are you sure? We should probably get out of here."

"Aeric, I normally defer to your decisions, but we need canned food and better clothing. We should be fine as long as we make sure to wipe the cans down really well. They're more insulated inside that concrete building than we are out here."

Aeric pulled at the bandana covering his mouth. It *would* be the perfect opportunity to get supplies where no one would bother them. How long had it been since the blast, five days? Six? He couldn't remember. Was that enough time for the really harmful radiation to have dissipated like Tyler said it did? He needed that book.

"If we go into the store, we can be selective about what food we take, instead of the ravioli shit that we got from that gas station," Tyler continued. "We could get better camping gear, ammunition and guns that haven't been touched. We could change our clothes. Hell, we may even be able to find painter's masks with filters to help with the ash and particles in the air."

The painter's masks sealed the deal for Aeric, whose mouth had already begun salivating at the thought of food other than the cheap, greasy pasta that they'd been eating for more than a week. He nodded silently and pushed the bike forward to get going before pedaling towards the store.

They passed the bodies of shoppers in the parking lot as they zeroed in on the front doors. It wasn't a far stretch to imagine everyone alive and carrying their groceries when they were killed instantly, with no idea what had happened to them. Some lay with bags in their hands, while others slumped beside overturned shopping carts. They were each different, once vibrant and full of life. Now they were dead and their colorful clothing was muted by the ash that covered their bodies.

Even here, where the town hadn't burned, the ash was prevalent upon every surface. Aeric wondered just how much of America had been caught up in the fires and he hoped that his parents were alright. *Springfield wasn't a large city, so surely it had escaped targeting by our enemies,* he tried to convince himself. The only way they'd be able to determine the truth was to complete the trip and they desperately needed supplies to be able to do that.

The Walmart's doors were closed when they got there and it took considerable effort on both of their parts to pry them open without any power. When they finally opened them, several bodies fell out onto the sidewalk and they were hit immediately by the smell of decaying flesh and drying feces. Out in the open, the smells had thinned and they no longer noticed them, but the stench of gasses escaping the human body, soured dairy products, rotting vegetables and spoiled meat had been trapped inside the sealed store for over a week.

Aeric gagged while Tyler tightened his bandana around his nose. "Breathe through your mouth, it's easier," the big man instructed.

"I don't want that shit in my mouth."

"Suit yourself. Let's go to the hardware section and see about those masks first."

The inside of the store held bodies, like outside. However, it appeared that these people hadn't died immediately like those in the surrounding town. As they made their way from the grocery side of the store to the hardware section, Aeric noticed that some of the people had dragged themselves along, knocking over clothing racks as they went. Mothers clutched the still forms of their children. It was terrifying. These people must have been slightly shielded inside the store, but still gotten a lethal dose of the radiation and died slowly.

"God, this is awful," Aeric muttered.

Tyler nodded silently in agreement. Once again, Aeric marveled at the mental change that seemed to occur in his friend when they had a mission to conduct. The normally affable, jovial Tyler became more focused and taciturn. He saw to it that whatever they were doing would succeed and Aeric was extremely grateful for the big man's presence.

They turned off the main aisle by the registers down a second wide aisle that separated the hardware and housewares sections. It was the strange juxtaposition of soft pillows and linens next to the plumbing fixtures and tools that Walmart used as their standard layout. They'd only gone a few feet down the aisle when they noticed movement and Aeric's heart was broken by the cruelty of man.

A young employee lay on her back. Her legs moved slightly as she tried to gain traction, but her efforts were hindered by the slipperiness of her own urine and blood. A dried trail of the mixture ran towards the back of the store where she must have dragged herself from when the bomb went off, tearing her flesh open on the concrete floor.

Aeric could tell that she'd been beautiful once, but now her features were twisted in pain and dehydration. She noticed the two men and reached out for them with crooked fingers. They rushed to her side and Aeric knelt beside her.

"He...help...me," she croaked, her voice barely audible in the stillness of the empty store.

Aeric grasped her hand in his gloved one and whispered, "Shh… You're going to be alright," he lied. They didn't have any way to care for her. They could try to give her some pain medication, but how would they even give it to her? The girl's body was so ravaged by the initial radiation burst, and now from the dehydration of five or six days without any food or water, he doubted they could force any pills down her throat.

He pulled out the bottle of water that he had in the side pocket of his pack and unscrewed the lid. Her lips quivered in pain as he dribbled a tiny amount of water between them. Aeric watched as her throat constricted, trying to swallow the fluid. It wasn't working. She couldn't do it lying flat.

"She's a lost cause, man," Tyler said over his shoulder.

"She's still alive, bro. Maybe we can save her."

"Look, I feel for her too. I really do, but what are we gonna do with her? We can't stay here in this town. It's fine for us to come in and get supplies, but long-term exposure to the radiation will kill us just as surely as it did to these people."

"We can't just leave her," Aeric protested.

"Well, we can't take her either. We have bicycles, remember?"

"I'm going to see what I can do for her."

"Suit yourself, bro. She's a goner, we need to get our supplies and get out of here." The big man turned away from Aeric and the girl. "I'll be in the hardware section."

Aeric decided that maybe he *didn't* like how mission-focused his friend had become. The girl was obviously in pain and the humanitarian thing to do would be to take care of her. She couldn't swallow, so he slid his hand under her back to lift her up.

Her body resisted his efforts to lift her because it was stuck to the floor, held fast with dried blood. Her back must have been a ragged mass of torn flesh from sliding along the floor. He looked around, behind them was the pharmacy section, she must have been trying to make it there when she couldn't go any farther. He cradled her head in the crook of his arm and poured more water in her mouth.

She swallowed and her yellowed eyes searched his face, but she wasn't able to focus. "Help…" she mouthed, her voice didn't work anymore. Aeric felt sorry for her and he hated the life that he was being forced to live. It wasn't fair. He was supposed to go to school, play baseball and have a legitimate shot at playing professionally. His life was supposed to be filled with fun times, girls and hopeful dreams for the future. Instead, he sat on the floor of a Walmart in the middle of nowhere trying to comfort a dying girl that he didn't even know.

He hated the thought of it, but Tyler was right. What were they going to do with her? Maybe they had a pull-behind cart in the sporting goods section, one of those things that he'd seen parents pulling their children behind them. Could he pull her all the way to Missouri? What did he do with her if she died—which she likely would—leave her on the side of the road? Bury her? She was a lost cause and all he'd end up doing was depleting his energy.

"I'm so sorry that this happened to you," he told her.

She squeezed her eyes shut, but she was so dehydrated that her body couldn't spare the liquid for tears. It was heartbreaking for Aeric. He knew that she wouldn't recover because the radiation had destroyed her body. It was a miracle that she was still alive as it was.

"What can I do for you to help ease your pain?"

"Ki...ki...mmm," she stammered.

Aeric realized what she was saying. The girl must have been in incredible pain over the last few days, wishing that her life would end, to stop the suffering with no way to do so. It wasn't fair that he wanted to try and keep her alive when she wanted to die. It wouldn't take much to put her out of her misery. Could he force enough pills into her to kill her or would he end up causing her more pain by pushing them down her throat? Maybe a quick gunshot to the head or one good knock from Tyler's baseball bat would be enough.

The pills would take too long and the baseball bat didn't seem humane. The gunshot would be quick and to the point, but that's what you did to an animal that was injured. She wasn't an animal. She'd been a living, breathing human being, energetic and active a week ago. Now she'd been reduced to a frail, pathetic husk of what she must have once been.

Then, he realized what he needed to do. The answer was right in front of him in the housewares section. It would be so simple. It wouldn't take much in her current state. It was the humane way to do it. "I'm so sorry that this happened to you, uh, Kami," he said as he read the name tag pinned to her deflated chest.

Aeric reached over and grabbed a throw pillow off the shelf in front of him. It was a ridiculously happy, fuzzy, purple pillow with pink flowers and butterflies, meant for a little girl's room. He adjusted his leg so he could use it as a stable base and lifted her higher.

He looked into her eyes and whispered to try and comfort her. "You're going to a better place, Kami. Somewhere where the pain will end and you'll always be happy. I wish I could have met you before all of this. You're an amazing person and everything will be over in a few seconds. Goodbye, Kami."

In truth, he didn't know if she was an amazing person, whether she'd been nice or if she'd been mean and spiteful, but it made him feel better to tell her those things before he killed her. He placed the pillow on her face and pressed down hard over her mouth and nose, all the while whispering into her ear that she was going to a better place and how sorry he was.

Kami didn't have enough energy to fight him and it didn't take long for her to die. Her soul fled quickly from the ruined body that it had been trapped in for the past week. Aeric cursed the people responsible for this. It didn't matter if the Vultures had initiated the attack by hacking into the nuclear network. The governments of the world had developed the weapons that did this. They were ultimately to blame for what happened and he was glad that they'd blasted each other into oblivion.

Aeric moved his legs and gently set her lifeless body on the concrete floor. As an afterthought, he put the pillow under her head like she was resting, instead of lying dead on a Walmart floor after a week of suffering unimaginable pain and loneliness. He didn't know anything about her, but he knew that she didn't deserve what had happened to her. He opened a package of bedsheets and covered her with it in a final, futile show of respect for her death.

He walked woodenly over to where Tyler made noise in the hardware area. He'd taken a cart from someone and had a small pile of gear in the basket. "Alright, let's do this and leave. This place is evil," Aeric muttered.

Tyler looked up at him and nodded curtly in understanding of what Aeric had done. "Sorry, man. We can't save everybody."

He surveyed Tyler's haul. He'd found the painter's masks that they desperately needed for defense against the radiation and ash particles suspended in the air. There were three full-face respirators and three boxes of filters. The masks were awesome because they didn't have the small eye goggles like the military masks that Lorelei's platoon wore. The entire face shield was hard, clear plastic, which would eliminate the glaring blind spot issues inherent in the military version of the masks. They also didn't look as heavy or bulky, but then again, the military masks were designed for prolonged use in a nuclear, chemical or biological environment, whereas the respirators were designed to keep airborne paint particles out of painters' lungs.

Aeric started to set the third mask back on the shelf thinking that Tyler had gotten it for Kami, but decided better of it and put it back in the cart. They might run across another survivor somewhere who needed one or they might even need to replace their own if it got damaged. He searched the shelf and grabbed another mask and box of filters.

"Whoa, where do you think we're gonna store all this stuff?"

"I had an idea," Aeric responded. "Let's go to the sporting goods section and get two of those pull-behind carts for the bikes. We can put a lot of gear and supplies in them."

"You mean like those little trailers that people put their kids in to pull behind them?"

"Yeah, one of those," he answered. "If we take advantage of the empty store here, we could get a few weeks' worth of supplies and not have to risk going into another store for a long time."

"That would be helpful. We could set up, like, bug out bags in case we need to run quickly…" Tyler trailed off in thought. "We'd lose some speed hauling all that weight behind us and probably some maneuverability, but yeah, I think it's a great idea. Being in that Walmart in Corsicana was one of the scariest moments of my life. The less time we can spend in places like that, the better."

Aeric pumped his fist in the air and said, "Awesome!"

"We should set them up in here, where it's been shielded from a lot of the radioactive fallout. Plus, there will be tools here that we'll need."

They pushed their cart over to the sporting goods section and walked down the aisle. There were only two of the bicycle carts left on the shelf, which was all that they needed. The boxes were heavy, but they were able to maneuver them out to the larger back aisle where there was a little more light from the opaque skylights above.

They retrieved their bikes from outside and over the course of the next two hours, they put both carts together. One was red, the other yellow, and they both had reflective tape all over them. A few cans of black spray paint from the hardware section made quick work of that problem though and soon they were ready to continue shopping.

They added a lot more everyday equipment to their shopping cart that they never would have thought about without the added carrying capacity of the bicycle carts. Tyler found four bicycle locks which they could use to lock all of their tires to the bikes for the night, which would help to avoid the theft of their gear. He also added a set of medium-duty bolt cutters so they could cut locks if they needed to. Two smaller backpacks, two pistol holsters, several coiled lengths of rope, four tarps, a camouflaged rain coat for each of them, two tire pumps, more spray paint, padlocks with matching keys for the trailers, two collapsible fishing poles with some lures, a shotgun that promptly got the barrel sawn off with a hacksaw and then filed down, and lots of ammunition rounded out their shopping list in the sporting goods section.

They'd done a good job of getting the essentials in the camping section of the first store that they'd visited, so they didn't need much more. However, both men looked wistfully at the hunting bows. The silence that they offered would be nearly unbeatable, too bad neither of them had ever learned to shoot. Aeric had tried several times as a kid in high school gym class. The bowstring had constantly hit his forearm and he didn't like it, so he stopped taking the class. His coach tried to get him to use a forearm guard, but he'd already decided to quit so it hadn't made any difference. Nothing could be done about it now.

They picked up a can opener on the way towards the food section and once again, the smell of rotting vegetables and soured dairy products assailed them. Aeric opened his respirator mask and put it on. Amazingly, the smell almost disappeared completely behind the mask. He gave Tyler a thumbs up and his friend followed suit.

Behind the masks, the world seemed distant, like they were insulated from the dangers it posed. Their ears were still uncovered, so hearing was unimpeded, but the face shield would keep the floating ash—likely radioactive—away from their eyes and help to keep them from breathing it in. Once they bundled back up in some clothing, they'd be able to keep their skin mostly covered and they should be fairly well insulated against the worst of the radiation particles as long as there weren't any more missiles.

"I think we'll be good to go now," Aeric said. His voice sounded detached from his body. It was a strange sensation because he heard how he normally sounded in his head, while simultaneously hearing the muffled words from behind the mask.

"You sound funny," Tyler laughed.

"So do you!" he responded and then examined the signs hanging above the grocery aisles. "Ok, canned goods are this way."

"Got it, let's get as much of the stuff as we can fit in the carts and then get a few changes of clothes, and then we'll get out of here."

"Aren't the clothes gonna have radiation on them too?" Aeric asked. He was fine with the jackets and gloves that they'd picked up, but those weren't next to his skin. Did the fabric retain the radiation that had killed these people?

"I don't know," Tyler admitted. "The killing radiation that a nuke emits immediately has a half-life of a few seconds. The other types of radiation that stick around for a long time are distributed through fallout. Since we're inside a sealed building, there shouldn't be any of that other type of radiation."

Aeric regarded his friend. The guy had obviously watched way too much television. "Okay, we can pick up some clothes for temporary use and then go to a clothing store somewhere down the road. A place that only sells clothes will probably not be as dangerous as a grocery store."

"Yeah, okay. Food first, then the clothes?" Tyler asked. Aeric nodded in agreement and they turned down the canned goods aisle.

They picked out canned vegetables, canned meats and more of the canned pastas that they'd grown sick of. As long as they wiped the lids to ensure no accidental radiation transfer, they would be fine with the contents of the cans. They piled the carts full of more canned goods than they thought they could eat in several months, but they both knew that the future was uncertain and that they needed to take advantage of the empty store. Thankfully, the water filters that they'd picked up in Corsicana made it so they didn't have to pile the carts with heavy cases of water.

Finally, they grabbed some changes of clothing, focusing where they could on fabrics that were sealed or covered in plastic. When they were done, the carts easily weighed the same as each of them, essentially doubling the weight that they'd be forced to carry on the bikes. The extra weight was worth it, though, to avoid the constant need to raid grocery stores for supplies. The less interaction that they had with people in the near future, the better off they'd be.

A few quick adjustments of some nuts and bolts on their bikes and they had the carts firmly attached. Aeric decided to keep the few tools that they'd used for the job so they could disconnect the trailers if they needed to. He also thought they needed some type of quick disconnect system so they could ditch the carts in a hurry, but he was stumped as to how to do it. They had a couple of weeks to think about it as they rode, so maybe something would come to him on the road.

They hopped on their bikes and began to pedal. It was tough to get the heavy contraption moving initially, but once it was rolling, it wasn't too much of an effort on the flat surface of the parking lot. Aeric knew that when they made it to the mountains, it would be a different story and the simple mountain bikes that they rode would struggle to pull all that weight. He thought they'd likely end up pushing the bikes on the long, curving uphill slopes and riding them down the backsides into the valleys.

Looking back on it, he'd been foolish to believe that they could make it to Missouri and back in two days when he left Veronica's apartment. Of course, they had no way to know that there would be a nuclear war that fried all of the electronics across America, but he should have thought about the likely shortage of fuel. So much had happened in only a week since he'd left her that he felt like he'd been a child back then.

He didn't feel like he was a hardened killer, but he hadn't hesitated to shoot those men in Corsicana, and he sure as hell would have fought with Tim to make it around Tyler instead of being turned away. He'd even killed Kami, but that was an act of mercy, not one of anger, he told himself. Aeric hoped that he hadn't gone too far down the path towards chaos to return. Surely the madness would cease and then the world would need people who weren't completely consumed by it to help rebuild society

*****

"Stop!" she screamed to her driver as their Humvee topped the hill and almost slammed into a car resting on its roof sideways across the highway. Lieutenant Lorelei Griffith stared in shock at the devastation that used to be her home. Her platoon was still fifteen miles from the Killeen/Fort Hood area, but she knew that there was nothing left of her base except for the swirls of ash that obscured her view into the valley below.

Her little convoy of vehicles skidded to a halt behind her and one by one, her soldiers began to step out of their vehicles to see the wreckage for themselves. They were still too far away to tell for certain, but she knew. She knew that her husband was dead, her neighbors and their families were gone—vaporized in an instant. She'd prepared herself for it while they sat on that goddamned checkpoint, but seeing it with her own eyes was like some cosmic asshole was tearing the bandages off of her emotional wounds and she began crying again.

The general lay of the land had the installation in a very large bowl, which must have stopped the worst of the bomb's blast pressure from making it far. She thought back to the mandatory classes that she'd been subjected to in ROTC back at Wisconsin University and decided that the base must have been hit with a small-yield ground burst. It would have wiped out everything in the immediate area of the impact, but the ground burst meant that the terrain had a much greater effect on how far the damage spread.

Her platoon, 1st Platoon, Bravo Company from the 115th Brigade Support Battalion, had sat at the checkpoint for more than a week after the one-day war that had killed millions, possibly billions, before she decided that they'd followed orders long enough and packed up the checkpoint. They'd only seen but a few people since the war, and no military traffic whatsoever on the interstate, so they'd completed their mission.

During the week, her communications sergeant was able to determine the reason that their hardened military radios still worked, but weren't able to communicate with anyone. The explosions had knocked out all the communications relays in the area, so they couldn't talk beyond their line of sight—which basically meant that all they could do was talk to each other and didn't have any further instructions than what she'd been given almost a month before by her commander.

When she made the call to leave the checkpoint that morning, it had been difficult for her. The platoon still had enough food and water on hand that they could have stayed for another week or longer if they rationed their supplies properly. She'd gathered her soldiers together and laid out the situation. She didn't think that their higher headquarters even existed anymore and most of the troops had agreed with her. She wasn't the only one with family at Fort Hood that had been wondering what happened to them.

The trip back would have taken about three hours on a good day, but they'd been on the road the entire day. They were forced to travel back roads to avoid the massive pileups on the larger highways and were flagged down multiple times by people asking them if they were part of the government response to provide relief. Each time, she'd had to break the news that as far as she knew, there wasn't a larger government response being organized. Of course, she had to caveat her answers each time with the fact that she didn't know anything about what had happened beyond the first several detonations. Each of those had been a singularly devastating event, combined, they were catastrophic.

What really tore at her soul was the way the population looked at her. At first, she was heralded as a savior of some type, the harbinger of salvation. Then, when they discovered that she was just as in the dark about events as they were, the men and women would stare daggers at her. On one occasion, they'd even been shot at after it was discovered that they weren't there to provide relief.

Lorelei pulled her protective mask away from her face and wiped the tears from her cheeks. It wouldn't do for the troops to see her crying, regardless of her personal feelings of sadness and loss about her husband. She tried the radio uselessly for a minute, more a show for the men and women gathered around her truck than in the actual hope that they'd find anyone. After a few unsuccessful tries on multiple emergency radio frequencies and then with the radio scanning across all frequencies, she sighed and opened the heavy door on her armored Humvee. It was time to face her platoon and decide what they were going to do.

"Alright, Bulldogs, gather round," she called out. Her platoon sergeant shouted out her orders so everyone could hear. She waited while everyone except two men from the rear truck who were on security formed a semicircle around the hood of her Humvee.

"It's as bad as we thought it would be," she started. "We figured that there wouldn't be much left of the base since we hadn't heard anything from them. Well, it looks like there's *nothing* left.

"I know that about half of us had families either on post or in the community, but there's no way—" She took a ragged breath to steady herself before continuing. "There's no way that they survived...that."

Lieutenant Griffith gestured weakly over her shoulder towards the bowl below them. "It looks like Fort Hood got hit with a ground burst nuke, which means all of this shit in the air is probably radioactive, so keep your gear on."

One of her soldiers made an exaggerated point of removing his mask and tossing it to the side. Private Foster's face was beet red from crying. "Foster, put your mask back on, didn't I just say that this stuff was toxic?"

"No, ma'am," he said. "My wife and kid were down there. If they're dead, then I don't care if I live or die."

"Foster, put your damn mask back on. Committing suicide won't honor their memories," the platoon sergeant, Staff Sergeant Jimenez, ordered.

"Maybe you don't think so, Sergeant, but I do. I'm not putting that mask back on."

Lorelei waved her hand at her platoon sergeant and said, "It's fine. If he wants to develop cancer and die a horribly painful death in a few weeks, let him. We need to figure out what we're doing."

Sergeant Jimenez looked at the thirty soldiers assembled and then said, "I think we should drive as far into the wreckage looking for survivors as we can, ma'am. It will help the platoon feel like we did everything that we could. If we find anyone, we take them with us—wherever we're going—and if we don't find anyone, then be thankful that you weren't one of the casualties in the blast."

"I read a lot, Sergeant, I think the lucky ones were the people who died right away," Sergeant Cantrell stated.

"Fuck you, Cantrell! That was my family down there," Foster shouted.

"What the fuck did you just say to me, Private?" Cantrell yelled back.

"At ease, both of you!" Sergeant Jimenez thundered. "Tensions are high, I get it. We all lost friends and family, if not here at Hood, then probably back home as well. There ain't shit that we can do about it right now, so shut your damned mouths."

The lieutenant waited a moment before speaking, "I'm sorry, guys. Like Sergeant Jimenez said, we all lost loved ones, but we're soldiers and we have to keep moving. I've been told about another community that might need our help. We can travel there after we search the wreckage."

"Oh, not that bullshit those two were trying to sell you a week ago," Cantrell moaned.

"Sergeant Cantrell, I swear to God, I will beat your ass in front of everyone if you don't shut your damned pie hole," Sergeant Jimenez threatened. "Let the lieutenant speak."

"Thank you, Sergeant," Lorelei replied. "Yeah, it's the same place. San Angelo is a pretty small city with a very small Air Force base right next to it where they train airmen on intelligence gathering. They may have information about what the status of the nation is. Hell, if nothing else, it's our duty to try and report to another military command."

"How do we know that they didn't get nuked too?" one of her female soldiers asked.

"We don't. I hope that it's small enough to have escaped targeting. Fort Hood was the home to America's largest armored force, so it makes sense that it was targeted, but that little Air Force base? I don't know. The only thing we can do is go there and see."

There was some grumbling from the group, but overall, the chain of command still held firm and they mounted up in their trucks to go search for survivors before traveling further west. The drive would be slow through the valley since the devastation was complete.

They couldn't make it any closer than Harker Heights before the roadways became too clogged with debris and wreckage. The platoon split up—three trucks in each group—and went cross country both north and south of the main highway, but both returned quickly when they couldn't go any further. They backtracked as a group and tried several other roads to get closer to the base, but everything was hopelessly blocked.

Their search for survivors, even on the perimeter of the devastation, proved to be useless. They saw lots of bodies. Some of them crushed, twisted and generally mangled beyond belief, all of them were burned from the massive fireball that must have spread outwards from the blast. After several hours of witnessing the carnage, Lieutenant Griffith finally called off the search and directed the platoon to head back east so they could work their way around the blast zone outside of the valley.

The platoon suffered its first casualty as Private Foster abandoned his truck and ran westward into the wreckage to search for his family. They tried to call him back, but he was gone and Lorelei had to make the hard decision to leave him so they could move out of what was surely a heavily contaminated area.

It was a tough choice to abandon the disturbed soldier, one that made her sick to her stomach. It was a vital decision, though. She wanted her troops to know that the safety of the entire platoon was more important to her than one individual. It was a lesson that she would rely on in the coming days as the discipline in her platoon threatened to tear the organization apart in the wasteland.

EIGHT

The miles disappeared rapidly on their first travel day after they made camp a few miles from the Red River Army Depot. Southeastern Arkansas along Highway 41 was mostly flat, resembling its southern neighbor until they reached the town of De Queen and got onto Highway 71 north. The terrain began to change slowly. The long, gently-rising foothills told them that they'd soon be in the mountains.

De Queen was small, only about a mile across in the main section of the town. Highway 71 took them through the smaller eastern side of town, but Aeric could feel the eyes of the survivors in town watching him. The streets were vacant and silent, there weren't even any dogs barking as they rode by the abandoned buildings. When they passed a large construction supply store, all hell broke loose as people started shooting at them.

They put their heads down and pedaled as fast as they could. They only had to sprint for a block before buildings obscured them from the view of those shooting at them from the construction building. Thankfully, the people hadn't given chase and they continued on unmolested through the quiet town.

Running quickly through an ambush was a technique that Aeric's uncle had told him that they used in Iraq and Afghanistan when they got hit by an IED or ambushed. Leaving the area in a hurry made the most sense instead of trying to stop, seek cover and engaging in a pitched gun battle with people who knew the local area better than you did. Plus, they could have booby trapped the sides of the road, so it was just best to high-tail it out of the area.

An hour's ride past town, they found an old forest road off of Highway 71 and made camp in the tree line. They marveled that neither of them had been hit. The people at the construction yard must have been interested in scaring them off rather than actually causing any damage, otherwise they would have been riddled with bullet holes at that close distance.

After De Queen, they decided that it was best to keep a watch at night instead of both sleeping at the same time. It was inconvenient, but a necessary requirement after their long days of riding. They could always rest longer and leave an hour later each morning since they weren't on anyone's timeline other than their own. Arriving in Springfield a few hours later likely wouldn't make any difference.

The terrain became rougher with each mile they traveled past De Queen. The inclines were just shallow enough to keep the men from walking their bicycles, but the change in elevation was enough to leave them heaving for breath by the end of each stretch. The painters' masks didn't help either. They'd considered them a godsend when they found them. Full face shield, double filters, easy to don and doff. Now they hated them. The filters that blocked out the harmful ash—whether radioactive or not—also made it difficult to breathe and it was especially difficult to take deep breaths when they exerted themselves on the uphill climbs.

Over the next few days, their daily mileage decreased, but they still made much better time than they would have without the bicycles. They'd done a decent job of avoiding towns until they came to Mena. They spent a full thirty minutes pouring over their well-worn road atlas to see if they could skirt the city. Nothing presented itself that didn't involve either miles of backtracking or routing them through potentially bigger cities, so they decided to follow the highway through town.

Mena wasn't a large city, maybe four miles across with a prewar population of about six thousand people. Their route took them directly through the heart of town with buildings pressed up close alongside the road. De Queen had been a larger city than Mena, but they'd been able to avoid the majority of the town's structures and population by staying on the highway. After the near disaster there, they weren't excited about the prospect of going into the city during the daytime.

They timed it so they'd break camp and travel through town at first light in order to try to avoid most of the residents. Their hope was that people would be slow getting around in the mornings without the use of alarm clocks. Aeric had the final watch that night and spent his time filling pockets with ammunition and rechecking bolts and straps on the two pull-behind carts. When he thought the dawn was about fifteen minutes away, he woke Tyler and they took down the tent.

Once the tent was tied to the top of Tyler's cart, Aeric looked at his friend and asked, "Are you ready for this, bro?"

Tyler pulled the pistol from the shoulder harness that he'd picked up at the Walmart in New Boston and pulled the slide back slightly to ensure that a round was in the chamber. Then he slid it back home in the nylon pocket and snapped the strap across it. "Yeah. Let's do this."

Aeric gripped the big man's hand and shook it firmly. He wanted to say something about Tyler's steadfast loyalty and how the man didn't need to follow him on his quest to find his parents, but the words wouldn't come and seemed much to fatalistic.

Instead, he nodded his head, dipping his chin sharply and then got on his bike. Maybe one day Aeric would be able to tell Tyler how much his companionship meant to him.

They pedaled out from their campsite, easing the bikes with their carts onto the pavement. Within minutes, they passed a sign telling them that they were entering the city limits of Mena. They increased their pace to go faster than they normally would have, but not at such a breakneck pace that they couldn't stop if they had to.

They began to head steadily uphill once again, minor buildings passed by alongside the road with long-abandoned cars in the parking lots. The first of the detonations had happened sometime in the late morning, so it made sense that there'd been cars already at the various businesses after they'd opened. Their pace slowed considerably as they pedaled hard against the weight of their overloaded carts and Aeric's sense of dread that something would happen increased.

Eventually, they made the top of the rise and their bikes began to pick up speed as the road stretched before them at a downward angle. They had to use their brakes liberally to veer around cars that had stalled in the road and been left for eternity where they'd died. They made extremely good time on the downhill and the buildings thinned out, causing them to believe that they'd made it through the city unscathed.

By the time the road had leveled out again, they realized that they weren't out of town yet as another Walmart loomed off the road to the left and a squat, ugly strip mall sat on the right side. Cars had been pushed across the entrances and exits of the

Walmart parking lot along the highway, effectively ringing the front of the building in steel.

White bed sheets were spread across the sides of the cars every few feet. They'd been spray painted with the words, "**GO AWAY!**" and phrases like, "**OUR SUPPLIES, YOU WILL BE SHOT!**" It was more than enough to cause Aeric to nearly panic at the thought of being stuck out in the open once again.

Then his worst fears were realized as the pavement three feet in front of his lead tire splintered upwards and the distinctive *ping* of a round ricocheting echoed into the stillness of the early morning. "Go! Go! Go!" he shouted as he buried the pedals.

More rounds hit close to them, carving long, straight divots from the pavement perpendicular to the Walmart. The thousand feet of highway along the front of the store where they could be seen was the most scared that Aeric had been in a while, even more so than when he and Tyler had snuck out of Veronica's apartment to kill the band of thugs in the parking lot.

When they finally cleared the line of sight, they passed another construction supply center on the left and his sphincter tightened once again. "Keep going!" he gasped as he tried to suck in air through the respirator's thick filters and continued the fast pace to get out of town as quickly as possible.

Soon, they came to the long, northward curve in the road that Aeric knew from their map recon to be the actual end of the town. He allowed himself to slow the bicycle down to his steady and sustainable pace while his heart hammered in his ears, threatening to pound his brain into mush.

They passed a few small houses and some type of medical park and finally Tyler said, "I could hear them. Those assholes were laughing at us."

Aeric glanced over at his friend. "Are you serious?"

"Yeah, they were laughing like hyenas. I don't think they were actually trying to kill us. They could have nailed us with the rifles they were using. I think they were just trying to have fun with us and fuck with our heads."

The thought of a bunch of drunk rednecks taking pot shots at them from the roof of the building infuriated him. What was the point of shooting at people? What purpose could it possibly serve other than pissing people off and starting a war? He certainly was mad enough to turn around and sneak up on them from the side. They could kill them all before they even knew that they'd been duped.

"Not worth it, man."

"Huh?" Aeric asked.

"I can tell what you're thinking. It's not worth it. Let's just get away from this place and leave them behind. They did their job of making us go away, we survived. It's a win-win and we should count our blessings that nobody was hurt—on our side or theirs."

He took a moment to regain his composure and let his blood pressure drop while he pedaled slowly. "Okay, you're right. I guess I just can't get used to the messed up world that we're living in."

"It *is* a fucked up situation, isn't it?"

Aeric decided that if they weren't going back, then he didn't want to talk about it anymore. "What's our next turn?"

"Hell, we've got thirty or forty miles to go," Tyler replied. He stuck his hand inside the flap of his jacket and pulled out the

Arkansas map that he'd folded to their little area so he could look at it while they rode. "We probably won't make it today, looks like the terrain begins to get really mountainous soon."

"Tell me about it," Aeric muttered as the peaks of the Ouachita Mountains loomed ahead.

"Actually," Tyler muttered as he slowed his pedaling to a crawl and brought the map up close to his face. "Okay, I was wrong, we're gonna turn off of Two Seventy-One in about, what, twelve miles? We'll turn left onto Seventy-One towards Fort Smith and then we'll turn right on Two Fifty. That will take us as far as my map fold can show without stopping."

"So we've got a ways to go still, right?"

Tyler chuckled, "Yeah, think of it as Coach Harris' rapid weight loss plan."

Thinking about their baseball coach, who was likely deceased now, made him sad. There was a possibility that he was still alive though, since he lived in Austin and besides the gang violence, the city had survived relatively unscathed. It probably wouldn't stay that way, though. There were too many people and not enough food to go around. It had been over a week, so even the most timid residents were probably fighting for resources to keep their families safe and fed.

The line of thinking about the state of affairs in Austin made him wonder about Veronica. Was she alright? When they left, she had enough food and liquids to last her several weeks if she rationed her supplies like he'd recommended. Had her father come to the city from San Angelo to take her back home like she was convinced that he would? Obviously, he wouldn't know and he longed for the capability to just pick up a phone and call. That would have made everything so much simpler.

Of course, that also brought up the issue with San Angelo. Veronica had made it seem like the perfect place and a location that they'd be able to possibly go to for safety as time wore on, but if she was gone and didn't vouch for them, would they be turned away? Like the setup in Tyler, if San Angelo was actually secured, they'd likely have guards far from the town to keep the vagrants away.

Vagrant. A wanderer. Was that what they'd become? The two of them were on a fools' errand across the lower half of the country to ensure that his parents were alright. What did he expect after that? He didn't know if his parents would be willing to leave their home to make the return trip with him and he sure as hell didn't plan on staying in Missouri with all the nuclear winter stuff that Tyler talked about.

He sure as hell didn't have all the answers—not *any* of them, actually. What he did have was a bicycle and cart, a good companion and a long way to travel, so for now, he would have to be content with making it through each day, and deal with events as they came.

*****

The days flew by as they struggled up the rough Ouachita Mountains and then once they were past those, the Ozark Mountain Range loomed ahead. Battling the mountains took a constant physical toll on their bodies. The uphill stretches were brutal and they often had to push their bikes until the crest in the road. The downhill jaunts were terrifying as the overloaded carts threatened to tip over at the speeds that they traveled.

Aeric was concerned about the brakes, they'd been abused on the mountain roads and he wasn't sure that they had enough padding left to be effective. The combined weight of each man and his cart were easily pushing five hundred pounds. The brands of bike that they sold at the Walmart where Tyler had picked them up were never designed for that kind of weight or sustained use. They needed to switch out the bikes with newer ones and they got their opportunity in Eureka Springs.

The northern Arkansas tourist town of Eureka Springs was famous for the quaint Victorian style houses that had been built there in the 1800's. The entire town had been listed on the National Register of Historic Places before the war. Everywhere they looked as they topped the final hill that led down to the city had an older home or brick business. Capping it all off was a massive white hotel on the top of a hill overlooking the city below. It was the picture-perfect postcard town and Aeric could imagine that the city was experiencing its first snowfall as they gazed down instead of the ash that drifted from the sky.

It was easy decide that the city was harmless as they looked down on it from the ridgeline. Maybe it was the way it reminded them of what an older American town was supposed to look like, a glimpse into the past before all the modern inconveniences that were now useless pieces of junk. The Victorian village set against the brilliantly colored fall leaves was breathtaking.

They were ready for a break. They'd been relatively alone for over two weeks and most everyone that they'd ran across had tried to kill them. *Surely not everyone in the world was crazy, right?* Aeric hoped. Hell, it might have simply been the fact that the town had been spared the massive amounts of ash that covered most everywhere else that they'd been.

Whatever the reason, they pushed off the hilltop and set out on the winding road down to the town, intent on actually interacting with the residents of Eureka Springs. When they reached the city limits, there weren't any sentinels guarding the town or groups of people staring at them with hatred. Instead, they were greeted warmly by a widely-varied group of people. The town had been in a seasonal lull when the nukes went off, so most of the people were full-time residents. Some of them were obviously tourists who'd gotten stuck in the town and weren't able to get out, but they made it clear that everyone would be welcome.

Regardless of whether they were permanent residents or recent transplants, everyone was hungry for news of the outside world. According to the group assembled, no one had been through since the war and they had no information about what was going on. Unfortunately, Aeric and Tyler could only relate their own firsthand experiences and didn't have much else to tell the residents of Eureka Springs about the global scope, beyond what Lieutenant Griffith had said.

Even without the details that they'd hoped for, the people were grateful to learn that there were other survivors out there besides the small communities spread throughout the mountains and at least they had a little bit more information to chew on. They threw a small party in Aeric and Tyler's honor and several of the local street musicians played on their banjos and guitars. There was even an accordion and one guy had bagpipes. The music sounded strange and foreign to the two men who'd traveled in silence for so long.

At the end of the night, they were given a free room in the world famous 1886 Crescent Hotel, which, like the rest of the town, was known for its Victorian styling and for being one of the most haunted locations in America. Despite the lack of power or fresh supplies, and their total isolation, the hotel was still an amazing sight. They had a roaring fire in the lobby's fireplace that the few guests who'd become stranded huddled around to talk in the evening. Both Aeric and Tyler were hesitant to stay in the supposedly haunted hotel, especially after some of the guests regaled them with tales of what they'd seen since they'd been stuck there.

Eventually, the need for sleep overcame their reservations about staying overnight in the haunted building, so with the assistance of the hotel bellman's cart, they unpacked the bicycle carts into their room and locked up the bikes for the night. They heard all sorts of noises throughout the night, but everything could be explained away by a skeptic—or by two travelers who didn't want to be scared shitless—and they convinced themselves that the strange shadows that they saw and the scratching on the ceiling were really just echoes of the creaking trees outside as the moon shown through the clouds of ash.

In the morning, they traded their bikes with the worn out brakes and an entire carton of cigarettes for newer bikes from one of the defunct tourist shops in town. The residents saw them off with a meal of freshly cooked eggs and bread. They wished everyone the best of luck, knowing that they'd likely never see any of them ever again.

As they left town, they were surprised to see a giant white statue of Jesus with his arms outstretched on a hilltop to the east.

They had a long theological discussion about the nature of the war and if it was the proclaimed end of times like in the Christian Bible. Aeric had been raised Catholic and had very little understanding about the Book of Revelation, but Tyler had been dragged to church every Sunday with a fire and brimstone Baptist congregation, and had heard the story multiple times over the years.

Their current situation certainly seemed like it was following the tale of the Four Horsemen of the Apocalypse. The first of the horsemen in the story rides the White Horse and he's known as Conquest, or Pestilence, depending on which interpretation one followed. Tyler had been thinking a lot about it during their journey and his interpretation was that the "pestilence" was actually the spread of the disease of terrorism. The actions of the terrorists which had led to this moment certainly seemed to infect everyone like disease would. The people had responded by throwing the government's inability to stop the terrorists back in their faces, which led to further tightening of security and harsher penalties for everyone.

That infection over time had given birth to the Red Horseman, War. Tyler wasn't aware of any other interpretations for what this rider was supposed to represent. The Vultures had followed quickly on the heels of the riots, police state actions and social reforms, which allowed their group to believe that initiating a global nuclear war was an acceptable thing to do. The belief that the war was the end of things couldn't be farther from the truth.

Next came the Black Horse, Famine. In the Bible, the rider brought with him the scales that indicated how food would be weighed in times of famine. One of the thoughts about what this meant was that the rider also judged the rich versus the poor, since historically the rich would be fine while the poor and destitute of the world were the ones who suffered. The passage mentions how luxury products would continue to be produced while a simple thing like food for the poor was neglected. It was easy for them to see how they were entering a time of famine and lack of resources as the city dwellers that couldn't produce their own food would likely begin to starve if they didn't begin growing their own produce.

Finally, the Pale Horse of Death closed out the story. Simply put, if you didn't die in the war or of starvation, then Death would wipe you out anyways. This notion is where Aeric and Tyler had their first disagreement.

"So why are we struggling to survive if we're going to be killed anyways?" Aeric asked.

Tyler breathed roughly through his mask. He'd been doing most of the talking about the Horsemen and needed some extra oxygen. "Because we have to. If we give up, then we lose all chance of making it to Heaven."

"Are you kidding me, bro?" Aeric asked incredulously. "Do you really think that there's a Heaven after all of this?"

"Everything about me originates in some form from how I was raised. I was taught to believe that there was a Heaven and a Hell, and that the Devil was real and he wanted your soul."

"But how can you say that any of it is accurate when Christianity itself disagrees with your sexuality, something that you have no control over?"

"Christianity doesn't believe that homosexuals are evil, it doesn't say that in the Bible. People's different interpretations of

Christianity say that it is. But you're right, am I supposed to go to Hell for the way I was born? That's not what I believe and I don't think God punishes people for being gay. It's just the way I am."

Aeric stopped pedaling and let his bike slow to a halt. He wasn't sure how the conversation had devolved from the Four Horsemen to the Church's opinions on sexual orientation, but it was on his friend's mind, so he was willing to keep on talking about it. "I think that once people's opinions get involved, things are automatically going to be screwed up. I agree. There's no way that God would abandon you for being gay after He made you that way."

"Thanks, man. I'm just… Ah, who the hell am I kidding? Everyone that said shit to me when I was growing up is dead anyways. They told me that I had to repress my feelings and marry a woman if I wanted to go to Heaven. I wonder if that's where those bigots are now."

So that's what it was about, Aeric thought. Tyler felt guilty for not being home with his family when they died. "You don't know that, they might have—"

"Nah, man. Don't try to make me feel some type of hope. Do you know how many nuclear missile sites are in Nebraska?"

"Well, no," Aeric responded truthfully.

"Hundreds. Yeah, sure, the enemy targeted the bigger cities across America, but they also targeted those missile silos. Those things were all over the place around Omaha. There's nothing left of my home, my parents or *any* of my family. I'm the last of the Nordgrens, man."

"Shit, I hadn't even thought about that. I mean, I'd wondered about why we weren't going to try to find your family like we're going to Missouri, but I really thought that you'd decide to continue on to Nebraska once we were there."

"There's nothing left to go to. You're the closest thing to family that I have left."

Aeric was touched by the big man's sentiment. "You're like a brother to me, too, Ty."

"Thanks, man. I appreciate that." He started pedaling his bike and Aeric leaned against the handlebars to get his moving as well. From behind, he heard Tyler mutter something about the big, stupid statue.

*****

"I hate that building. It's useless, ugly and a reminder of the old world's consumerist greed. They thought all that glass was beautiful, reflecting the sun and throwing it back in God's face. I want it gone, take it down."

"Yes, sir," Greg said and turned to relay the orders to his troops who were waiting for their next mission since they'd recently invaded a few of the larger apartment complexes to gather the residents' food supplies. Justin needed the population entirely dependent upon the Vultures in order to maintain control. They needed to learn of their leader's benevolence, but first, he had to set the conditions.

Justin smiled as he watched the man go. Captain Greg Sanders had been on security duty along Interstate 35 with the mission of keeping it clear for military use when the war happened and Fort Hood was wiped off the map. Justin had seen the opportunity and seized upon it. He offered to allow Captain Sanders to keep his command and become the defender of Austin with all the benefits associated with being a member of the Vultures. Now, he was one of Justin's most trusted advisors.

With the Army company's leadership in his pocket, the rest of Captain Sanders' men had quickly followed suit. Then it had been a simple matter of purifying the minorities from the organization, and now Justin had an entire company of tanks and a platoon of self-propelled artillery at his command.

He'd used his soldiers to assist the police who remained alive to wipe out the Latino gangs, earning him their adoration and ultimately their own vows of service to the Vultures. It was a simple matter to tell the city's leadership that he was officially in charge. Once they realized that they'd been effectively isolated by the nuclear blasts and that he had the loyalty of the police force, they handed over responsibility *willingly*. The Vultures took the former Texas governor hostage and set up shop in the capitol building.

He smiled again. His kingdom was expanding and besides the few military vehicles that remained, the Reset had wiped out all of the electronics. The Cleanse was in full effect and soon everything would be complete. Of course, there had been a slight alteration to his plans as more than half of the hackers in the Vultures had tried to leave the organization after the EMPs. They helped to orchestrate the Reset, but they'd thought that their own computer systems would be safe from the purge. They were useless social shut-ins anyways.

He'd orchestrated public executions of some of his closest friends and that brought the others in line. As an added bonus, it increased his following amongst the local population. In conjunction with seizing the population's food supplies, when they learned that he had multiple warehouses hidden throughout the countryside full of food, his position of power in the region was solidified.

With the adoring support of the population, he could afford to do the little things that he wanted to do, like bring down that glass monstrosity that stretched its way towards the heavens. Everything was going perfectly for him. He leaned back and rubbed his fingers across his nipples, the feeling of power was arousing. Maybe he'd order Cassandra to have sex with him again. The sexual release was the only way to keep from going mad with power. He knew that if he went crazy, the other Vultures would descend upon him like— well, like vultures.

He'd set up his headquarters in the former Texas State Capitol Building. Its palatial feel suited him well and he'd even gone so far as to set up the House Chamber on the second floor as his own throne room, where he held public court. He kept the entire third floor to himself so he could overlook the proceedings on the second floor from the galleries and used the third floor's north wing as his bedchamber. The Vulture's *palace* had a very medieval feel to it that appealed to him. It helped to solidify in the minds of the people that the Vultures had the real power in the city.

He shook slightly with the need for the release, but he had some business to attend to first, which actually added to his own sexual satisfaction. "Bring me Harris," he bellowed into the hall's openness. The courtiers in the audience clapped approvingly. They loved to watch him abuse the old man who'd ruined his life. He smiled and waved for the crowd, his eyes lighting on one particular beauty. Justin beckoned her forward, maybe she could take Cassandra's place next.

The clinking of chains soon told him that his second favorite pastime was arriving. He excused the beautiful woman, asking her to go to his bedchamber and wait for him while he dealt with Colonel John Harris.

"How are we feeling today, Colonel?"

"Fuck you," the naked man managed to say. His bottom lip quivered slightly, whether from cold or from fear, Justin couldn't tell. It didn't matter.

"Ah, I'm sorry, my dance card is full. I've already arranged that meeting with the lovely Annie later this evening." He paused as the crowd applauded his wit. "You're looking much healthier, Colonel. I'd say you've lost at least, what, ten pounds? Maybe a little more."

"Not eating for a week will do that to you, bastard."

"True. But I wouldn't want my mentor to die, so from here on out, you'll be given food and water—*uncontaminated* water." He looked up to the courtiers assembled and said, "See, ladies and gentlemen, I am compassionate towards my guests. This man ruined my life before the Reset, but I will not kill him and hang his head from the flagpole as he deserves. No, I will care for him, feed him, clothe him…and make him regret ever crossing the Vultures!"

The crowd went wild. They shook guns and knives in the air, chanting unintelligibly about whatever the hell they'd decided was their mantra of the day. Justin didn't bother to learn them since they changed almost as often as he fucked one of the women in the crowd. Once the official chant was decided upon by the masses, then he'd take the time to learn it.

"Okay. First things first, Colonel. My friends demand a little torture each day. Just a little bit," he held up his thumb and forefinger inches away from the colonel's face. "Maybe a fingernail, possibly an entire toe—you'll never miss your pinkie toe, it's actually kind of useless. Not like your pinkie finger, which is surprisingly important.

"Did you know that there was a book over at the LBJ Library that had pictures and text about all the forms of medieval torture? I made sure to save that book before I burned that place down. Isn't that wonderful? It's more than three hundred pages long. I think we can make it all the way through each and every one of them together. In fact, I've already got my engineers building several of the non-lethal machines. Ever heard of the rack, or the picquet? I'm so very excited, Colonel, I've been planning to spend this time together with you for as long as I can remember."

He grinned like the madman that many had claimed he was before he killed them. "So, what's it gonna be, Colonel, fingernail or toe? Ooh, maybe a nail through your penis?" he said excitedly.

The old man broke down to blubbering, but didn't give him an answer. He held up his hand to his ear in an exaggerated expression for the assembled crowd. "What was that? I couldn't quite hear you."

"I'm sorry! You did the right thing. I shouldn't have ruined your life."

"There you go! I forgive you. Wait," he thought about what the colonel had said and then about their exchange when he was captured. "Do you remember *why* my life was ruined by you?"

Panic flashed across the old man's face. "I kicked you out of the Army."

Justin rolled his hand for more. The prisoner looked him up and down and said, "You went AWOL and I kicked you out."

Justin's face contorted in anger. "You don't even know who I am, do you?"

"Justin," the old man replied.

He picked up his water bottle and threw it into the crowd. "I am the leader of the Vultures!" he screamed. "Does that help you figure it out yet?"

"The computer hackers?" the colonel asked, confusion clearly setting in on his face.

"That's how we started. But we've grown beyond that, so far beyond those early days. We are now an army of men and women, loyal to God, carrying out his wishes to purge the earth of humanity's petty squabbles and materialistic ways. We are the *future*!"

The crowd erupted in another cheer and he looked down on Harris. "I was your lead defensive computer systems operator at CyberCom. We defeated a major threat because I disobeyed your stupid orders and sought out the real attack while my team dealt with the diversion."

Realization dawned on his face. "Rustwood? Holy shit."

"Holy shit is right. I was set to promote to staff sergeant, but instead you busted me to E-4 for disobeying you and then got me reduced to E-1 for a bogus weapons charge and kicked me out. I spent years bouncing between menial jobs trying to recover from what you did to me. Years. Do you realize what that does to someone?

"No, I—"

"Well, I've had a lot of time to think about what I'd do to you, Colonel. Now that I have you, you will beg for death. You will cry out to your false gods for forgiveness and an end to your suffering.

But I will keep you healthy and won't allow your body to quit on me. Together, we will get those *years* back, my friend."

He glanced off to the side where his men stood and shouted. "Bring me the pliers!"

The crowd roared their approval at his decision. Finally, the talking was over, it was time for some action.

NINE

It took them another week to make it to Springfield. From a distance, it looked as if it had remained intact without taking too much damage, but they found out that the residents tore the city apart without any help from the nuclear missiles. The ash was much thicker here than it had been in the mountains, which was likely due to the obliteration of both Kansas City and St. Louis on either side of the state less than two hundred miles away. The destruction of Little Rock to the south had ensured that no matter which direction the wind blew, the ash would make its way to Springfield.

While the nukes hadn't hit the city, it hadn't been spared the effects of the EMP. Abandoned, useless vehicles filled Highway 65 and they were forced to dismount their bikes to walk around massive pile-ups at many points. Once, they had to roll vehicles off of a bridge in order to get around the choke point. That involved breaking a few windows and forcing the cars into neutral, then pushing them into the median. One of the newer trucks wouldn't go into gear without the keys, so they had to work around that newly-minted permanent addition to the bridge by moving several more cars than they'd planned, finally clearing the span after several hours.

Ultimately, they made it to Aeric's hometown and then to the street where he'd grown up. He was shocked at the transformation of the city. It had only been four or five weeks since the nukes went off, but people were already starving to death. Residents called after them as they rode by, offering to sell them anything they wanted in exchange for food. Women and girls—even a few men—

huddled in heavy coats offered their services for bread or canned goods. It was evident that Springfield had been hit hard by its lack of preparedness. They were flashed on multiple occasions by the prostitutes, filling Aeric's mind with promises of ecstasy in exchange for a simple can of soup.

Neither of them wanted to contemplate what it would be like farther along in the winter, but the prospect was grim. Before the war, his hometown had a population of more than three hundred thousand and the fact that they were isolated from the blasts meant that most of those people likely survived at first. All of those survivors had quickly depleted the food supply and now they were doing whatever they could to stay alive for one more day. What surprised him the most was their chance meeting with his ex-girlfriend, Kate.

They'd become relatively immune to the constant barrage of humanity begging for mercy on their long trip to the heart of the city where his family lived. When they turned onto his street, they only saw one person on the lonely street standing in the cold, huddled against the windblown ash. Nichols Street was quiet, almost serene in comparison to the busier parts of the city that they'd rode through to get there. Gunshots and wails of anguish still echoed in the background, but his street, the avenue where he'd learned how to ride a bike, played roller hockey with the neighborhood kids and walked down every day on his way to school, was quiet. He couldn't tell much about the person as they walked near them other than it was a woman, buried under a layer of blankets against the cold.

They pedaled past her, trying to avoid catching her attention, but she yelled for them to stop. "Please, mister! I'll let both of you fuck me if you have any food. My family is starving to death!"

Aeric thought he recognized the voice, so he slowed down and glanced over. She saw him look and opened her coverings to reveal shriveling breasts and a stomach that was beginning to protrude slightly, either from pregnancy or starvation. He'd seen those breasts many times throughout high school and they'd always seemed so firm and well placed, now they were sunken inwards and at an odd angle. Her body was literally eating itself.

Aeric squeezed his brakes and stopped. She misinterpreted his move and started over towards him, swaying her hips seductively. "Katie?"

She stopped and looked him over. Kate took in his size and she tried to see his face through the mask, which was now covered with a short, curly beard. Her eyes widened in recognition and she pulled her blankets closed in embarrassment. "Aeric? Is that you?"

He put the kickstand down on his bike and dismounted. Out of the corner of his eye, he saw movement as Tyler raised the sawn-off shotgun to his shoulder. Aeric flipped his own rifle off his shoulder and pointed in the direction that Tyler had. Three men stood a few yards off the road on the opposite side of where Kate had stood waiting for her next trick. The men had obviously intended to jump the two of them from behind while they were distracted by her. His head rotated rapidly back and forth between his former girlfriend and the would-be muggers.

Kate held up her hands and the blankets fell open once more to reveal a patch of hair that she hadn't had while the two of them dated. "No! It's okay, I know him!" she yelled.

If the message was intended to stop the three men, they hadn't heard. The one in the center reached under his jacket and the roar of Tyler's shotgun shattered the silence of Nichols Street. Two of the men went down immediately and as Kate screamed, Aeric pivoted around towards the fight. He sighted down the barrel at the torso of the third man who held a pistol. He squeezed the trigger and the man fell backward onto the ash with a rapidly expanding crimson stain across his chest.

Aeric turned back to Kate with his rifle still pressed tight against his shoulder socket. She'd fallen to her knees, sobbing tears that her body couldn't afford to lose. "What the fuck was that?" he demanded.

She didn't answer him. Instead, her hands clenched and unclenched in the filthy layers of ash. "Is this what you've become? You're a whore who robs people?" he screamed as spittle flew against the inside of his mask's face shield.

"And you're a murderer!" she screamed. "Why did you come back here? There's nothing for you here but misery and death."

He dropped the rifle to his side as Tyler stalked forward to check the bodies to ensure that they were dead. It certainly wouldn't do to be shot in the back while he played catch up with his crazy ex-girlfriend. "I came back to make sure everyone was alright."

She looked up at him and he saw her eyes pass over his shape again. "You came all the way back from Texas?"

"Yeah," he said. "I came to see what I could do, but now I know that they have to come back to Texas with me."

Kate sniffed hard and sat back on her heels. She used the back of her hand to wipe away the snot and tears from her cheek and twitched her shoulder so the blanket slipped down around her waist. "You seem to be doing well for yourself."

A strange mixture of disgust and pity overcame him. "Cover up, Katie," he muttered. A few faces had appeared in windows along the street as some of the survivors wanted to see what was going on outside. He didn't like the attention that their gunfire had brought on them and felt the need to get off the street. They had a lot of food and an angry mob would quickly overwhelm them.

She nodded her chin towards Tyler and squeezed her shrunken breasts together. "You've obviously been eating okay. I'll do you both for some food."

"He's not your type."

Kate stood up quickly and he started to raise the 30-30 again, but she slid in close and pressed against him. "We were so good together, baby. You know, I never got over you."

"You had a funny way of showing it," he retorted. "You practically turned the entire school against me, and I was one of the stars of the state championship team."

Her hand slid down and cupped his dick. "I miss this," she purred.

"Katie, I—"

"Take me with you!" she pleaded suddenly. "We can have sex every night. You'll never have to worry about that. I'll take care of you so well, baby!"

"Who were those men that we killed?"

"They were— They helped keep me safe out here."

He pushed her hand away from his crotch. "Did you make them the same type of promises?"

She glared at him and said, "You have no idea what life here has been like. I watched my mother get beaten to death for three cans of vegetables and some bottled water. They bashed her brains in with a tire iron. I still have a bruise on my side where they hit me." She paused and pulled her blanket open to reveal a large greenish-brown patch of skin, obviously a bruise that was in the process of healing, further diverting calories away from her body. "I've done what I had to do to keep me and my sister alive."

"Julie," he answered with a start, remembering the vibrant middle schooler that he'd known since she was born. "Where is she?"

Kate smiled. "Oh, you're gonna love this!" She stepped in and grabbed both of his ass cheeks to pull him in close and then leaned in to whisper into his ear, "When my mom was killed, we went to the only person that I knew who could help us. There was only one person in Springfield that I could trust."

The pit of his stomach dropped out. He already knew the answer, but asked anyways, "Katie, where do you and Julie live?"

"With your mom! Isn't that exciting? We can be one big family again and you can protect us!"

Aeric sighed as he felt a massive headache forming behind his right eye and he turned towards his house at the end of the street.

*****

He walked stiffly up the stairs to the old, worn porch that he'd spent so much of his youth playing on. The paint on the cement floor was chipping once again and Aeric allowed himself a moment of nostalgia. He and his father used to scrape away the old paint every two or three years and then repaint it. They'd spend two days posted at the front door keeping the mailman off of the porch to let the paint dry completely. At the time, it had been tedious and boring, but Aeric would have given anything to have those days back again.

His hand hovered inches away from the door to knock. It seemed strange to knock on the door to his parent's home. The door had never seemed like a barrier to him before, now it stood as a symbol of the fact that he'd grown up, he no longer had the right to come and go as he pleased in someone else's home.

He looked over his shoulder to where Tyler and Kate stood. Tyler's head was on a swivel watching the street. He knew that they were being watched and didn't like it either. Tyler passed back to the left and he noticed Aeric looking at him. Their eyes locked and the big man smiled behind his mask. Kate was smiling too, but hers didn't warm him the way that his friend's did. When he saw her smile, the only thing it did was remind him of the story of the scorpion and the fox.

His own smile faltered with that sobering thought. In the story of the scorpion and the fox, both animals are trapped on one side of a river. The fox begins to swim to the other side and the scorpion, who can't swim, begs the fox to ride on his back across the river. The fox refuses because he's afraid that the scorpion will sting him. The scorpion promises not to, so the fox agrees to carry the scorpion across the river. Halfway across, the scorpion stings the fox, dooming them both. The fox asks the scorpion why it had stung him and condemned them both to drowning. The scorpion's answer is simply, "Because I am a scorpion." The moral of the story is that a creature may be able to hide its true nature for a while, but it always comes out in the end.

Kate was the scorpion. She was a poison that would derail his plans and their situation had suddenly become a lot more complicated because of her.

Aeric turned back to the door and let his knuckles fall heavily onto the sturdy wood three times. The sound echoed along the silent street and Aeric was reminded that they needed to get their supplies hidden quickly. The peep hole darkened and a woman called out from inside, "Who is it?"

"Mom, it's me, Aeric!"

"Aeric?" The curtains on small side windows parted and his mother's face appeared. He took off his respirator and waved at her, suddenly feeling very much like a boy again.

Her eyebrows shot up in recognition and the sound of furniture being pushed to the side sounded through the door. The muffled turning of the deadbolt and what sounded like several chain locks sliding out of place followed the sound of the furniture, making him wonder how much else had changed in his home. *Everything*.

The door swung inward and his mother appeared. Her hands covered her mouth and tears ran down her cheeks. "Oh my God, Aeric. I... I can't believe that you're actually here. I thought... Never mind what I thought, you're here!"

She reached out to hug him and he stepped back. He placed both hands on her shoulders and leaned down to kiss her. She looked hurt at his actions. "I'm sorry, mom," he said. "I'm covered in radiation. I don't want you to hug me until I can take these outer layers off."

"Oh... Radiation?"

"That's what all this ash is. There was a nuclear war and the cities burned, some of them are probably still burning."

She glanced past him at Kate and Tyler. "I see that you found Kate. Where are her goons?"

"Dead," he replied. It was better to let her know up front what kind of person he'd become. He and Tyler wouldn't hesitate to kill someone if they were threatening them or anyone that they cared about.

"Did *you* do that?" she asked.

"Yes, momma. We killed them. They tried to jump us."

His mother nodded her head. "Good, those men were evil. They used her, they did awful things to us. I'm glad that they're dead. Thank you."

"Can we come in?"

"Yes, of course!"

She turned to go inside and he stopped her. "Mom, we need to bring the bikes inside too."

"Can't you just leave them outside on the porch, son?"

"Mom, we *need* to bring the bikes inside," he repeated with emphasis.

She seemed to take his meaning, "Oh, okay then. Bring them inside."

It took a little bit of maneuvering to get the bikes and their carts full of supplies up the five concrete steps, but they eventually made it and wheeled them inside. He locked the deadbolt and then noticed the five chain locks screwed into the doorjamb at various points along its length. Those were all new additions. Once the chains were in place, he and Tyler pushed the hallway cabinet back in front of the door.

Aeric appraised his boyhood home. Everything seemed like it was in shambles compared to the way he remembered it. The front windows were blocked by the grandfather clock and the china cabinet from the dining room and all the pictures were gone from the walls. A small, meager fire burned in the fireplace and there were mattresses on the floor near it. The couch cushions were lined up along the wall where the couch had been, but there was no sign of the furniture itself.

He walked back towards the kitchen as his mother trailed him hesitantly. The island was covered with dishes stacked high to the ceiling and little Julie stood there holding a crowbar. A clawed hammer and thick flathead screwdriver rested on the counter underneath the partially demolished upper cabinet. They'd been burning the cabinets for wood, simply prolonging the inevitable. This place wasn't his home. They needed to leave. The only thing for them in Springfield was a slow death.

Julie's eyes widened in surprise when she recognized him. "Aeric? Holy crap!" The twelve-year old ran over to him and started to hug him, but he held up his hands and took off his overcoat, letting it drop to the floor. Then he wrapped the little girl in an embrace.

"I'm so glad you're here!" she cried into his shoulder.

"Everything will be okay now, sweetie," he lied.

Finally, Julie let him go and he hugged his mother. "Oh, I've missed you so much, Aeric," she cried into his shoulder.

After a few moments, he leaned back and said, "Mom, where's dad?"

She stared at her feet for a moment and then up at him. Once again, tears glistened on her cheeks. "When he heard about the dorm fires at the university, he bought a plane ticket and went down to look for you."

"He's in Austin?" Aeric asked. That was more than ironic, it was a cruel twist of fate.

"No, honey, your father is dead. His plane crashed."

The sense of happiness at completing the first leg of his journey crashed away and he felt like he'd been punched in the gut. His father was gone because he'd been trying to find him. If Aeric had only stayed local for college, then he wouldn't have gotten mixed up with the dorm fires and his father would still be alive.

And Aeric wouldn't have met Tyler and likely would have ended up either dead or some type of thug, robbing people to keep his family fed. His father wasn't dead because of him. His father was dead because of the Vultures. The world was dying because of the Vultures. He hated them. They were the true evil in this world and he knew that at least one of them was in Austin. He'd find that sick bastard and make him pay for everything that he'd done.

"I'm sorry, son." His mother brought him back from his thoughts. "You've come all this way and everything is different than what you were expecting."

"I'm fine. Of course I'm sad, but… I'm fine. I'm just glad that you're alive."

His mother squeezed him tight and then asked, "Who's your friend?"

"Oh, I'm sorry. Mom, this is Ty."

His mother took Tyler's hand and he said, "Nice to finally meet you, Mrs. Gaines."

"Please, call me Beth," she said.

Aeric introduced Julie and then formally introduced Kate to Tyler. "So, you guys want some dinner?" he asked.

"We don't have anything to eat, Aeric," his mother moaned. "Those druggies followed Kate one day and forced their way in. They've eaten or sold all of the food that your father and I had."

The sadness in his mother's voice filled him with despair. From the little that she'd said on the front porch and now, he was certain that they should have taken much longer to kill those men. They deserved so much more than the quick death that he and Tyler had given them. "It's okay, mom. It's over, we're here now. Those men will never bother you again."

She began to cry again and Aeric wrapped his arms around her. "Mom, it's okay. Tyler and I have a lot of food. We can make you lunch today and then we're leaving Springfield first thing tomorrow morning."

Kate slid up close to him and put her arms around his waist. "I'm so glad that you came back to us, baby!"

He started to step away from her, but decided against it. What was the point in creating a rift in their new group? He didn't trust her at all, but he couldn't leave her and Julie to starve to death here. She would continue to be a prostitute and probably drag Julie into it as well, if she hadn't already.

"Go get some clothes on, Katie. You can't walk around naked all the time."

Kate's grip on his waist loosened slightly and once again for the sake of unity, he swallowed what he wanted to say. Instead, he said, "The ash that's falling from the sky is radioactive. You need to keep your exposed skin to a minimum."

That seemed to put her unease to rest and she gripped him tightly once again. "Okay, I'll go get some clothes." She reached up and pulled his head down, kissing him on the cheek.

When she'd gone upstairs, he went to the carts and got two cans of chili and an unopened package of flour tortillas. They needed to eat the tortillas anyways because they were going to begin molding soon. His mom put the feast into a pan and took it to the fireplace.

Tyler walked over to where he stood watching his mother prepare the food. "I don't know about your friend Kate," he whispered.

"She's not my friend," Aeric answered. "She used to be my girlfriend—since middle school actually—but we broke up our senior year and she turned the entire school against me. She's got a major vindictive streak in her, so it's better if you don't get on her bad side."

"What, like killing her pimps?"

"Yeah, something like that," Aeric chuckled. "Although, hopefully, that was a 'friendship' of convenience, and not something else."

"Just watch your back around her. The way she switched from what seemed like hatred to all super-lovey and mushy… That girl is a user, bro."

"Yeah, I know. I just don't know what to do about it."

"I can arrange an accident."

Aeric looked at his friend in horror. It was one thing to kill people in self-defense or in defense of others, but Tyler was offering to kill Kate as a matter of convenience. Was that what happened when you killed people? Was it true that the more often you did it, the easier murder became and you could justify reasons for it?

"Uh, no. We'll just keep an eye on her. There's no reason to kill her."

"Okay, you're right. I just want you to know that the option is there. I can get rid of her."

"Noted," Aeric replied. "We need to find some bikes for them, though."

"We should ask your girlfriend if she's seen any on her trips."

Neither of them noticed Kate come down the stairs and she squealed, "Girlfriend? Oh, Aeric, I knew you still loved me! What we had doesn't just go away over some stupid misunderstanding."

Aeric rolled his eyes towards Tyler when she wrapped him in a hug from behind. "Hi, Katie."

"Oh, I missed you so much," she said with a squeeze.

The rest of the day passed quickly as Tyler and Aeric helped the girls pack clothing into various bags that could be secured to bicycles. Katie stuck to Aeric like a mushroom growing on a tree stump and on several occasions she'd made it known to him that she would satisfy every sexual desire that he'd ever had as long as he kept her and Julie safe.

Aeric couldn't get over how much she'd changed. The last time that he'd seen her was right before graduation in June. It was November now, only a little over a month since the war, and she'd been almost completely transformed. True, it was likely all an act to keep herself alive, but it was definitely strange to have her hovering around him.

He hoped he wasn't dooming their small group by telling Tyler that he could handle her. She was an opportunist, but she wouldn't outright betray them if a better opportunity came along, would she?

*****

As night descended, the girls made quite a fuss about ensuring that everything was locked tight and all the lights were extinguished. They told them about the criminals who came at night, the rapists, murderers and slavers, who were attracted to places with light. The men who'd moved into the Gaines house uninvited had been mean and taken their own liberties with the two older women, but at least they'd kept them alive and defended them against the worst of the sadists that roamed the streets at night.

Tyler and Aeric weren't deterred by their stories. They needed to go find bikes for the girls. They wouldn't be able stay together if everyone wasn't mounted and the speed that bicycles offered them greatly outweighed the dangers of them going out into the city to get the bikes tonight.

Tyler watched as Beth Gaines grasped her son tightly and held him for a full minute before letting him go. "We can go to find some bicycles tomorrow morning and then leave. I've lost your father and I thought you were dead. I don't want to lose you again."

Aeric placed both of his hands on her shoulders and looked down into her eyes. "Mom, we've survived on our own, in and out of cities, all the way from Texas. Me and Ty are more than capable of taking care of ourselves. I promise."

She nodded her head and allowed Kate to say her goodbyes as well. Tyler rolled his eyes as Aeric suffered through her attentions and then went through the motions of appeasing her. Their small group definitely didn't need to be fractured from the very beginning. Tyler thought that it would come to a head soon enough, but for now, Kate was going to stick around.

Their plan was to travel by foot to the campus of Drury University, ten blocks away, with their bolt cutters. There should be plenty of bicycles at the university. They'd find three that were suitable to their needs and steal them. As an added bonus, Central High School was on the way, so if there were any smaller bicycles there for Julie, they'd grab one of those.

The idea of stealing bikes would have horrified Tyler only a little while ago, but now it was just part of how things were done. They didn't have to take them, they could barter for them tomorrow somewhere, but what was the point of giving up their precious supplies to someone who'd likely be dead within a few weeks? They had a place to go, away from Springfield, instead of staying here in the city waiting for the government to rescue them or for some other savior who wouldn't appear.

They left one of their pistols with Aeric's mom and went out the back door, so they wouldn't be observed from the street, and headed west towards his old high school. Aeric said that he'd walked Nichols Street hundreds, maybe thousands, of times over the years and knew every house along the route. They used those houses and buildings as cover to move from shadow to shadow down the street.

Twice they saw people breaking into homes and both times they had to turn away. They didn't need to get involved, they had a mission to do and distractions would only derail their plans. It was a moral dilemma for them, but they couldn't save everyone and at some point, their interference would get them killed. There were three women who were relying on them to keep them safe. The people in that house would need to fend for themselves.

Tyler was worried about their footprints in the ash leading someone out looking for victims back to the Gaines house. The wind constantly whipped the ash into swirling clouds that covered tracks within a few hours, however, it was plainly obvious when someone had been out recently and their tracks led directly to the back door. Scavengers out looking for an easy score would go someplace where the occupants were out scavenging themselves. The old adage about no honor among thieves applied today more than ever, as people didn't possess the means to feed themselves yet. Those who survived the coming winter would be much more prepared and hardened to face life in the new world.

There was nothing that could be done about the footprints, so they pressed on. They'd given Beth a pistol and she knew how to use it. The women had survived on their own for the last month and like everyone else, they'd have to defend themselves for the next few hours if anything happened.

It turned out that they didn't even have to go all the way to the university. There were a lot of bikes in the bicycle racks at the school. The nukes had hit during class, so the administrators likely hadn't released the kids until their parents walked to the school and picked them up. Which meant that a lot of the bikes were abandoned at the school. They found two full-sized mountain bikes and a smaller bike that would be perfect for Julie on the same rack. Their bolt cutters made quick work of the bicycle chains and they were on their way back in minutes.

The bikes made it impossible to hop from shadow to shadow as they'd done on the outbound trip. Their return route took them in front of one of the houses that they'd saw the predators enter only a few minutes before. A woman's screams drifted from the gaping front entrance and Tyler couldn't stand it. "I'm going in, man. It killed me to walk by the first time. You've got the bikes, take them back and I'll meet up with you."

Aeric shook his head, "No way. We're a team, we stick together."

Tyler began to protest, but the look Aeric shot him through the respirator's face shield quieted him. "Thanks. I'm glad that I've got you to watch my back, Aeric."

He waved his hand, "Eh, stop with the mushy shit. Let's go put those fuckers in their grave."

They set the bikes quietly against the dying bushes and crept up the steps to the house. Tyler pulled his baseball bat from the modified arrow quiver on his back and Aeric pulled the large hunting knife from the sheath on his belt. They'd try to do this quietly without drawing any more attention to themselves, but both of them had their guns in case they couldn't keep it quiet.

They stood on either side of the doorway listening as the cries of a child mingled with the woman's pleas for help from upstairs. It drove both of them crazy to allow her to continue screaming from the upper level, but they needed to ensure that the lower level was clear before they went upstairs. They wouldn't be able to help anyone if they were hit from behind while they were trying to sneak upstairs.

The first floor was remarkably similar to Aeric's own house. It looked like the family had been breaking their furniture to burn in the fireplace and mattresses lay in a semi-circle around the hearth here as well. On one of the mattresses, the body of a man slowly oozed blood from multiple stab wounds, including both of his eyes. He wasn't going anywhere.

A loud curse and then an audible slap echoed down the stairwell followed by something small hitting a wall. The child stopped crying, but the woman's screams took on an intensity that told Tyler that the child had probably died in view of its mother. Cruel laughter and mocking voices drifted through the house and his hatred of the people upstairs grew.

They cleared the bottom floor quickly without any incident and went up the stairs as softly as possible. The rough slapping of skin against skin as they raped the woman disguised the creaking of the old wooden stairs as they gained the landing. The bedroom door where all the noise came from stood ajar, so they went in the opposite direction to make sure the entire floor was clear except for whatever was in that room.

By the time they'd finished the other two rooms and the shared bathroom, the woman had stopped crying. They could hear muted whimpers of pain, but not the screams that had brought them into the house initially. Both of the men readied their weapons and crept to the door. It looked like there were two men inside, one standing with his pants around his ankles stroking his erection, while his partner plunged into the woman on the bed.

Tyler indicated that he'd hit the one standing up and that Aeric should stab the rapist. He nodded once and then they rushed into the room. The baseball bat crunched into the side of the stroker's head as he turned to see what the noise was.

Aeric had a little farther to travel and realized too late that the man on the bed had been holding a pistol. He stopped mid-thrust and tried to bring it around, but Aeric's knife plunged into the back of his neck. The pistol exploded, lighting the room like electricity for an instant and destroyed their night vision.

Tyler's eyes had never fully healed from the flash burn and the bright light caused him to go completely blind for a moment. He could hear Aeric struggling with the man and fuzzy shapes began to form on the bed. He saw a head pulled backwards and then an arm raise. There was a gurgling sound and both men collapsed. "Aeric!" Tyler yelled in a near panic.

"I'm okay, buddy," his friend moaned.

At his feet, the stroker's legs began to kick as he started to come to. Tyler stepped back and brought the bat crashing down into his face. He flinched as blood splattered against his exposed neck. Thankfully the respirator's face shield had stopped it from getting into his eyes. He smashed the bat two more times until the man's legs stopped moving. Then it was over.

"My...my, baby!" the woman cried weakly.

"Aww shit. She got shot, bro," Aeric said from over near the bed. They'd fucked up their rescue attempt.

"How bad?" Tyler inquired.

"Is my baby..." the mother's voice drifted into oblivion.

His vision was still blurry and he saw Aeric place his fingers against her neck. "Pretty bad," he answered. "She's dead."

Tyler used the sheets to wipe off his mask and neck. Then he cleaned the bat and put it back into the sheath on his back. "Well, two more rapists are off the street."

"You don't think we fucked up this rescue attempt?" Aeric asked.

"It wasn't about a rescue. These people were dead anyways. They were barely surviving the first part of this winter. It's just going to get worse and they wouldn't have lasted much longer. This was about destroying evil."

Tyler could tell that his friend contemplated his words. Had he truly not cared about the family? Was that what he'd become? He was losing his humanity. The callous nature of his response proved it. His heart, once so big and open to love, was shriveling inside his chest, dying a little more each day in this world. He needed something to look forward to, a reason to keep going, otherwise, he was just as bad as the rest of these people. He needed a miracle.

*****

Aeric considered the meaning behind Tyler's words. It made sense to him that they couldn't always be the rescuer. People had to look out for themselves. The only thing that they could try to do was the right thing, in this case it was to kill those two raping, murderous motherfuckers.

"Alright, then scratch two more assholes," he replied with a shrug. "Let's go check their pantry and take what we can get. With all those extra mouths to feed, we need everything we can get and these people don't need it anymore."

"Yeah, about your girlfriend," Tyler sighed." She's gonna fuck us, you know that, right?"

"She's not my girlfriend," Aeric answered. "What can we do?"

"We could leave her, or refuse to share our food. That would make her go away."

Aeric considered it for a moment. "I can't do that to her, man. She played some bullshit high school games with me, but she hasn't done anything worth being condemned to die."

"Alright, then she comes with us and we keep an eye on her."

"I know it sucks and I'm probably gonna regret it, but—"

The whimpering of a small child cut him off. Across the room, the toddler sat up from the heap it had lain in. Both of them thought it was dead, but it obviously wasn't.

"Mommy!" the little girl screamed.

"Fuck—uh, I mean, darn!" Aeric muttered.

Tyler rushed across the room and picked up the squirming girl. She screamed at him and he tried to soothe her. "Shh, we're not gonna hurt you. What's your name?"

She continued screaming and tried to pull away from him, so he pulled his mask off and smiled at her. She kept crying, but he didn't seem to terrify her anymore. He bounced her slightly against his hip and Aeric wondered where the gentle giant in front of him and come from. "There, is that better? You're okay, we're nice. We're the good guys, like police officers. We stop bad people, honey. It's okay. What's your name?

She crammed her hand in her mouth and mumbled something that sounded like "Ketchup" to Aeric.

"She's got a large bruise on her face where those animals hit her, but I don't think she has any broken bones," Tyler remarked with a quick glance towards Aeric.

"Mommy!" Ketchup screamed and tried to claw her way out of Tyler's arms to the bed where her mother's body lay.

"I'm taking her downstairs," Tyler said. "She doesn't need to be around any of this. See if you can find any backpacks or anything to carry some of her clothes and—"

"Whoa!" Aeric said with his hands up. "We can't keep her! We don't know how to take care of a baby."

"Not your decision, man. I'm making this one, she goes with us," Tyler said as he pushed past Aeric towards the stairs. "Our goal was to destroy evil in this world, not create more by abandoning a child to starve to death."

Aeric stared at the man's back as he whispered softly to the little girl while he walked down the stairs. "Fuck," he muttered and began rifling through the pockets of the men they'd killed. Besides the pistol, which went into his waistband, they didn't have anything of value. He found a large duffle bag in the master bedroom closet and went down the hall to the little girl's room.

The name 'Kayla' was painted on the wall and Aeric grabbed a bunch of warm clothes out of the closet. There were probably more downstairs where they'd been living so they'd grab those too. As he started to go, he noticed a large stack of diapers and baby wipes on the dresser.

He sighed audibly and crammed those into the bag as well.

*****

Aeric's mom was ecstatic about baby Ketchup, as Aeric called her. Beth thought that Kayla was about two years old, which meant she would be able to eat solid foods. Not needing to find formula or even jars of baby food was a major plus, but Aeric was more than a little concerned about the group adopting a child.

First off, she'd already demonstrated the inability to be quiet when ordered to and she'd be taking up more than half of their room in one of the carts. The diapers alone took up so much space that he wondered how the hell the settlers had done it in the old days. Of course, they had horses and entire covered wagons to haul their gear and his group just had the power in his and Tyler's leg muscles.

It had taken him and Tyler a month to go the route by themselves, now that they'd added the women and baby Kayla, he could easily see it stretching to six weeks or more. That would put them firmly into winter in the mountains and he decided that it wouldn't work to be exposed like that. Their presence alone would make predators and scavengers curious. Add in wintery conditions on the mountain roads and it was a recipe for disaster, in his mind.

Aeric finished rearranging the pull-behind carts and repacking everyone's backpacks for the third time. He had to talk to Tyler about their plans. He walked into the living room where Julie and Tyler played with the baby on the floor. "Hey, Tyler. We need to talk about our route."

The big man looked up and shrugged his shoulders slightly, "Alright."

"I don't think the way we came is going to be the best for the group. Those mountains were tough on just the two of us, and now that winter is starting to actually set in, I think it would be dangerous on those roads, what with the instability of the carts and the potential for snow and ice added to the ash."

Tyler stood up and walked over to his bike where he had the map stashed away after the first rearrangement of supplies and pulled it out. He examined the map for a few seconds and then replied, "Okay. We can swing west into Oklahoma and then south into Texas."

"That has us avoiding the mountains?"

He brought the map closer to the single candle that burned in the living room and reexamined it. "Yeah, I think that will have us bypass most of the bigger mountains. There may be some foothills and stuff, but it shouldn't be any of the big mountains like it was in Arkansas."

Aeric nodded his head. "Okay, let's take that route, then. I really wanted to go back to Eureka Springs and spend some time there, but it's just too much of a risk in those mountains."

"Yeah, honestly though, I think the best thing that we could do for them is to allow them to remain isolated. Could you imagine how they'd handle men like the two who'd killed Kayla's mom and dad?"

Aeric chuckled. "I don't know. Up until all of this went down, I didn't think you had it in you to be ruthless. You've proven to me time and again that you're a badass motherfucker."

"Aeric!" his mom scolded him.

"Sorry, mom. Sorry, Ketchup." The child looked over at him and smiled. Maybe the kid would be alright.

"Okay, we should try to get some sleep before we take off tomorrow," Aeric announced.

"Good idea," Tyler agreed. "The carts are packed and ready to go. All we need to do in the morning is to pack up the bedding and then we can take off."

"Alright, good night everyone," Aeric said as he walked over to blow out the candle.

Beth and Julie snuggled together on one of the mattresses while Tyler lay beside Kayla. He blew out the light and jumped when Kate grabbed his hand and led him over to the third mattress. The girl was insufferable.

"It's dark enough, they won't be able to see anything if you want to do it," she whispered into his ear, running her hands across his chest and cupping the muscles underneath his shirt.

He sighed. Her nonstop quest to get him in bed was already getting old and it hadn't even been an entire day yet. Part of him said, *why not?* What good was denying himself a little bit of pleasure? He had no clue how long he'd be alive, why not allow himself a little bit of enjoyment in the time that he had left?

"Kate, I don't feel like it tonight. I just killed a man and inadvertently got Kayla's mother killed."

She molded her body to him. "Oh, baby. I'm sorry. I wasn't thinking about your feelings. You're right. I'll just hold you and keep you safe."

He laughed at her choice of words. The girl had gone full-on crazy because of her own need to be safe and here she was telling him that she'd keep *him* safe. "Thanks, ba—uh, Katie."

He lay there in the darkness listening to the cacophony of gunshots, screams and shattered lives that drifted around the furniture blocking the windows. Springfield was a dead town. It just didn't realize it yet.

TEN

The days and weeks flew by quickly as the group traveled back towards Texas. They ended up following roughly the same route that Aeric had taken to Austin in his car the previous summer. They had to alter course after McAlester because the road led to Dallas after passing by the ruins of the ammunition plant.

They explored the remains of the ammunition storage buildings to see if they could find any food to replace their dwindling supplies, without any luck. Whoever had cleaned up the area after the disaster had cleared everything of use so they continued south.

They were near Antlers, Oklahoma when it began to rain. It was the first time that any of them could remember it raining since the war. At first, they raised their hands to the sky to soak up the rain, but it quickly became apparent that the shit falling from the sky was poison. Everywhere the gray sludge touched their skin it burned, so they decided to leave the highway to seek cover during the storm. It didn't take them long to find a house set off the road that looked abandoned.

After knocking for several minutes, they decided that it was empty, so they went inside. They found the former residents in the living room. An obese woman sat in a recliner, two empty bottles of pills were beside her on the side table. Next to her, the remains of a man occupied a second recliner. He'd taken the shotgun in the mouth route, painting the walls behind him with his brain matter.

Aeric and Tyler dragged the bodies outside and then searched the house for useful items. In the kitchen, they found plenty of canned goods and giant balls of mold growing on something in the sink. The canned goods went into their carts and the shotgun was added to their growing arsenal of weapons.

They also found a few replica swords and a battle axe. The wheels in Aeric's mind began to turn. Over time, they'd probably run out of ammunition, maybe they should learn to use the medieval weapons for that eventuality. The swords that the couple had would likely not hold up to any type of pressure since they were just cheap replicas, but they could still get the motions down with them.

He told Tyler about his thoughts and the big man reached back to pat the handle of his baseball bat. "I've got this, I'm good. Besides, there's plenty of ammo in the world, we'll be fine."

"Yeah, you're right, I guess. I'd probably just end up cutting off my own leg."

"Hey, man. If you want to learn, then go for it. I'm not gonna tell you that you can't do it."

"Maybe when we're not on the road," Aeric answered. He gestured towards the back room. "I think we're gonna take advantage of the guest bedroom while we've got the opportunity."

Tyler frowned and said, "Go get 'em, tiger."

Aeric had stopped denying himself the pleasure of Kate's affection after their first night in Springfield. Katie had been more than willing and had shown him that over the short time that they'd been apart she'd learned a lot about pleasing others. At his core, he knew it was stupid and reckless, that she was using him simply because he offered her the protection to stay alive, but in reality he was using her too. The thought that they'd be dead any day overrode his common sense and drove his need to satisfy the desires of his body.

Of course, Tyler didn't approve and let him know on multiple occasions. At first it was the base argument that the girl was a poison, then when that didn't work he switched it to saying that Kayla didn't need to hear them humping into the night. Finally, he'd just said that *he* didn't want to hear their moans of intimacy.

Before everyone went to bed for the night, they gathered in the kitchen to discuss their options and treat the chemical burns on the skin that had been exposed to the weather. Even though they'd moved the couple's bodies outside, it was an unconscious agreement to avoid the living room.

They debated whether to post a guard for the night as they had every night, ultimately deciding that since the home had remained unmolested for as long as it had, it was highly unlikely that anyone would brave the acid rain and come to the house. They all needed a good night's rest. Aeric and Tyler had been traveling for almost two months straight on a limited diet, and the girls had gone from the outright terror of daily life in Springfield to living on the road. The group was weary in both the body and the soul, so the break would do them good. As a precaution, they piled furniture up around the doors before they turned in and went to their separate rooms for the night.

There were several cases of bottled water in the home's pantry, so everyone took the luxury of using the water in the toilet reservoirs to bathe. To Aeric, it felt luxurious to scrub away the dirt and grime of the road. As he scrubbed with a washcloth, he laughed about how his perception of luxury had changed. He was using toilet water to clean himself for Pete's sake.

When they went to bed, Aeric and Kate took the guest bedroom while the other four stayed in the master. The pattering of the rain outside combined with their newfound cleanliness added to the intensity of the sex between them. For the first time since getting back together with Kate, Aeric truly enjoyed himself, turning off his mind and just getting lost in the moment.

The rain continued for three days, so the group stayed in the house in Antlers that long. By the time the weather cleared, they were well rested and ready to get on the road once more. Their carts and packs were full of the supplies that they'd pilfered from the home's pantry and they even had several books that they'd been reading, which would have been a luxury that they couldn't have afforded themselves before the break.

They made their way back to the Indian Nation Turnpike and turned the front wheels of their bicycles south. The dawn of the new day was still dreary and overcast with a mixture of ash and rain clouds, but to the travelers it seemed to beckon them onwards with the promise of renewed beginnings, and they allowed themselves the opportunity to hope for a future free from suffering and weariness.

They also allowed themselves to become complacent. Their decision not to post guards at the suicide house had opened the floodgate to their own demise.

*****

The group stayed far to the east of the Dallas-Fort Worth metroplex as they continued southward. They knew that Tyler was going to be an issue, so they avoided it altogether and traveled between Tyler and Corsicana, where they knew chaos had already set in more than a month prior, hoping that the insanity had smothered itself out in the region.

They stuck primarily to the back roads and smaller highways, finally making it to Austin a little more than two months after they left Veronica's apartment. They knew right away that things were different in the town. The immediate transformation that they noticed from far away was the Tower at the University of Austin was gone. Just…gone. And several of the high rises in the downtown area looked to be pockmarked with massive holes. The Frost Bank Tower, the large, easily recognizable 33-floor, all-glass building, was nothing more than jagged remnants of the structure that had been there before.

The military force that had ringed the city the last time they were there was also gone. The missing vehicles made Aeric wonder if they'd gotten word of the nuclear strikes before they occurred and left, or if the military vehicles—which are shielded against EMPs— drove back to their base.

One thing that was not missing from Austin were the bodies. When they'd left, corpses were relatively uncommon, even though they'd seen their fair share of them on their walk from the hospital that first day. Now, as they stood near the 45 toll road to the northeast of Austin, they saw piles of bodies and skeletons several feet tall. They appeared to have inadvertently come upon the city's dumping grounds for its dead. That likely meant that somebody was in charge and trying to keep the city free from disease.

After discussing it amongst themselves, they decided it was best to continue with their original plan to find out about Veronica and then continue to San Angelo. The broken skyline told them that Austin obviously had problems that they were unwilling to get involved with, so the sooner they could leave, the better.

They traveled a few blocks from the dumping grounds and made camp in the burned-out shell of a small gas station. The four concrete walls allowed them a small bit of protection against creatures of the night. Cities naturally made them uneasy nowadays and seeing the damage brought upon their former city made them even more uneasy.

The entire group was restless that night and sleep came hard to everyone, even young Kayla. There were still several hours until dawn when they decided to break camp and move towards the center of town where Veronica had lived. They couldn't shake the feeling that they were being watched as they left the night's sanctuary.

They made their way through the sleeping city and the feeling that they were being watched increased, making them believe that they were being followed as well. Aeric chalked it up to paranoia and pressed onward. *It was four or five in the morning, bad people were asleep at this time of day,* he told himself as the pavement passed quickly under their bicycle tires. While he tried to convince himself otherwise, he was thankful for the darkness that helped to hide them from the city's watchers.

Signs of a major battle were evident along their route. Entire sides of buildings were collapsed in on themselves or the bricks had sloughed off like mud sliding down a hillside. Glass littered the sidewalks and blackened char marks painted the sides of structures where fires had kissed them. The city looked like a proverbial war zone, but it had been spared from the actual nuclear war. What could have happened?

When they made it to Guadalupe Street and turned south, it became more apparent that Veronica was probably not going to be in the city. Smoke drifted from multiple places downtown and Aeric called a halt to the group. He indicated another burned-out building and hastened everyone inside. They searched the first floor quickly to make sure that it was vacant and then gathered back in the front room.

"I don't want to take everyone down to Veronica's apartment," Aeric stated, letting the group know the thoughts that had built in his mind on their journey through the city. "It's better that we split up, you guys stay here and I'll go down to check it out."

"Absolutely not," Tyler replied.

"Look, pal. You have Kayla to look out for. You need to keep her safe and following me blindly everywhere I go is not in her best interests."

"That's a pretty low blow, Aeric," he responded. "I can watch after both of you."

"Not this time, man. Just do me a favor and keep the girls safe until I get back."

"I'm not staying here," Kate interjected.

He threw up his hands in dismay. "What?"

"I go where you go," she replied.

Aeric placed his hand on her shoulder. "Katie, I'm positive that something isn't right in Austin. It'll be dangerous. The best thing is for you to stay with Tyler and my mom until I get back."

He was surprised when she grabbed his wrist and jerked him towards the corner of the room away from the group. When they got there, she whirled on him and whispered, "Look, I'm not stupid. I know you and Tyler say shit about me and that I'm only out for myself. It's true that I let my sense of self-interest get in the way last year when I broke up with you and then you went away to college. Look what happened when you weren't around."

She took a deep breath and held up her palm towards him, indicating that she wasn't done. "I did what I had to so that Julie and I could survive. That doesn't mean that I haven't changed. Aeric, this is going to sound crazy when I say it, but this past month, just being with you out on the open road and spending our nights together has been the best time of my miserable life. I'm not about to let you walk away and get yourself killed. If you're going to meet up with this woman who knows the way to a safe place, then I'm going with you."

Aeric opened his mouth and then closed it. He didn't know what he'd expected Kate to say, but it certainly wasn't what she'd just said. "I, uh—"

"Shut up. It's not up for debate. I'm going with you or else you're not going. You need someone to watch your back and Tyler needs to stay with baby Kayla to protect her."

"Katie, that's not necessary, I'll be fine."

"No, you won't. I'm not going to put up with any shit from you, Aeric. I mean it, we're not debating this. I'm going with you."

What the hell could he do? The girl seemed intent to stay by his side, even when it meant that he'd be leading her into danger. Maybe she *had* changed for the better. Maybe she actually did care for him enough to risk her own life to keep him safe. "Fine," he said. "I appreciate the help."

She squealed like a girl getting asked to the prom and pulled his mask up over his face so she could kiss him on the lips. Then she settled it back loosely over his chin and pulled him back towards the other four members of their group.

He was still trying to adjust the respirator when she announced to Tyler that she was going to be his backup and that Tyler would stay with Kayla and Julie.

"Are you sure about this?" Tyler asked.

"Yeah, I think so," he replied. Then, with more confidence he said, "She can shoot. We made sure of that, so I'm comfortable with her watching my back."

"I don't like it. You need me there."

"Kayla needs you here. We're only about two miles from Veronica's place. We'll go in, see if she's still there or if she left the note like she said she would if her family came to get her. We'll be back before nightfall."

Tyler agreed grudgingly and bid Aeric and Kate farewell. Aeric hugged his mom and borrowed her bicycle so he'd be more maneuverable while Kate kissed her little sister. The whole thing felt much more fatalistic than Aeric had intended it to be when he'd decided to go alone. He believed that taking everyone to Veronica's was an unnecessary risk that could be avoided. But at the same time, he hoped that splitting up their forces wasn't a mistake.

*****

He watched the two of them pedal away. Tyler grudgingly had to admit that his buddy had seemed much healthier and in a better mood with Kate around. It didn't change his opinion that in the long run, the girl would find a way to screw everyone over, but for the time being, the physical contact was good for him.

"Well, I guess we just settle down in here and wait," he said as he muscled the burned metal frame of a refrigerator into place over the doorway.

"How long are we going to wait?" Beth Gaines asked. "I don't like being separated from my son again."

He shrugged, saying, "It shouldn't be more than twenty or thirty minutes down to the apartments, then another five or ten minutes looking around there and right back, so what is that, an hour? Maybe two at the most."

"Tyler, do you think he'll be safe?" Julie asked.

He turned to the teen, who was holding Kayla, and smiled. "Mr. Aeric will be fine. He's got a lot of experience in the city and even more from our time on the road. I wouldn't worry about him. Let's feed Kayla something to keep her quiet and settle in for the wait."

They spent the next few minutes preparing a small meal, something that would keep the toddler quiet in their hiding spot. He'd just opened a can of spaghetti rings when the pea gravel outside in the parking lot crunched under someone's foot.

Tyler stopped and held up his hand for everyone to be quiet. Had there been someone outside the door or was it just the wind blowing the gravel around? Aeric and Kate had been gone less than ten minutes so it was possible that they turned around for something or even changed their mind about going down to the apartment.

The sound of several people running across the gravel parking lot towards them filled the morning air. Tyler grabbed the shotgun, prepared to defend the girls when the front of the building exploded and brick went flying everywhere.

A large chunk of masonry hit him squarely in the chest and he heard Mrs. Gaines cry out in pain. He couldn't see what was happening because ash and dust that had been swept up combined with the murky light from outside to temporarily blind him. Pain flooded through his body, causing him to almost black out. Maybe he did, he couldn't be sure. It wasn't until a face appeared *above* him that he realized that he was lying flat on his back. The face belonged to a woman wearing both a combat helmet and a sneer.

"We got them, sir!" she yelled over her shoulder. "Gross! This one is ripped open like one of Justin's projects. She must have taken a grenade to the chest! Aw man, that's her stomach!"

"What were they carrying in those carts?" a man's voice ordered.

Tyler turned his head weakly and saw several people digging through their hard-earned supplies and the prone form of Aeric's mother. Some type of clear, bloody fluid poured freely from her ears and the ash underneath her was slowly darkening. "It's just food and worthless shit," the woman said.

"Wait. Weren't there two bike carts?"

"Uh…."

"You idiots! They probably took off with anything of value in the second cart. It has to be the little one that ran off. Go get her!"

Tyler smiled. *Julie was okay and running. Did she have Kayla with her?* He turned his head to the opposite side where he thought the second cart holding the little girl had been. Sure enough, the bicycle and cart were gone and there wasn't any sign of the child. But his shotgun was laying less than an arm's length away.

The group of people seemed to have forgotten him, so he steeled his resolve and prepared to move. He figured that could take out several of the fuckers before they killed him. Tyler tried to lift his shoulder off the ground to reach for the weapon and pain once again became the only thing that he was aware of. He screamed in agony as the jagged end of his baseball bat slid out of his back with a wet, sucking sound.

"Oh no you don't, big guy," the leader of the group said. "You know, we followed you and your friend because you looked like the men that Justin told us to be on the lookout for when this all began. What did you take from him that he wants so badly?"

"Captain Sanders!" a man shouted from the depths of the building that they stood in.

He turned away and said, "What?"

"The little bitch must have gone out the back door. It's wide open, but there's no sight of her."

"Where's she going, Mr. Baseball Player?"

Even through the pain in his back, Tyler recognized the wrongness of his statement immediately. He hadn't told this man that he played baseball. Did he think that because of Tyler's bat or was it because this "Justin" person knew what he looked like?

"I... We didn't have a plan besides waiting here until our friends got back."

"You expect me to believe that you've survived more than two months of this shit without making back-up plans? Tell me, where's she headed off to?"

"I promise, I—" A rifle butt landed hard against his face, cracking his nose, which filled his sinus cavity with blood.

"Don't lie to me!" the captain screamed. "Where was she going?"

"We..." he stopped and used his swollen tongue to push a tooth out of his mouth. "No pwan, we wewe gonna wait hewe fow them," he mumbled through his broken mouth.

A heavy boot landed on his ribs and he instinctively curled to that side, sending more spasms of pain through his body as the gash in his back stretched wide. He used his splayed fingers to try and protect his head as the blows rained down from all around.

He blacked out and the darkness mercifully swallowed him.

*****

Pain. It never ended, never lessened. There was only the constant pain of burning flesh and the maddening feeling of fluids dripping slowly down his body as boils burst, scabs tore and his own bodily functions betrayed him.

Aeric hung suspended by his wrists, chains wrapped around them and kettlebell weights tied to his ankles to add to the mass of his own body. He'd been beaten and tortured by the Vultures. The most brutal and long-lasting of their tactics had been a simple set of chain links from a swing set that had been heated in a fire. They laid it across his body, burning him repeatedly, no place was spared from the torture. The crowd of people that seemed to constantly be present in the torture room had started calling him "Tracks" because of the crisscrossing chain burns across his body.

He wasn't sure how long he'd been there, a few days, maybe a week. Time ran together and really held no meaning for him anymore. When he could muster the energy to contort his body, he could see that some of the boils on his skin had burst and scabbed over, while others still contained their fluid. It was excruciating and humiliating to swing naked in front of so many people, but at least he wasn't dead. He thought about the things that they did to Coach Harris, and Katie's betrayal. Aeric wished that he would die.

Almost immediately after they'd set out from the building in north Austin, they'd been attacked by a large group of what appeared to be a mix of soldiers and civilians who were armed to the teeth. He'd considered fighting, but his desire to keep Kate safe had stopped him from acting foolishly in the face of such overwhelming odds. Now he wished that he would have.

They were beaten and taken to the State Capitol building, which was now the headquarters of the Vulture gang. Somehow, they'd made the leap from computer hackers to a powerful group of thugs who controlled the city. Aeric still hadn't worked that part out. It had something to do with the food and drug supplies in the city.

The leader of the group was a man named Justin. He said that he knew Aeric and his big friend were in the city and that Tyler would be joining them soon if he survived the attack. So far, Aeric hadn't seen Tyler or his mother, so he hoped that the gang leader was just lying to him. He did see poor Coach Harris a few times, though.

The first time he saw him, he noticed the man had lost a lot of weight, his skin hung off of him in saggy flaps. He was stretched across some type of wooden machine that held all of his limbs apart and there were gears that could be turned to stretch him further. As Aeric and Kate had been paraded around the room full of people in handcuffs, Justin told them that they intended to torture Aeric the same way for being one of the social rejects that worshiped at the altar of consumerism. They planned to keep them alive a very long time so the crowds would stay entertained.

Katie hadn't even lasted the tour of the facilities before she was offering her services to Justin. The steady source of food and exercise on their long trip from Missouri had done wonders for her figure and even with a black eye and bloody lip, she was still the beautiful prom queen who knew how to work a crowd. Justin had her stripped naked and examined her body. The gang leader saw something in her that he liked and spared her the same fate as him. Now, almost every time Aeric saw Justin, Katie was at his side. Tyler's belief that she would slip out on the first chance she got had come true and he felt like a fool for believing her.

He'd thought that she really did love him and that she'd only acted the way she did in Springfield because she was trying to survive. Hell, that's all that she was doing now. She was taking advantage of the situation to survive. He hated her for it, but at the same time, he couldn't blame her. She took the smart way out to avoid getting tortured simply for being around Aeric when he was captured. Becoming Justin's whore was the part that made him the angriest. She willingly slept with the man who ordered his daily torture.

When the torturing had first begun, he'd felt sorry for himself and cried out in pain until he passed out. Then, somewhere over the course of the sessions, he stopped feeling the pain. It no longer mattered to him. His best friend was dead, he was the last of his family, the woman he thought he loved had betrayed him and the people that he'd sworn to protect were all dead.

Aeric Gaines was gone. In his place was Traxx, the wretched hunk of flesh that would *never* give the Vultures the satisfaction of hearing him scream again.

ELEVEN

The trip westward sucked. Julie's legs still burned badly near the end of each day as she pedaled the bicycle, pulling the cart and little Kayla. For such a small child, she was a heavy little thing. After almost two weeks on the road alone, there wasn't too much farther to go and she was ready for the trip to be over, one way or another.

When the grenades had blown the front of the building apart in Austin, she'd been in the middle of feeding Kayla. The door had been on the opposite side of the room and both Mrs. Gaines and Tyler were laying on the floor bleeding. Before the dust settled, she made the split-second decision to grab Kayla and the bike. She tore through the building and unlocked the back door. They were racing away around the corner before the men even figured out where she'd gone.

She knew that they had to get out of the city before she could really think about things. Tyler and Mrs. Gaines were either dead or just as good as dead in the hands of the people who'd attacked the shop, and Aeric and Katie were probably going to get ambushed when they came back. There was nothing that she could do, though, so she made her way onto the highway and ran.

It was about an hour later when Kayla's cries of hunger brought Julie back to herself and she stopped. The baby needed to be changed and fed, so she practiced the fieldcraft that she'd learned from Aeric and Tyler, hiding the bike up in the trees off the road before doing anything. Once there, they ate and she took stock of the supplies that had been in the cart when she took off.

They had a lot of food and some water, both of the water purification systems, one sleeping bag and Aeric's large backpack. Everything else had been in the other cart because of Kayla. Inside Aeric's bag, there were changes of clothes, a map of Texas, a folding knife, a whole bunch of cigarettes, multiple calibers of ammunition and a pistol. Also inside was a worn out scrap of paper with Veronica Delgado's address in San Angelo.

After she fed and changed Kayla, she mapped out how to get from Austin to San Angelo and then took off once again. If Aeric and Kate hadn't gotten ambushed, then they'd eventually make their way to San Angelo like they all planned to do originally and she'd meet up with them there. If they *had* been ambushed, then she hoped the citizens of the city would take her and the baby in.

That had been two weeks ago. Two weeks of struggling to keep the larger bike upright and pull everything along. She'd passed a sign saying San Angelo was two miles away and she could see the few skyscrapers standing darkly against the overcast sky. Her legs pumped slowly, driving the bike up a slight rise in the highway. When she reached the top, the road stretched on below them for what seemed like miles, leading to the city.

Less than two football fields away sat a checkpoint. It was situated on the reverse slope of the hill where she couldn't see it until she'd topped the hill and exposed herself and Kayla. The people manning the checkpoint saw her and began moving behind barricades. She had the distinct feeling that guns were pointed in her direction and she sighed. There was nothing she could do about the city's defenders. If they were ever going to be safe, they had to make it past the checkpoint and find this Veronica Delgado woman.

Gravity carried the bike slowly down the hill to where the men and women waited for her. They called out for her to stop when she was about twenty feet from the barbed wire stretched across the road.

"We ain't taking no more stragglers," a male yelled out and then quickly yelped when he was slapped by one of the women.

"I'm going to come out there to meet you," the same woman said. "Are you alone? Do you have any weapons?"

Julie held up her hands and replied, "I have a pistol and a few knives. Nothing else."

The woman glanced behind her along the road and asked, "Are you alone?"

"Yeah. My group got separated and the people I was with were killed."

She approached Julie warily. "No grenades or bombs or anything?"

"Huh? No, of course not, lady!"

"What's in the cart?"

Julie had wondered how to answer that question on the entire trip from Austin. She'd finally settled on a response. "My baby sister and some food."

The woman's body language changed and the wariness seemed to go away. "Oh my God! You have a baby with you?"

"She's two, but yeah."

"Can I see her?"

"Yeah, sure." Julie turned around and said, "Kayla, this is Miss…."

"Oh, I'm sorry. My name's Shellie."

Julie smiled and said, "That's was my mom's name too! I'm Julie."

The woman stuck out her hand and shook Julie's. "Nice to meet you, Julie."

Shellie bent knelt down to see Kayla and exclaimed, "Oh my gosh, isn't she precious? Mind if I take her out?"

"No, go ahead." Julie watched the older woman bend down to unlatch the harness around Kayla's shoulders. When she stood upright with the baby on her hip, she was smiling and looked like she'd lost ten years. Julie realized that the woman probably wasn't that much older than Katie had been when she died.

"Hi, Kayla. My name is Shellie, just like your grandma." She bounced the girl for a moment and then looked up at Julie. "My daughter was only a couple of weeks old when…when everything happened." Shellie wiped away a line of tears and continued, "She didn't make it. The water we were using for her formula was contaminated."

"I'm sorry, ma'am," Julie said.

"Oh, please, call me Shellie. I'm probably only six or seven years older than you. We buried her out in the city cemetery…" She trailed off for a moment and then refocused back on Julie. "Sorry. Anyways, you guys are welcome here in San Angelo, although you'll probably have to get some sort of job—the mayor has everyone over the age of fifteen working across the city. That way we can try to keep ahead of the radiation, keep the population fed and defend what we've got against raiders."

"Yeah, we ran into some of those raiders in Austin."

"You've been to Austin? How long ago?" Shellie asked. "We've been looking for info about the group there called the Vultures."

Julie nodded her head. "Tyler and Aeric talked about the Vultures a lot. They're the ones who set off the nuclear missiles."

"Huh? I thought they were a street gang, how'd they get nukes?

Julie shrugged and replied, "They hacked into the computers and launched them is what I was told."

"Okay, you need to come with me to see the mayor."

"Wait," Julie said as she reached across and took Kayla. "We're here to meet a friend of ours. I need to meet up with her and see if the rest of my group arrived yet. Do you know Veronica Delgado?"

Shellie shook her head. "No, there's a hundred thousand people in San Angelo, or there was before the fighting. It took a few weeks for the mayor to reestablish control and a lot of people died during the panic after the missiles hit Dallas and Houston."

"I have her address."

The older woman held up her hand and said, "Wait a minute. Hey, Charlie, what's the mayor's daughter's name?"

The other defenders had abandoned their spots behind the barricades and sat around a table playing cards. One of the men— Charlie, Julie assumed—looked up and said, "I don't know. Victoria, Veronica, something like that."

"Thanks," she called and turned back to Julie. "Maybe your friend is Mayor Delgado's daughter. He went to Austin to get her right after the nukes hit, which is why it took so long for him to get things back under control."

Julie jumped up and down. "That *must* be her! When Aeric and Tyler left Austin a few months ago, she told them that her father was on his way to get her."

"Okay then. I'll take you to see the mayor *and* his daughter. I'm sure she'll be happy to see you."

Julie frowned and stared at the ground. "I don't know. I've never met her before. Aeric and Tyler knew her. Tyler died when we were ambushed in Austin and I have no idea what happened to Aeric or my sister Kate. I didn't know what else to do, so I followed our original plan to come here. Now that I'm here, I feel kinda stupid. I mean, Veronica doesn't know me at all."

Shellie shrugged. "Well, you've come all this way. Let's go see what she has to say."

Julie nodded. Shellie was right. She'd traveled a long way, more than half of it by herself with Kayla. It was time to meet the woman whom she'd hung the possibility of her survival upon. "I bet she's going to be surprised to see us," she muttered.

*****

Thumping on his bedchamber door woke Justin. He sat up rapidly and his hand blindly found the pistol that sat beside the bed. He disengaged the combination trigger lock by feel and aimed the weapon loosely towards the door.

"What is it?" he shouted.

Movement to his side told him that his worthless whore, Kate, was finally waking up. She could fuck really well and was finally starting to fill out with all the food that he fed her, but he was sick of her whining and annoying talking. Why the hell did she always want to talk? He thought about cutting her tongue out, but then decided against it since it would limit her sexual abilities.

"My lord, its Greg Sanders. May I come in?" a voice on the other side of the door asked.

He glanced down at Kate's exposed breasts and briefly considered letting the captain come inside so he could see Justin's conquest. Instead, he replied, "No, I'll come out. Give me a moment."

Justin put the safety mechanism back on the pistol and set it on the nightstand. He didn't trust Kate. Even though she fucked him, she'd probably try to kill him if he left any weapons around. Hell, he would try to kill her if the situation was reversed. Once he was dressed, he walked across the thick rugs that had been piled on the floor to ease the chill in the air and opened the door to his bedchamber.

In the hallway, the former Army captain, who'd since become his most trusted henchman, was already dressed in his battle fatigues for the day. He'd done away with the silly gray digitized version that he'd been wearing the day the war started and he decided to join forces with the Vultures. Instead, he now wore the different version that the military had used in Afghanistan, which blended in much better with the various earth tones of the city's rubble.

"What is it, Captain Sanders?"

"Sir, we've received word of a major attack against our forces near Buda."

"Buda? Is that some sort of Hindu mosque or some shit?"

"Uh... No, sir. It's a town south of Austin along the interstate. That's been our unofficial boundary where we collect stragglers coming up from the wasteland of San Antonio."

Justin's hand whipped out lightning fast and slapped Sanders across the face. The man bristled, but the bedchamber guards were enough to make him stand down. Justin decided that he'd have to watch the man closely. He was a valuable resource, but a resource that obviously needed reminding of who was in charge. "I know where Buda is. I was making a joke."

The captain smiled, but the blood on his teeth made it look more like a grimace. "Of course, my lord. Forgive my stupidity."

He waved the man's apology away. "Come to the map room and tell me what you're talking about."

They made the quick trip down the stairs to the map room, which was adjacent to where he held court every day. Inside, they had a large-scale map of the city of Austin and the surrounding communities. The Vulture's secret warehouses were also marked on there. If word of their locations ever reached the populace, then his grip on power would be loosened.

"As you know, we have several tanks guarding each of the main entrances to the city," Captain Sanders indicated on the map where all the major roads came into Austin.

Justin yawned and told one of the guards to go get him coffee. "Yes, I know about your tanks," he replied dismissively.

"Of course, my lord. The team in the south near Buda was attacked by a massive pack of what they're calling wolves and—"

"Wait a minute," Justin interrupted. "You woke me to tell me about a pack of dogs?"

Sanders cringed at his words, which brought a smile to Justin's face. "They weren't regular dogs, sir. They tore through the ranks, killing twenty men. The tank crews buttoned up inside their vehicles and used the machine guns to kill the creatures."

"So a pack of vicious, hungry dogs killed some of our men. What's the big deal?"

"I would agree with you, my lord, but the survivors say that the wolves—the *dogs*—were crazed and much stronger than anything they'd ever encountered." Sanders swallowed the spit that had built up in his mouth and continued, "Sir, the men are worried about mutations. It would be of great value if you could visit them and ease their fears."

"Mutations? How the hell am I supposed to ease their fears about something that will probably happen?" Justin drummed his fingers on the map table. "Okay, fine. I'll make a trip down there and see these animals for myself and pat a few of my soldiers on the back."

"Thank you! I know the men will be excited to see you."

The guard returned with his cup of coffee. "I need this in a travel mug, you idiot! God, I swear that I'm surrounded by morons!"

Once the coffee fiasco was sorted out, he mounted up into the captain's Humvee and they drove to the edge of the city. Along the way, Justin commented on the subtle layers of defense that Sanders had put into place. The city was a fortress that could withstand any attack. Their only long-term problem would be the lack of food production. He took a note on a scrap of paper to find out if any of his people had been chemical engineers before the war. He would get them working with the farmers on how to balance out the acidity of the soil so they could grow crops. Once the city was producing its own food, they would be the ultimate power in the region—maybe even in the entire world.

They came upon the battle ground after a twenty minute drive. Sure enough, the dead and wounded were scattered across the checkpoint. It had been dogs that attacked, some of them had giant tumors while others had clearly been burned and injured beyond recognition not long before. A few of the dogs even had the remnants of collars around their necks.

He bent down to check the tag of a particularly nasty beast. It had made the journey from Seguin, Texas which was about forty or fifty miles away. "How much do we know about San Antonio?"

"I'm sorry, my lord?" Sanders asked.

"We've always assumed that San Antonio was nuked based on the explosions to the south. Seguin is a suburb of San Antonio. If this dog survived, how do we know that the city was wiped out?"

"I'll send a force right away," the captain responded. "We'll find out about the city."

"Do I have to think of everything, Captain?"

"No, sir. I just assumed that it was vaporized like everything else around us."

"What if it wasn't and there's an army preparing to invade us? Or what if it was hit, but with a smaller bomb like at Fort Hood? We could be seeing more of these mutated creatures soon."

"Yes, sir. I'll send a team immediately."

"Do that." He walked to the corpse of another animal. The bitch's tits were swollen with milk and she clearly had more of the tumors across her body. Justin stared southward in the direction of the animal's attack. Would the genetic mutations start after only one generation? What had this thing given birth to out there?

The thought of something lurking in the ashy murk made his skin crawl. "Captain, I think we may be too far spread out. We should collapse our forces back towards the city and begin building earthworks."

"Uh, earthworks, sir?" the man asked.

He sighed. "You don't know what earthworks are? You were in the Army for Christ's sake. Earthworks are fortifications around a base or a town. Basically, they're like walls.

"These things were just crazed, hungry dogs," Justin continued. "But the radiation *will* cause mutations and the things that come hunting for food will get nastier and nastier over time as the domestication is bred out of them. We need to build fortifications against those things before it's too late."

The captain saluted and said, "Yes, sir! I'll work with your engineers to determine the best places for the city's walls."

"I want the river to be the heart of the city, not outside the walls. We'll need to figure out a way to block access to the city by the river while still allowing the water to flow. Figure it out and then brief me this afternoon."

"Yes, sir. I'll send out the patrol to San Antonio and devise a plan to shrink our perimeter."

"Good. Now take me back to the palace. All this talk about mutated creatures and invading armies has stressed me out already this morning. I'm in need of something that's upstairs."

*****

Katie watched as the torturers dragged the unconscious Colonel Harris from the throne room and then the housekeepers rushed in to wipe up the blood from the marble floor. Justin had ordered the coach castrated in front of everyone because he'd refused to call him "Lord Justin" today.

She'd spent almost a month in his constant company, so she didn't understand why Justin had made such a big deal about the man refusing to obey this one time out of probably thirty or forty appearances before the leader of the Vultures. It was yet another example of his insatiable cruelty that seemed to know no bounds.

The former prom queen sat beside the hideous man every day, laughing at his stupid jokes and allowing him to rut inside of her multiple times a day with his tiny penis. She was only biding her time for the opportunity to present itself so that she could rescue Aeric and Tyler.

Katie hoped that they hadn't broken mentally. She'd been able to convince Justin early on that keeping the men alive would be much more rewarding than killing them outright. It was up to them to keep it together in their minds until she could formulate a plan of escape. She'd seen the broken and battered body of the military man who'd kicked Justin out of the Army. By the time they were brought to the Vultures' headquarters, the coach was missing most of his fingers, toes, even his ears had been mutilated. She knew that if that type of damage was done to either of the two men whom she'd traveled with from Missouri, then they might go crazy. The daily burns that her poor Aeric endured were her idea. It would at least keep him whole enough to attempt an escape.

The way that her former lover stared daggers at her during his torture broke her heart. A few weeks ago, he'd stopped talking altogether and simply stared at her as his daily torture was administered. He was either going batshit crazy now, or his hatred for her was complete.

There was nothing that she could do about it though. So far, Justin hadn't trusted her enough to allow weapons within easy reach and she was still escorted everywhere she went outside of the bedroom, including the bathroom. But that all changed this morning when he went to oversee some type of operation down on the south side of the city and didn't take the folding knife that now rested in the sole of her shoe.

Once Justin came back from the operation, he'd been in the mood for sex and she'd obliged him, not wanting to ruin her opportunity for later that evening. Then he'd wanted to see the colonel and the man's public refusal to submit to the leader of the Vultures ultimately led to his fate. Maybe the man was tired of fighting to survive and had hoped that he would be killed for disobeying. *What a messed up world we live in*, she thought.

"Bring me the baseball player!" Justin ordered.

"Which one, my lord?" the jailer asked.

Katie's heart skipped a beat and then increased in rhythm while she waited for Justin's decision. Given the mood that he was in, all of her hard work at distraction and subterfuge to keep the two men alive might have been for nothing. If he ordered Aeric to call him lord and the man refused to talk, would he curse him the way he had the colonel?

She felt Justin's eyes on her and she glanced over. He was staring at her and she smiled. "Bring me the man they call Traxx," he said quietly.

Of course he knew that Aeric and Kate had been lovers, he even knew of their long-term relationship. When they'd first been taken prisoner, she told Justin about Aeric's past in an effort to keep him alive, hoping that the madman cared enough about her to honor her wishes. It had worked so far, but there had been levels of depravity that she'd been forced to partake in that made her sick when she thought about them. Several times, Aeric had been chained to the bedroom wall while Justin had sex with her and another girl—Annie—then the man had ejaculated onto Aeric's naked body. It was disgusting beyond belief.

The slow dragging of bare feet and the clinking of chains announced Aeric's arrival in the throne room. Normally, the torturing occurred in the east wing of the former Texas State Capitol building, but the colonel's castration in the throne room had proven that it could happen wherever the hell Justin wanted it to take place.

"Ah, Traxx. How are you today?"

Aeric stared straight ahead, not answering Justin, which was now the typical response that the crowd had grown to expect from him. Katie worried that today was not the day to test Justin. *Something* had happened earlier today to get him all riled up and set him on edge.

"You know, Traxx. I really enjoy your girlfriend's attentions. She has such a calming effect on me."

Aeric's eyes shot up, flickering briefly on Justin and then settling on Kate. The look in his eyes made her change her mind. Now she hoped he would remain quiet instead of answering Justin's barbs.

"You taught her how to move perfectly." He stopped and switched his tactics, "Do you know what that jerk coach of yours tried to do today? No? Well let me tell you, he refused to bow down to me and to call me Lord Justin. Something he's done ever since I first brought him here to the palace. He wouldn't cooperate, so I took his testicles."

A genuine look of fear flickered across Aeric's scarred face and Justin noticed it. He clapped his hands excitedly, "Ah! So now we know what you're afraid of. You don't want your boys to go missing. That's understandable. I empty mine every night into your girlfriend, so I would be devastated if they weren't there anymore."

Justin surged up from the large wooden seat that had been liberated from a Catholic church and brought into the capitol building to be his throne. As he walked forward, guards flanked him and he gripped Aeric's testicles. First he pulled them hard towards himself and then he squeezed.

Aeric's lip quivered slightly, but he still didn't cry out so Justin released him and took a police baton from one of his men. He hit Aeric hard in the backs of his legs, causing him to collapse to his knees. "Finally! You kneel before me. You think I'm being cruel, Traxx, but I'm not. I'm molding you into a stronger individual. You will look back on this one day and thank me."

He waited expectantly for an answer that wouldn't come. "Oh, fine. Take him away. He's no fun. His big friend always offers us some entertainment, bring me the big Swede!"

"No!" Aeric's thundering response caused everyone in the throne room to look his way. "Leave him alone. He's suffered enough."

"Oh, *now* you speak? I've been torturing you for weeks and you haven't said a damn thing. Fucking your woman in front of you and you couldn't be bothered to curse me. Now I talk about hurting your friend and you suddenly find your damned tongue?"

"He hasn't done anything to you."

"He is part of the problem! You are a part of the problem. The old world burned because of people like you. Self-centered, egotistical, pop culture junkies who could hit a ball and became instant celebrities. Millions of people died because of your vanity—

no, make that *billions*. You two have absolutely done something to me."

"The Vultures are the ones who launched the nukes, not the common people who followed popular culture as a way to escape their daily grind. People like you are the—"

The police baton crashed hard against his ear and Aeric collapsed sideways. "Blasphemy! Where is that other one?" Justin screamed.

"Craig went to get him, my lord," one of the guards answered.

"Who the fuck is Craig?" Justin asked in confusion. "Never mind, hurry up!"

The guard in question returned with a shackled Tyler in tow. "Ah, thank you, Craig!"

Justin walked rapidly to the fire pit that had been erected in the throne room. It was little more than a ring of bricks sitting on the floor where they burned wood to take some of the chill out of the air. He grabbed the poker that sat in the fire and walked back to Tyler.

"Hold him," he ordered. "I am not the problem, Traxx. It's men like you and your big friend here."

He plunged the glowing hot poker into Tyler's eye. Katie turned her head and covered her ears as the super-heated metal popped the mucus layer on Tyler's eye and sizzled against the fluid inside. Tyler screamed for a few seconds, throwing the smaller guards around and then passed out.

Justin pulled the poker away and jabbed it roughly into Aeric's ribs where it sank several inches. "Take these assholes back to the torture room."

He fought visibly to control his emotions of anger and smoothed his hair into place before walking back to the throne. "I have tried to help those men repent for their sins against the old world, but they have refused. I can't do anything else for them. At dawn tomorrow morning, we'll have an old-fashioned hanging. These men will pay the ultimate price for their sins."

The crowd murmured in approval of his decision and he turned to Katie and grabbed her by the wrist. "Come on, I need another release."

TWELVE

Katie lay still underneath Justin until he was done thrusting into her and finished his business. Then he collapsed on top of her body in a sweaty heap and nuzzled his greasy nose against her neck.

"Yeah, baby, that's what I needed," he said.

"Can I go clean up now?" she asked.

He pulled back away from her and asked, "Is something wrong?"

"No, my lord. I just don't feel well."

"You don't want Traxx to die, is that it?"

"Of course I don't want him to die. He was my first boyfriend. I just want him to be able to live his life in peace."

"He has about twelve hours left. Do you want me to send him a woman so he can go out with a bang? No pun intended of course." Katie frowned at his stupid attempt at humor.

"No, just make it quick so he doesn't suffer any more," she replied.

"As heavy as that guy is, his neck will snap like a twig. Promise."

She sighed and nodded her head. "Thank you, my lord. Can I go get cleaned up now?"

"Yeah, fine. Make it quick though in case I need some more."

Katie grinned mischievously at him. "You're insatiable today."

"There have been a lot of interesting developments that are on my mind and sex helps me think clearly."

She made an effort to push her lip out in a pouty expression. He noticed it and squeezed her breast, "Of course, being close to you is what *really* helps me out."

Katie nodded her head, saying, "That's right." She slid out of bed and bent down seductively away from him, giving him a full view of everything she had as she reached into her shoe. "This is what makes everything better."

She gave a fake squeal of delight as he slapped her hard on the ass. "Go to the bathroom, I think I'm ready for round two, baby," Justin said.

Katie walked quickly across the room to the bathroom and sat heavily on the toilet. She tried her best to get everything out of her, but she knew that there was still a part of him *inside* of her and it made her want to throw up.

Her hands shook as she unfolded the knife that she'd taken that morning. The thought of Justin touching her again made her sick, but the idea of taking a human life was worse. She'd been forced to do absolutely horrible and disgusting things to stay alive and to keep people away from her younger sister, but could she actually kill someone? Besides the few times when he'd forced her to have sex with a few of the palace women and humiliated her in front of Aeric, he'd been gentle enough with her. Did she have what it took to kill him?

The blade locked in place with a soft click. She'd watched that man in the next room beat people, torture them, cut off body parts and repeatedly commit murder. If what Aeric and Tyler had told her was true, then his gang was responsible for the nuclear war. There was no doubt in her mind that he was evil incarnate. She could do this.

She stood and hid the knife along the back of her forearm before opening the bathroom door and walking out. "Oh, good, I was starting to wonder if you were taking a crap or something."

Katie exaggerated the sway in her hips as she walked towards the bed, allowing the candlelight to play across her cold-hardened nipples. "That's not very sexy, my lord."

He threw back the covers to reveal his small, semi-erect member and asked, "Is this sexy?"

She placed a knee on the bed and grinned. "Yeah, baby. You know I love it." She bent over seductively and suppressed a gasp of pain as the knife's tip dug into the skin on her arm.

"You know what I want first," he ordered.

Katie nodded and slid the hand with the knife under the covers while she bent down over him. It took a few minutes to get him to where he wanted to be, but he finally told her to climb on top of him. She positioned herself and he leaned his head back in ecstasy.

She grabbed a pillow and pressed it hard against his face while she stabbed savagely into his neck. Blood spurted towards the ceiling when she pulled the blade from his artery, spraying across her naked body. The knife lifted and fell again and again, leaving jagged wounds across his chest and then in his stomach. The air filled with the smell of half-digested food and feces as the blade plunged into his intestines, spilling their contents. Justin's struggling stopped and the sheets turned a deep red as the last of the blood flowed from his bloody corpse.

Katie leaned to the side of the bed and threw up. Then she pulled the knife from his body one more time and ran it across the man's throat to ensure that he was dead. She'd already went this far, there was no sense in leaving herself open for a comeback.

She gently lifted herself off of him and used the bedsheet to wipe herself off. Then she settled down to wait.

*****

The clinking of chains woke Traxx and he looked around wild-eyed into the near darkness. He was used to the normal movement of Coach Harris and Tyler throughout the night in the next room over, however this was different. It sounded like the chains had fallen to the floor. In the morning, he and Tyler were condemned to death by hanging, but it was still the middle of the night. What were the guards up to this time?

The movement increased and then the twisting of his cell's door handle announced that someone had come inside. He attempted to see over his shoulder to determine what was happening. It was no use. He couldn't see anything in the half light of the hall's candles. It was probably another one of Justin's ways to fuck with him or one of the night guards coming to rape him one last time.

A flash of blonde hair appeared over his shoulder and he immediately saw red. Katie had been sent to him in one final twist of the knife in his gut. He understood her desire to stay alive, but it still hurt him more than he could have ever imagined that he'd been deceived by her so completely.

"Hold still," Kate said. "We've got bolt cutters for the chains."

Her words swam through his mind but they didn't process correctly. In an even crueler twist, Justin must have sent her to be the one who unlocked the chains before the hanging. Had the entire night passed without him realizing it and now the hour of his death had arrived?

A familiar face appeared in front of him. Dried, crusted blood and mucus covered his cheek and jaw where it had oozed unattended for hours after Justin had put out his eye. "Dude, Katie is rescuing us. We need to hurry."

"Tyler? Oh my God, I'm so sorry for what that bastard has done to you."

"Can't be helped. Let's get out of here."

Katie materialized beside Tyler and lifted the bolt cutters. The chain broke with an audible snap and he fell the several inches to the ground. Tyler held the kettlebell handle to keep it from hitting the floor and set it down between his feet. As soon as his vision cleared, Aeric reached out and placed his hands around Kate's throat to squeeze the life from her worthless body.

"You filthy whore!" he spat. "I'm going to kill you!"

Tyler's meaty hand wrapped around his wrist and pulled weakly at it. "Stop, she's helping us."

Traxx saw her eyes beginning to roll back in her head. A few more seconds and he'd be rid of her forever. She'd never be able to betray him again and he'd never be manipulated by her again, forced to do things in order to keep her safe. He'd never have to worry about her safety again, never have to wonder if she was alright, or if she was in pain….

He opened his hands and she collapsed to the floor. "Fuck. What have I done? Katie, are you alright?"

She sat up weakly, glaring at him and gasping for air. After several seconds she muttered, "You're welcome, you fucking prick."

"I'm sorry. I'm so sorry," he said and reached out for her.

She recoiled from his grasp and whimpered, "Don't touch me! We need to go before they find the bodies."

Traxx didn't know what the woman was talking about, but he knew better than to ask and delay the rescue attempt. "Do you know the way out?"

"I know how to get to the back door, but after that, it's all new to me," she admitted.

"We need weapons," Tyler said.

"What about Coach Harris?"

"He was in the same room as me. When Katie killed the guard and opened the door, we tried to get him to come with us." Tyler shook his head, "The dude's gone to Lala Land. There's nothing left upstairs, man. We cut off his chains, but he just curled into a ball and talked to himself."

Traxx nodded in acceptance. He'd been pretty close to losing it himself and coach had been in Justin's "care" for months longer than he had been. He glanced at Kate. She sat on the floor rubbing her neck. Maybe he *had* lost it and just didn't realize it yet.

"I'm not leaving until that bastard is dead. I don't care if they catch me again, he can't be allowed to live."

Kate accepted Tyler's outstretched hand and he pulled her to her feet. "He's dead. I was finally able to get a weapon and I killed him. Oh God, I stabbed him over and over. Then I slit his throat to make sure he was truly dead."

The look of pain and sorrow that crossed her face made his cold heart melt. Traxx realized that she'd been just as much of a slave in this place as he'd been a prisoner. She hadn't traipsed around the palace on her own, in fact, this was the first time that he'd ever seen her without a guard. She'd been forced to have sex with that madman and she'd been biding her time until the opportunity presented itself for her to strike.

He gestured towards her throat and said, "I know this doesn't help, Katie, but I'm sorry. I'm sorry for everything that you were forced to do. I'm sorry that I choked you. I'm sorry that I believed that you'd betrayed me."

Her lips pressed thin and she nodded. That was all he was going to get out of her for now. He looked over towards his friend, "We need weapons."

Tyler bent and picked up the bolt cutters. "I'll beat motherfuckers to death with these."

Kate pulled a bloody knife from the pocket of her pants. "You can take this. I don't ever want to use it again."

"I don't suppose you got any of our clothes, did you?" Tyler asked as he gestured to his naked, shit- and piss-covered body.

"No. You'll just have to get over your modesty for now, big guy," Katie replied. "We need to get going. They're going to find the guards' bodies soon and Captain Sanders always comes to brief Justin in the morning."

"What time is it?" Traxx asked.

"No idea. I had to wait a long time after I killed Justin…until the bedchamber guard went to the bathroom."

He accepted her explanation without comment and walked gingerly towards the open doorway. His legs were still wobbly from being chained for so long. It couldn't be helped. They had to get out of the Vulture's palace before they were discovered.

The bloody body of a guard sat in the hallway so he dragged it into the room. It had a knife and a pistol, so he grabbed both and then sized up the rail-thin body. There was no way that the man's clothes would come even close to fitting either of the two of them.

They closed the door and then stopped quickly at the one where Coach Harris was writhing on the floor as if he were in pain. His body jerked and he stretched out to his entire length, then back to a fetal position. It reminded Aeric of how possessed people used to look in the movies. The man had clearly lost his mind and wouldn't be going anywhere anytime soon.

Aeric started to leave him, but had a change of heart and went into the room. He knelt beside the pathetic shell of the man that he'd once looked up to and tried to talk to him. Coach Harris didn't even realize that Aeric was there. He had a choice to make and he didn't have a lot of time. He could leave the man there to be tortured further or he could end his suffering.

Aeric tried one final time to get the man to stop, to listen to the message that he was free, but the madman heard none of it. His body straightened to his full height as the blade of Katie's knife went through his chin up into his brain. Aeric left the knife in place until the body spasms stopped and then pulled it bitterly from the old man's brain.

Tyler nodded his head curtly in approval and the group left the torture room. They followed the hallway towards the stairs and crept quietly down to the first floor. At the base of the stairs, two guards sat playing cards, obviously bored of their assignment. Neither of them saw the two naked men descending on them. Tyler bashed in the head of one of the guards while Aeric stabbed the other in the throat. It was over before it even began.

They turned left towards the back of the building, creeping through the darkness, ready to do whatever they had to do in order to escape. When they arrived at the building's north entrance, they startled two more guards who were watching the doors to the outside to ensure no one tried to enter in the middle of the night. These two were vastly more attentive than the men at the stairs and recovered quickly from their surprise.

One of the guards blocked Tyler's swing with the bolt cutters. It shattered his forearm, but he was still able to fight and brought up his pistol. Aeric's target hadn't been as lucky. He dodged the blade aimed at his neck, but took it to the chest instead. The knife penetrated his lung and put him down so that Traxx was able to slit his throat.

The first guard's shot went wide of Tyler, striking a pillar on the far side of the rotunda and echoing across the great hallway. Aeric stabbed him from behind and grabbed his pistol. "Let's go! We need to move. *NOW!*" he shouted.

The group burst through the doors and raced barefoot across the pavement towards the single guard shack near the entrance from the street. They had no way of knowing if there was a sniper up in the rafters of the capitol building taking aim on them or if the late hour assisted them. Traxx cursed their bad luck at the guard who'd shot his weapon, probably alerting everyone around that they were attempting to escape.

There was nothing that could be done about it though. The governor's entrance was wide open, with no cover or concealment so they just ran full tilt. Tyler had trouble maintaining his balance due to the lack of depth perception with only one eye and stumbled multiple times. They raced past a giant circular hole in the ground and Aeric's mind flashed on what the hell that could have been for. It was clearly man-made with pillars and glass windows down below. It was mildly interesting, but not important enough to stop and read the plaque.

He sprinted ahead of the other two, grimacing as boils burst and scabs across his body ripped open. Aeric didn't even bother to see if anyone was in the guard shack, he fired three rounds into the glass doorway and continued running. The glass was bulletproof and it spider-webbed. If there were guards inside, the ear-shattering noise would likely cause them to keep their damn heads down until Aeric and his friends could make it past the structure.

No one returned fire from the guard shack and he immediately turned left out of the building, heading westward down old 15th Street. Traxx slowed to a walk behind the relative safety of a five-story building that blocked him from view of the palace. He allowed Katie and Tyler to catch up to him and then began jogging slowly. He needed to find a place to rest soon, though. His body was unused to the physical activity, nearly starved and he was battered and broken. Tyler seemed like he was in worse shape than Aeric was—which was saying a lot.

"I've got to stop soon," he admitted once they were several blocks away.

"Where can we go?"

Traxx ignored Katie's question and looked over to their large companion. He was clearly beginning to flag, but didn't complain or say anything. "How are you holding up?"

"We need...to get off...this main road," Tyler answered gasping for breath between words.

They crossed a large street and Aeric tried to determine which one it was. The moon was hidden behind the clouds of ash that still smothered the earth and there were no lights anywhere. "I don't know where we are," he admitted.

"Lavaca," Tyler replied. He pointed to the next street and said, "Guadalupe."

"Let's go north on Guadalupe," Traxx said. "In a couple of blocks, we can try to hide out."

They made it to 18th Street and then slowed to a walk once again. By the next block, they were looking for a place to hide. Then, the idea hit Aeric. "What if we go to Veronica's place? Either she's there or not, but her neighbor had clothes that fit us."

"How far?" Tyler asked.

"It was what, 27th or 28th Street, right?" Aeric asked.

"28th and Guadalupe."

"Okay, so we're only about ten blocks away, maybe less. Can you make it that far?"

"I'm good to go. Just need a goal to focus on."

"What do we do if this woman that you're so infatuated with isn't there?" Katie asked.

Aeric glanced at her. She was still jealous about Veronica, a girl that Aeric barely knew. He shook his head. He'd *never* understand what went through women's minds. They'd just escaped—hell, were still trying to escape—a cesspool of torture, murder and rape and she was jealous like a school girl.

"Then we steal whatever we can find and try to make it to San Angelo like we'd planned all along."

"Well, what if she *is* there?"

He stopped and looked over at her. "Are you serious right now? We're running for our lives and you're acting like a damned…" He sighed in frustration. Fighting amongst themselves wouldn't do any good. "I don't know what you're acting like, but knock it the fuck off. If she's there, then we'll find out why she's still there and not in San Angelo. Hell, for all we know, that place could be worse off than Austin."

She put both of her hands on her waist and cocked her hips out to the side. "You don't have a right to treat me like that—no, shut up." She held up her hand and Aeric could see the darkened lines on her skin where blood had dried in the crevices. "Yeah, you were tortured, but so was I. Maybe not to the extreme physical level that you were, but that son of a bitch abused me mentally and raped me two or three times a day. The only thing that kept me going was the thought that I'd be able to find a way to save you. Yes, I want to know what your obsession is with this woman. All you've ever talked about is how she was going to lead us to her family.

"I did have a relationship with you before," she continued. "But I was too scared of losing you to ask you the question. Now I want an answer, what does this woman mean to you?"

"You need to lower your voice. I think we're starting to attract attention," Tyler said quietly as he pointed to some of the buildings around them where a few faces had pressed near the glass.

"Can we talk about this when we're off the street?" Aeric asked.

"No, asshole. I want to know if you were just using me for sex before."

"Are you kidding me? *Me* using *you*? Don't you think that's like the pot calling the kettle black?"

"I want an answer. It shouldn't be that hard to get a straight answer out of you. Are you dating Veronica or what?"

Aeric sighed. "Look, I met her for one night. Sure, we hit it off, but there was nothing sexual about it, just friends. She told us about San Angelo and honestly, if it's even half as good as she said it would be, then it's a hundred times better than out here."

"That's it? You just want someplace safe to go?"

"Yeah, Katie, that's it. I'd been trying to find a place for my mom and me to go, but she—" Aeric glanced over at his friend. "She's dead now."

In truth, he didn't know what had happened. When he was being tortured for the first time, naked and afraid in front of everyone who cheered the men on, he'd seen Tyler's bloody and unconscious form carried across the chamber. Since no one else was brought in, he assumed that they were all gone.

In truth, he didn't know what, if anything, Veronica meant to him. She'd offered him a chance to go someplace that might have been unaffected by the war. Like Tyler, he just needed a goal to focus on. "Can we just keep walking? We need to get inside somewhere," Traxx said. "This town has changed. It's not the fun, beautiful city that it used to be. Now it's just a wasted shell where humans exist until they die."

*****

They ducked in and out of doorways, taking advantage of the shadows as much as possible as the morning began to lighten. Finally, they saw the building where Veronica lived and they rushed forward. Aeric snorted in derision as they passed three skeletons near the middle of her parking lot. Animals had eaten most of the flesh from the thugs that he and Tyler had killed when they stayed the night at Veronica's. No one had even bothered to remove the bodies to the piles that ringed the city.

The glass doorway to the back stairs was little more than a jagged frame of glass shards and metal. They didn't need to open it, they simply stepped through the door and made for the stairs. Aeric's sense of déjà vu was overwhelming as he pushed open the stairwell door and used the chair to block it once again when they were inside. It was as if the place had been totally abandoned and not touched since the night they left more than three months ago.

That wasn't the reality of the situation, though. There were dried blood stains in the stairwell that most definitely were not there the first time that they'd come through the apartment and the building had a much colder, abandoned feel to it. The concrete of the stairs radiated the early morning chill and a puff of steam appeared before their faces every time they breathed out. Their bodies would soon begin to cool after their run from the palace building. If they didn't get clothing soon, they were in danger of becoming sick—or worse.

The trip up the stairs to the seventh floor was unnervingly similar and horribly different at the same time. The blood and other bodily fluids twisted Aeric's recollections of that first night after the power went out into a bizarre mockery of his memories. When they reached the top, the hallway door stood slightly ajar due to an old shoe that had been used to prop it open.

They slid silently along the wall towards Veronica's apartment. Signs of fighting and property destruction littered the hallway. Bullet holes peppered the walls at various points and just about every doorframe that they came to showed signs of damage from being kicked in.

When they arrived at Veronica's door, it was the same story. Her door had been forced open at some point. Aeric wondered who could have systematically gone through the building, entering every apartment. Of course, after his time with them, the answer was obvious. The Vultures had probably come through to collect food and useful items, that way the population would have to rely on them for its survival.

He nudged her door open with the barrel of the pistol and entered Veronica's ransacked apartment. No one was in the living room, her television had been smashed, movies covered the floors, and even the couch cushions looked like they'd been ripped open with a knife.

They cleared the apartment rapidly. Her kitchen was predictably empty of any foodstuffs and the bedroom had been torn apart by the Vultures who'd been looking for anything of value. It made him sick to his stomach. The only bright spot that he could cling to was the absence of any blood or signs of a struggle besides the damage done by the animals' that'd searched the apartment.

Katie found Veronica's note crumpled on the floor behind the couch. She read it and snorted before handing it to Aeric. He glanced at her strange reaction and read the note.

> *Aeric,*
>
> *I hope you made it to Missouri and found your mom and dad. It's been eight days since you left and my father finally arrived this morning. I'm sure by now that you know about the nuclear war. His car stopped working and he had to find a bicycle to make it the rest of the way here, so that's what took him so long.*
>
> *Things have gotten worse in Austin. The Vultures seem to be everywhere and I hear gunfire constantly. I've tried to stay away from the windows like you told*

me to, but I've been tempted and seen some pretty bad things happen out on the street. Please, leave the city at once and go to my father's house at the address that I gave you.

My dad is checking for anything useful, one last time, before we go in a few minutes. Then we have to find a bike for me, it's too far to walk to... Well, you know where. God, I wish my horse was here!

Tell Tyler that I've been thinking a lot about the two of you and I can't wait to meet back up with you when you get there.

See you soon,
Veronica

She'd kissed the paper beside her signature with a purple lipstick. What the hell was that about?

He handed the letter over to Tyler who skimmed it and then said, "We should go get clothes before we rest," Tyler said wearily.

"Yeah. You're right," Traxx agreed. "Katie, I need you to stay here and keep this apartment secured while we go to the one next door and try to find some clothing."

Kate started to protest, but decided against it and nodded her head instead. "I risked my ass to rescue you two and killed two men. Don't mess around and get yourselves killed trying to get some clothing."

"It's just across the hall," Aeric replied. "It shouldn't take more than five or ten minutes. Once we get back, I'll knock twice. That'll be your signal to let us back in."

He considered just leaving, knowing that she'd probably been with that madman last night and hadn't had a chance to clean herself, but decided to suppress his emotions and gave Kate a quick peck on the cheek, saying, "We'll be right back."

"Yeah, and we're gonna talk about Veronica. Seriously, what kind of woman wears purple lipstick?"

Aeric suppressed the urge to sigh and went through the doorway behind Tyler. They crept across the hall and stood on either side of the door like they'd seen in countless police and military movies. It made sense to not get shot through the door if there was a trigger-happy squatter living in the dead man's apartment. When they were ready, Tyler knocked softly and they waited. There wasn't a response so he knocked a little harder.

The door pushed open with this knock and Aeric called inside, "Anyone home? We're from across the hall."

There still wasn't a response, so Aeric went inside, pistol first. This apartment had been ransacked much the same as Veronica's. No one was in the apartment, so they went back to the bedroom as they'd done all those months ago and grabbed as many changes of clothing as they could. They'd figure out what fit and what didn't once they were back in the apartment with Katie.

It took three trips to move the clothing and footwear from the other apartment. Once they were done, they locked the door with the chain lock and blocked it with the couch. They were mildly certain that they were secure, so Aeric and Tyler began trying on clothing while Katie went into Veronica's bathroom to use whatever was left in there to clean herself up.

"There are some wet toilet wipes that have moisture left in them and the toilet reservoir is still over half full," she announced when she returned. "You boys smell horrible, maybe you should go get cleaned up as much as possible. There's also a small first aid kit under the sink, so once you're cleaned, I can bandage the worst of your wounds."

"Thanks," Aeric replied. "Did you happen to find any antibiotics or Tylenol or anything like that?"

She shook her head. "No. If she had any, it must have been taken by whoever searched the place."

Aeric took a bowl into the bathroom so he could scoop out water for washing from the toilet basin without contaminating their only potential drinking source. He used a washcloth and tried to wash away the grime, dried body fluids and excrement as best that he could. He took special care around the hole in his side that he'd almost forgotten about until now. The cream-colored cloth quickly turned black with the nastiness. When he was finally done, he looked at himself in the mirror.

He was thankful for the poor lighting in the bathroom. He'd lost a lot of weight during the trip to and from Missouri, but he looked positively *skinny* now. The months in captivity, barely kept above starvation levels and the constant physical abuse had taken their toll on his body. At least he was mostly whole, Tyler looked much worse.

Aeric had to wake his buddy from a deep slumber so he could go into the bathroom to clean his own wounds. Once he was gone, Aeric asked Katie, "How are you holding up?"

"As good as can be expected, I guess. There was a lot of messed up stuff that happened at the Vulture's palace. The shitty part is that I've already become numb to the things that happen in this world now."

He thinned his lips in a grimace. It wasn't supposed to be like this. They were still kids, they should be out having fun, worrying about exams and making poor decisions on the weekend, not killing people and fighting off evil bastards.

"I'm sorry for what you went through. It shouldn't have been like that. You should have stayed with the others outside of the city."

"What, and then just left when you didn't come back? I don't think so, Aeric. I love you."

Well, there you had it. She still had feelings for him, even after he tried to choke her to death, called her horrible names and now the letter that Veronica kissed. "I didn't want you to get involved in all of this," he said. "I'm sorry."

She held up a hand to stop him. "Aeric, it's been a long time since we split up with your mom and…and Julie. But remember that day, when I told you that it wasn't your choice whether I went with you or not? I go with you wherever you go from here on out. Period. We'll deal with the whole Veronica mess when we get to San Angelo and can go to sleep without looking over our shoulder."

He smiled at her words and gritted his teeth. "Here, let me clean that puncture wound in your side." Katie indicated his ribs where Justin had stabbed him with the fireplace poker after he'd jabbed out Tyler's eye. "That's gonna get infected soon if we don't get it cleaned and covered up."

Aeric lay on his side while she used a generous amount of alcohol. His body had become so accustomed to injury that it barely registered with him. Her hands were gentle as she used paper towels to clean away the liquids that erupted from the injury. He thought about the hatred for her that had festered during his captivity and how wrong about her that he'd been. He felt ashamed of his actions and vowed to himself that he would do whatever he could to make it up to her.

Tyler returned from the restroom and she doctored him the best that she could. None of them knew what to do for his eye except to clean around the edges and cover it. Katie didn't want to use the alcohol down inside the socket like she'd done for Aeric's wound since she wasn't sure that would be beneficial. They needed a substantial first aid booklet that they just didn't have.

Besides the eye, Tyler was missing his right ear, both of his pinkie fingers, his nipples had been sliced off and he'd been repeatedly whipped with a metal-tipped flail. Aeric was amazed that the big man was upright, let alone that he had the energy to run for almost twenty blocks.

Almost as soon as they were done working on him, Tyler collapsed onto the ripped couch and passed out. They moved silently across the room and Aeric lifted the blinds slightly to look out onto the gloomy Austin morning. It wasn't a pretty sight and he dropped the slat back into place.

Katie came up behind him and wrapped her arms around his waist, resting her head against his back. "Can we go lay down?"

"Yeah, I'm really tired," he replied and then he looked around the room. The clothing that they'd pilfered lay in piles according to what fit whom. He was exhausted and needed to sleep, but the long months on the road had conditioned him to prepare everything to make a run for it in case they were surprised in the night. It took him a few minutes to make modified knapsacks out of a couple of long-sleeved t-shirts and then he stuffed everything inside. It would keep their clothing together while they ran down the stairs if it came to that.

Aeric and Katie walked awkwardly back to the bedroom. He thought about how he'd fantasized about having sex with Veronica in that very bed and what that meant for his relationship with Kate. They didn't bother to try to do anything, though. Almost as soon as they were horizontal, they were both snoring.

*****

The noise wouldn't go away. Had those bastards devised a new way of torturing him? He tried to open his eye, but couldn't see anything. His body registered that he was *lying* on his left side, had they laid him down for today's torture session?

Once again, the noise came, this time more clearly now that he was partially awake. It was someone's voice repeating the same phrase over and over, although it didn't necessarily sound like a normal voice. The message came again and he realized that he was hearing a speaker. Someone was actually using an electronic speaker to broadcast their voice.

Tyler sat up quickly and immediately regretted it as the world came crashing back into his head. It felt like it was going to explode and the pain where his eye should have been was excruciating. He staggered to the window and saw a short convoy of Army Humvees traveling slowly down Guadalupe. Seeing the trucks driving was strange enough, but the fact that their electronics worked was nearly enough to send him into shock—or maybe it was the blood loss that those assholes had caused.

The speaker on the lead Humvee continually repeated the phrase, "*Traxx… We know you're out here and we're coming for you!*"

He thought about it for a moment. They didn't know anything. They were just trying to spook Aeric into doing something foolish so they could find him. Austin was a big city and there was no way that they even knew what direction that they'd gone in. The key was keeping a low profile and not letting anyone see them who could turn them in for food.

Tyler thought about it for a moment and then made the decision to go talk to Aeric. He hoped that he wasn't interrupting the two of them having sex, but it was important to discuss their shared future. He walked down the hall, dragging his feet to make as much noise as possible and then knocked softly on the door.

After a second knock, Aeric replied, "Wha—?"

"Hey, it's Ty. We need to talk about what's going on outside."

"Outside?"

Tyler sighed, his friend was obviously still asleep. "Are you guys decent? It'd be easier to talk to you in person."

"Sure, come in, buddy."

He opened the door and saw that they were both still in bed. Katie's arms were draped across Aeric and she was still asleep. He was amazed that they were able to sleep through the announcements outside. They'd seemed extremely loud to him, maybe the two of them had a late night. After what Katie had done for them, he'd never begrudge her anything that she wanted. Ever.

"Did you hear the messages that the Vultures were playing outside?"

"No?" Aeric answered with a questioning lilt at the end of his word.

"They're driving up and down the street in those Humvees that they have calling out for 'Traxx' and saying that they know where you are."

Aeric slid away from Kate and started to throw on his clothes. "Whoa, hold on, man," Tyler said, placing a restraining hand on his friend's shoulder. "I've been thinking about it. They don't know where you are. They probably have groups of men searching all over the city and they're just trying to flush you out of hiding."

Aeric sat heavily on the bed and Kate pulled herself up close to his thigh. "Morning, Ty," she mumbled. Apparently, she was content to lay in bed with Aeric until they made a decision.

"Good *evening*, Katie," he replied. "I think the best thing to do is to lay low for a couple of days and let this thing settle down."

Aeric nodded his head. "Yeah, I think you're right. They probably don't have a clue where we are." He took a deep breath and continued, "And you're also right about holing up here for a while, although I don't want to. What are we gonna do for food?"

"I guess we'll have to scrounge."

"Kinda hard to keep a low profile if we're out searching for food, huh?" Aeric muttered.

"Maybe we can find stuff here in the building. It's doubtful, but it's better than the alternative of going out and interacting with people who might try to turn us in."

"This sucks," Kate moaned from behind Aeric. "I wish we could just leave and never come back."

"We will soon," Aeric assured her. "It makes the most sense to stay here for a few days while we let this thing blow over. Hopefully, there will be infighting soon to determine who will lead the Vultures and they'll forget all about us."

Tyler's stomach growled audibly, which caused all three of them to laugh. Once he'd stopped, he smiled to himself. It would be alright. They'd find food, stay safe and then make it to San Angelo. If San Angelo wasn't a viable option, then they'd keep going until they found somewhere safe. As long as they were together, everything would be alright.

THIRTEEN

It took a month for Aeric, Tyler and Katie to make it to San Angelo. They'd spent a full week in Veronica's apartment, combing the building for food supplies. In a strange twist of fate—or mass murder—the building was empty of residents. It didn't matter though, since most of the food had been stolen anyways. But there were enough crumbs and an occasional can of vegetables to keep them alive until the Vultures stopped looking for them.

They made their run for the north part of the city on the evening of their sixth day at Veronica's. Before they left the city forever, they went to the building where Tyler and the girls had been ambushed. Beth Gaines' body was gone and none of their gear remained. Austin's scavengers had swept in and cleaned everything out. Aeric and Kate paid their respects at the place where his mother had died and then they continued on into the night.

On their trip westward, they stayed in the Balcones Canyonlands Wildlife Refuge for three days because they were able to kill an emaciated deer and didn't have any means to transport the meat. They gorged themselves at each meal until there was almost nothing left of the beast and when they left the wildlife refuge they felt satisfied for the first time in months.

They were on foot until halfway between the ghost town of Llano and the small city of Brady when they stumbled upon a mass of dead bodies just off the highway. It looked like there'd been some type of gang warfare between two groups, one that wore all black and another that had Texas flag bandanas tied around their arms. The battle looked as if they'd each killed each other and whoever had been left alive fled the scene, leaving a lot of gear behind. So they were able to get bicycles, rifles and some heavier clothing, but they still had to scrape by for food and potable water.

The trip became much easier with the addition of the bikes, and after weeks on the road, their pace increased once they saw the few high rises on San Angelo's skyline. They unwittingly headed down the same highway that Julie and Kayla had taken seven weeks prior and topped the very same rise where she'd encountered Shellie.

Aeric's small group topped the hill's rise and saw two military Humvees resting on the reverse slope. They hadn't been able to see them on the opposite side of the rise. One of the vehicles was tan, like Lorelei's had been and one was green. Both had machine guns mounted on the top that were aimed at them. The guards were much more prepared for strangers now than they had been when Julie came through and fired two warning shots off to the side of the road. Experience had taught them to scare off the wanderers early or else they could quickly overwhelm the guard force.

"That's far enough," a man yelled. "We don't have any food and you're not welcome here. Go back where you came from."

"Please, we've been on the road since the beginning of all this," Aeric shouted back.

"Well, then just go around the city and keep on travelin'. You wanderers are worthless and all you do is take, take, take until you use something up and then you move on to the next place. We ain't got the resources for your kind."

Aeric opened his mouth and then closed it quickly. He hadn't anticipated meeting the motley mix of military and civilian guards, especially not so many of them. He wondered about the city's resources, if they could afford to have so many people on one guard shift at only one of the many roads leading to the city. Were they all as heavily guarded or was it simply because this was the road that led to Austin?

"We're not wanderers," he finally managed to say. "Yeah, we've been on the road, but we had a destination to go to and San Angelo is where we'd planned on going all along."

"Look, boy, are you deaf? I said we ain't acceptin' no new residents," the man yelled back at them.

"We were invited here by one of the city's residents before the war started." He didn't have anything to lose, so he took a shot and said, "Miss Veronica Delgado told us that she had a place for us to stay. Have you heard of her? She lives on Briarglove Lane on the south side of the city."

There was movement among the guards and finally a woman called out, "Come closer."

They walked their bikes slowly down the slope until they were about fifty feet from the guards and their military Humvees. "What's your name?" the woman asked.

"I'm Aeric Traxx," he replied automatically taking the name that he'd been given from all of his scars. He indicated his friends, "This is my friend Tyler Nordgren and my girlfriend, Kate Hampton."

"Holy shit, you survived! We thought you were dead."

"Huh?"

The squeal of metal scraping against the asphalt pavement filled the morning silence as the makeshift gate that had been placed across the road was moved out of the way. A single figure wearing a gas mask came out from behind the gate, walking rapidly towards them.

"Aeric! It's me, Lorelei," the woman said as she came closer.

"Lorelei? Oh my God! I... I don't know what to say."

She wrapped him in a hug that took him by surprise. "You were right about San Angelo. The Air Force base here was spared and they only had a small Security Forces element, so they welcomed our expertise in military tactics." She lowered her voice and said confidentially, "The Air Force guys had no clue how to run security. Even my group of Army mechanics is better trained than those clowns."

"Wow. I can't believe that you're actually here," Tyler said as he also hugged the lieutenant.

"That goes triple for me. I can't believe that you guys made it all the way to—where was it again?"

"Missouri," Aeric answered.

"Damn. Yeah, Missouri and back. That's crazy. You've been out there this whole time?"

Aeric held up his hands and said, "We were taken prisoner in Austin by the Vultures. They tortured us."

"We've heard stories about them. How did you escape?"

"It wasn't easy," he indicated Tyler and continued, "and both of us are horribly scarred from it. Katie actually rescued us. She killed their leader, Justin, and then helped us escape."

Lorelei's blue eyes flicked over to observe Kate. Aeric could tell that she was measuring the woman up and that bit of information had just made Kate a very dangerous addition to their group in the lieutenant's mind. "Good job, Katie. That's some good news that we haven't heard about yet."

"Thanks," Kate replied and busied herself with a piece of loose leather on her bike's handlebars.

She looked back to Aeric and asked, "The Vultures tortured you?"

"Yeah. They put out Tyler's eye and cut off his ear and some fingers." Tyler pulled off his sunglasses to reveal the new, bright pink skin that was growing together where his right eye had been.

"Oh, man. I'm so sorry," she said. "Okay, you guys are clear to come through our checkpoint. I think Miss Delgado will be surprised to see you. I've met her a few times and actually told her that you were the ones who recommended that my platoon come here if Fort Hood was destroyed."

"Is it?" Tyler asked as he put his sunglasses back into place.

"Yeah, it's gone. Looks like a small ground burst nuke took it out. The damage was mostly contained by the terrain around the base, so not much outside of the bowl that it sat in was damaged. Helped keep the radiation in too."

"I'm sorry, Lorelei," Aeric said. "I know you were hopeful that it would be there."

She nodded her head and the rubber of her protective mask made a swishing noise as it rubbed against her clothing. "Yeah… It can't be helped. We've all lost someone. The only things that we can do are to honor their memory and try to be the person that they wanted us to be."

She didn't elaborate and Aeric wasn't going to push her for who she'd lost. Maybe one day, they'd be able to get together and talk about what had happened. Instead, he focused on what they'd been talking about before he became sidetracked with Fort Hood's demise. "So Veronica is here? We weren't sure."

"Yes, sir. Just like you said she'd be. And like I said, she's going to be surprised to see you guys. That little girl that lives with her told her that you were dead."

"Huh? I guess I missed that part of the story," he admitted.

"There's a teenager who showed up a month or two ago with a baby. She said that she'd been traveling with you and that you were all dead."

"Julie?" Kate blurted out.

Lorelei looked over to Kate once again. "I don't remember her name. Cute little baby though. They split time living with Veronica and her dad and one of my guards when she's not on duty."

It was a miracle and they all hugged each other, even Tyler and Kate, who'd developed a tenuous friendship after she'd proven that she wasn't simply using Aeric to stay alive. Julie and Kayla were alright and they were here in San Angelo with Veronica. Aeric marveled at the way everything worked out. The only person who hadn't survived the trip was his mother, which was odd since the entire point of their trip to Missouri had been for her and his father.

"Julie is my little sister," Kate told Lorelei when their embrace ended. "We thought that they died in Austin on the day that we were all taken hostage."

"Oh, wow, that's awesome!" the lieutenant said. "Okay, I know you guys have been on the road for a long time. You're probably tired and hungry, so we've got some food—"

"Lorelei, if you don't mind, we'd like to see Julie and Kayla first," Aeric answered for the group.

"Oh. Of course," she made a gesture like she was slapping herself in the forehead, reminding Aeric that they were only a few months removed from television, electricity, cell phones, pop culture and the like. It all seemed like a lifetime ago that those things were a daily part of their lives and now it was all so different.

"Let's go. I can lead you down to the mayor's house."

"Mayor? No, we want to see our friends," Aeric insisted.

Lorelei looked at him funny and then asked, "You don't know? Well, maybe not. Veronica is the mayor's daughter. She lives with him now."

"Oh. No, we didn't know that."

The guard shrugged her shoulders and gestured for them to follow her. "They're alright," she announced to the other members of the guard force. "They're friends of mine—and the mayor's daughter—so they're gonna be staying in the city."

"Why do we admit your friends and turn away other people?" one of the guards grumbled.

"Shut up, Cantrell," Lieutenant Griffith ordered. "If you had friends or family that showed up, then we'd admit them too. That goes for all of you. You know that we're fair, but we can't take every asshole that walks over that rise."

"I still don't like it."

"Then get the fuck out, Cantrell. You don't like anything about San Angelo, our mission here or any of us. You've been nothing but a complainer for the past four months and I'm sick of it." She pointed back down the road that they'd just traveled and continued, "Austin is that way. I hear they need a new leader for the Vultures since this young lady killed him. In fact, take my bike. I'm sick of you."

"What?" Cantrell asked.

"You heard the LT asshole," a large Hispanic man said as he grabbed Cantrell's rifle. "You've been fucking up my platoon for a long time and now that Lieutenant Griffith has given the okay, you're out, man."

"Sergeant Jimenez, please," Cantrell pleaded. "If you guys kick me out of here, I'll die. You've seen some of those freaks that live out there."

"You've had plenty of chances, Cantrell," Lorelei said. "I'm sick of you. You're a cancer and I don't want your attitude spreading to the rest of my platoon. Fill your backpack with food and you can have my bike. Good luck."

Aeric and his friends watched the action in shock. Cantrell was the same guy who the lieutenant kicked off of her truck when they were on the Army checkpoint back at Richland. He'd seemed like an asshole then and apparently it hadn't gotten any better with time. He was right. Sending a single person out into the wasteland without a weapon was the same thing as killing him.

Cantrell lunged towards Lorelei and the sergeant—Jimenez?—punched him in the back of the head. He collapsed like a rag doll and the man took his gas mask off. "I'm keeping his mask, Lieutenant. He can wear a bandana like everyone else around here and one of ours may become compromised."

"Good idea, Sergeant Jimenez. I'm going to take these three to the mayor's house. When Cantrell comes to, send him packing. We don't need that kind of filth around here."

The sergeant stood upright and saluted, "With pleasure, ma'am."

She returned the salute quickly. "Alright, folks. Let's go."

As they pushed their bikes through the checkpoint, the lieutenant picked up a bicycle of her own and said, "Sorry you had to witness that. It's been a long time coming."

"Banishment means death," Aeric replied. "You should probably just shoot him outright and avoid suffering."

"I've thought about it, but I can't do it. I'll shoot those freako bastards, but I don't know if I can just shoot a man who wasn't shooting back."

Tyler shrugged, "I'll do it."

She glanced sidelong at him, "You guys are safe here. I know that you've been through a lot out on the road and when you were in captivity, but that kind of attitude will get *you* banished from here also. We can't just go around killing people."

"Just sayin'," he answered.

They mounted their bicycles and pedaled slowly towards the city's skyline. "You and Cantrell both said something about freaks. What do you mean?" Aeric asked.

"We've been seeing some really strange things," Lorelei answered. "People who are so screwed up that they're basically animals. I don't know if it's radiation or if they're just crazy, but they're ridiculously dangerous. Plus, there are packs of wild dogs and rabid animals that attack everything that moves, I'm surprised that you guys didn't run into any of them."

"Yeah, we've seen a lot of stuff out there, but it's mostly been bad people who made the choice to become evil, not these other things that you're talking about."

"Well, for now, you're safe. The mayor will probably tell the colonel that you guys shouldn't go into the guard rotation for a few days to let you recover from your journey."

Aeric was genuinely interested in the leadership structure of their new society and asked, "So the Air Force base commander and the mayor work together?"

"Yeah. The appointed base commander, another colonel, was gone at a conference when everything happened, so the training wing commander became the base commander. It's probably easier that one of them was gone, that way there wasn't some type of fight for power. Anyways, the colonel and the mayor work well together. The military handles all the defensive missions while the mayor handles the administration of the city."

"Seems like it's pretty efficient, then," Aeric stated.

"It works."

"So, what do you think our job in the community will be?"

"If it were my decision, I'd recommend that you guys lead our resource recovery teams. We have food here—actually, we have a whole lot of military rations that were stored at the base—but it's not sustainable. So, we send out teams to try and recover as much food as possible from the surrounding area to get us through until the ash settles out of the atmosphere and we can begin farming."

Tyler stuck his hand up like he was asking permission to speak. "I'll do it. I'm pretty good at gathering supplies."

Aeric laughed, "He means that he's good at killing whoever has what he wants so he can take it."

Lorelei skidded to a halt. "Are we going to have a problem with you guys? We don't just go around killing people here and that's the second reference to it since you've been here."

Aeric held up his hands in a placating gesture. "No. No, Lorelei, we don't go around killing people for no reason. We've become extremely efficient at doing it, but only to people who deserved it. I was just making a joke about taking other people's stuff. We haven't ever done anything like that."

"Are you sure that you can go back to living in a normal society?" Lorelei asked. "We have laws, rules and social norms, just like before the nukes hit. The standards are simply adjusted for our new way of life."

"I can vouch for them," Kate said. "If either of them get out of line, then I'll kick their ass. You won't have any problems from us."

The lieutenant stared at them for a moment and then nodded. "Okay. We've banished more people than Cantrell from the city. That's not a threat, so don't take it that way. It's a statement of fact."

"We won't be a problem. Don't worry," Aeric promised.

"Okay. My platoon and I are only here because of you, so I trust you guys. Just, keep down on the references to killing. The city went through a few weeks of chaos right after everything went bad. About a third of the population died and people are sensitive to that sort of thing."

"You're right. Being out there," Aeric gestured behind them towards the countryside, "made us insensitive and callous. We'll rein it in."

She nodded and put her foot back on the pedal. "Alright, let's go reunite you with your family."

As they fell into line behind her, Aeric had to suppress the butterflies in his stomach. He'd been looking forward to getting the opportunity to talk with Veronica again for a long time. He had no clue what was going to happen and he was in love with Katie. It was finally time to find out how Veronica fit into the picture.

*****

Mayor Delgado shook their hands and thanked Lieutenant Griffith for bringing Aeric and his friends to meet with him. Aeric watched the mayor's face intently when both he and Tyler took off their bandanas, revealing their substantial scaring, but to his credit, the man didn't blink an eye. "I know my daughter will be very excited to see you folks," he stated. "She took it hard when Julie showed up and told us that you'd been killed by the Vultures."

"Do you know where my little sister is?" Katie asked.

The mayor shuffled around some papers on his desk until he found the calendar. "Let's see, today is December 31st—a Tuesday in case you wanted to know—so that means she and Kayla are at Shellie's house. The girls split time between our house and living with Shellie, one of our city's guards."

Christmas had come and gone, they hadn't even known. It used to be his favorite holiday. His parents would always decorate the house with lights and tons of little knickknacks everywhere. They'd have his aunts and uncles over with their children and invite the neighbors for dinner. There was always an abundance of presents and food, good tidings and cheer, the works. His memories of the holidays with his family were some of his favorite. This year, it hadn't even been a passing thought for him.

"Is Shellie's house far?" Katie pressed the mayor, stirring Aeric from his brief nostalgia.

"No, it's only a couple of blocks away," he answered. "Veronica can take you there when she gets back."

"Sounds good," Aeric said. "Lorelei said that you might need help with your gathering squads?"

"Yes, we need experienced people who can go out into the surrounding area and bring in supplies to the community. We started doing that last month once we fully took stock of our provisions and realized that our current population could only be sustained for about six months with what we had in warehouses across town.

"We've had a terrible time with losses to the gathering groups, mostly because they are inexperienced and the people who currently own the goods don't want to give them up. The after action reports almost always have a clue as to what went wrong and if there'd been an experienced, level-headed leader with them to make the decisions, then things might have gone better. Would you be interested?"

"I don't know," Aeric replied. "You have the military base right here, why not ask them for leadership?"

"Well, that's a tricky subject. Sure, they have manpower, but the base was mostly a training installation with a lot of students and very few experienced leaders. Look, I don't know you from Adam, Mr. Traxx, but I know that you led your group through the wastelands, out in the open, for more than three months. Plus, you faced the Vultures, who are already starting to encroach on what we view as our scavenging land, and survived. There's no way that you made it without having the ability to know when to talk your way out of a fight and when you needed to stand up to someone. San Angelo needs that type of leadership."

"Not everyone in my group survived," Aeric muttered.

"Maybe not," the mayor admitted. "But most of you did. I've lost entire groups of people with no clue what happened to them. Twenty men and women at a time. We need whatever it is that you have, whether that's skill or just dumb luck, you know how to survive and I want that capability with our gathering squads."

"I wouldn't be alive right now if it wasn't for Tyler and I'd still be chained in the Vulture's palace—or hanging from the wall—if it wasn't for Katie. Our strength comes from our ability to work as a team. I'm nothing special, these guys are the reason we were able to make that journey and survive."

The mayor nodded his head in approval. "I know that. We're only as good as the people that we surround ourselves with. We need all of you."

Aeric looked at his friends and asked, "Well, what do you think?"

"I go where you go, buddy," Tyler responded and Aeric bumped knuckles with him.

Kate shook her head. "Aeric, I don't think I can go back out there. This place seems so...*normal*. I want to settle down and start a family. My days of fighting are over."

He did a double take and asked tentatively, "A family?"

She nodded her head. "I can't go back out there. Not right now."

"Oh shit," Tyler mumbled.

"Are you saying that you're pregnant?" he probed, ignoring Tyler's comment.

"I'm pretty sure. I... I want to keep it. I can't explain it." She glanced at Lorelei and Mayor Delgado, who'd made themselves busy by studying the art on the walls and shuffling papers around on the desk respectively. "Even though it's Justin's, I can't bring myself to get rid of it. I already love it. We could pretend that it's yours and no one except you and Tyler would ever know. Please, Aeric."

For a moment, anger rose up inside of Aeric, a rage that made him want to break everything and everyone in the room. There was no way that she was pregnant with his child, they had only tried to have sex one time since Austin and that had ended with her crying uncontrollably. No, if she were pregnant, it would be from that raping madman. He couldn't allow the seed of that man to grow into a child. He thought about the old days of coat hanger abortions in the back room, or maybe he could kick her repeatedly in the stomach, anything to cause her to abort the baby.

Then, he felt embarrassed and ashamed that he'd considered doing anything to her. The rage subsided and he thought about the millions of people who'd adopted children before the war. It wasn't Katie's fault. She'd been a victim, biding her time until she could stand up for herself and rescue the two of them. If she asked him to, could he raise Justin's child? Could he show it enough love and support to overcome Justin's genetics?

It was a lot to ask of an eighteen—make that nineteen—year old kid. It was a major burden that he wasn't sure he could carry. And then the memories of his father flooded through him. Sure, he'd been one of those helicopter parents, always hovering and heaping praise upon Aeric, but the man had been a *good* father. Could he live up to his father's legacy?

"Uh, we'll need to talk about this later," he answered her and then made up his mind as he spoke. "I'm with you, through thick and thin. We'll work through this, but this isn't the time to talk about it."

She took his meaning and smiled. "You're right. We'll talk later."

Aeric felt her fingers intertwine with his own as he looked back to the mayor. "Okay, I'll do it. If I've got Tyler with me, I know that I can be successful."

The front door to the house opened and closed. "Good, I'm sure we'll make a great team, Mr. Traxx. Sounds like my daughter is here."

"Hey, dad. The guys down at the soup kitchen said you wanted to see me," Veronica's voice drifted from the foyer.

"We're in the office, honey."

They waited a few moments while she made her way through the house. She opened the door and looked the three newcomers over momentarily and then glanced at her father. She didn't even seem to notice Lorelei over in the corner. "What's up?"

The mayor smiled and then asked, "You don't recognize your friends?"

Her eyes narrowed slightly at his words and she looked back to Aeric and Tyler. Veronica studied them for a moment and then she haltingly said, "Aeric?"

He grinned and felt the scars across his face tighten and stretch with the effort. "Hi, Veronica. We made it."

"Oh my..." her voice trailed off and she rushed across the room to wrap her arms around him. After a few seconds, she let go and threw her arms around Tyler. "I thought you guys were dead! Julie said that you died in Austin."

"We might as well have been," Tyler replied. "We were taken prisoner by the Vultures and Katie rescued us."

Veronica released Tyler and stuck out her hand to Katie. "You must be Katie. Are you Julie's older sister Katie, or am I confused?"

Kate took her offered hand and shook it lightly. Aeric hoped that there wouldn't be some type of territorial showdown or something like that. "No, I'm Julie's sister. God, I'm so glad that she's alive."

"She's such a huge help in the soup kitchen for us. We don't make her work since she's still a kid, but she jumps right in there and never asks for any special favors. She's a trooper."

"I can't wait to see her again," Katie answered enthusiastically.

"Okay, I can take you guys over to Shellie's house in a few minutes," Veronica stated. "Shellie likes having Kayla around. It helps her take her mind off of things that have happened."

Aeric sensed that there was a story there of some kind, but he knew that this wasn't the time or place for it either. "So, how have things been?" He felt foolish trying to make small talk with a woman he barely knew in front of everyone.

"Well, after you left Austin, the shootings and gangs started getting out of control," the younger Delgado replied. "Then, the nukes hit all over the place and wiped out everything electric that was still working after the power had been shut off. It was a really scary three or four days until my dad got there. We rode bicycles all the way from Austin to San Angelo—of course, that was before the crazies started coming out of the woodwork in the wastes.

"Since then, we've established a centralized feeding point for the city over on the old Angelo State University campus. It's pretty much in the center of the city, so we can help keep the food supplies safe and it's about the same distance for everyone to get their daily rations."

Veronica snapper her fingers and said, "Hey, I just had a great idea. Since you know your way outside in the wastes, maybe you should train our gathering squads. We could really use your expertise."

"Ah, you're just like your old dad, honey," the mayor stated. "I've already asked them and they both said yes."

She nodded her head, "Smart. If you've got a useful skill, then you'll be a huge help to the community and not a burden like a few of our residents who lived here before things went to hell."

"We would never be any kind of freeloader or something like that," Aeric assured her. "We pull our weight and then some."

Veronica poked him lightly in the ribs and teased, "Looks like you've lost a lot of that weight since the last time I saw you. I didn't even recognize you two."

He chose to keep the mood light and not mention the month of constant torture that they'd endured at the hands of the Vultures. Instead, he answered, "Yeah, we spent a lot of time pedaling away on bicycles too. My old baseball coaches would be proud of how thin I've become."

"I didn't know you were a baseball man, Traxx. I used to play too," the mayor said. "What position did you play?"

"I was a shortstop. Tyler was a first baseman. We both played for the Longhorns."

"Eh, I was an Aggie myself, but I won't hold the fact that you went to a party school instead of a real academic institution against you boys."

Aeric grinned to himself. Even in post-apocalyptic America, sports fans ribbed one another over their alma mater. Humans had messed up this world, possibly beyond repair, but there would always be good people who tried to make the most of the situation.

Aeric wanted to be one of the good guys and he decided that he'd start by making a difference in his new community.

EPILOGUE

"And that, children, is the story of Aeric Traxx, your great-great grandfather," Aiden said with a wide grin. "Because of him, we are who we are. Our family has thrived for more than one hundred and fifty years while others have faltered and died out. He laid the foundations that we have built our empire upon."

Varan glanced around at the ramshackle family homestead with its fourteen houses built around a central meeting area. Beyond the houses were the family crops and further still, the walls that the Traxx family maintained to keep away the Vultures and creatures that roamed the darkness. It didn't resemble much of an empire to him.

"Grandad, why did we leave San Angelo?" Varan asked. "If Aeric journeyed all that way to get to the city, why don't we still live there?"

The boy was much smarter than his older brother the old man thought. Caleb would have been content to smash demonwolves with a hammer all day long instead of applying critical thought to wonder why they attacked and making an effort to change things. "San Angelo fell to the Vultures when Aeric was an old man. My father and I fought to save the city, but there were too many of them. They were much more disciplined back then, not nearly as wild and unorganized as they are today. The Vultures were able to mass their forces and destroy the city. Not for plunder or for food, simply for revenge."

Caleb's eyes lit up at the word. "Was it Campbell?" he asked.

The old man yawned and stretched his arms skyward to loosen his aching shoulders. He shouldn't have sat as long as he had that night. Aeric's story could have been told over the course of two nights, but he'd been delighted to see the looks on the children's faces as he described the events of the past that had been passed on to him by his own father and grandfather, Traxx himself.

"The story of the Vulture's revenge is best left for another night, young ones. It is late now and you must go to sleep or else you'll be worthless at sword practice in the morning."

The grumbling of the children brought a smile to Aiden's weathered face. Now he was certain that he'd done a good job telling the story. The children rarely seemed enthusiastic for anything that didn't involve learning new ways to trap or kill and he was delighted that he'd been able to relieve their burdens, even if it was just for one night.

Little Tanya placed her hand on his knee and asked, "Grandad, did Aeric marry Katie or is Veronica our grandmother?"

"Ah, child, you are so observant. I *didn't* tell you who he decided to be with, did I? Aeric married—" He stopped himself from giving away the answer. He'd enjoyed himself thoroughly this night and wanted the feelings to be repeated so he kept them wanting more.

"You know, my little Traxx warriors, the story of your great-great grandmother will have to wait for another night as well. But know this: Aeric Traxx loved her until his dying day.

"Now, off to bed, young ones. Your fathers will beat me and throw me to the demonwolves if you sleep late tomorrow morning. Go!" he shooed them away with both hands, only giving up the fight when Tanya wrapped her arms around his neck.

"I love you, Grandad," she whispered in his ear.

"And I love you, baby girl. Run along, I'm getting tired myself and will probably fall asleep in this chair before too long. Your grandmother would strangle me if I don't come to bed, though. I don't want to get in trouble either," he said with a wink.

The small child patted his knee affectionately and then ran to her house. Once she was safely inside, the old man picked up his sword and walked stiffly to the house that he shared with his wife and their youngest son's family.

Behind him, the fire continued to crackle, sending large flakes of gray ash skyward to mingle with the remains of the old world suspended in the heavens above.

To be continued in *Fireside, Book Two of The Path of Ashes*

If you enjoyed this book, please leave a review! It sounds trivial, but the number of reviews helps other readers discover my work and adds to the chances that the book will be recommended in online searches. Thank you for your support!

ABOUT THE AUTHOR

A veteran of both the Iraq and Afghanistan war, Brian Parker was born and raised as an Army brat. He moved all over the country as a child before his father retired from the service and they settled in a small Missouri town where the family purchased a farm. It was on the farm that he learned the rewards of a hard day's work and enjoyed the escapism that books could provide.

He's currently an Active Duty Army soldier who enjoys spending time with his family in Texas, hiking, obstacle course racing, writing and Texas Longhorns football. His wife is also an Active Duty soldier and the pairing brings its own unique set of circumstances that keep both of them on their toes. He's an unashamed Star Wars fan, but prefers to disregard the entire Episode I and II debacle.

Brian has authored several books across multiple genres, including horror, post-apocalyptic fiction, paranormal thriller and children's fiction. He self-published four books before signing a 4-book contract with Permuted Press. His novels *GNASH* and *Enduring Armageddon* were previously self-published and will be re-released by Permuted beginning in June 2015 along with two previously unpublished works, *REND* and *SEVER*.

FOLLOW BRIAN ON SOCIAL MEDIA!

Facebook: www.facebook.com/BrianParkerAuthor

Twitter: www.twitter.com/BParker_Author

Web: www.BrianParkerAuthor.com

Enjoy this exciting free preview of
Fireside, Book Two of The Path of Ashes

The ringing of the family alarms woke Aiden from a fitful sleep. He'd gone to bed late last night after telling the story of Aeric Traxx, the family's patriarch, to his grandchildren. The old man had dreamt of the destruction of the city of San Angelo when he was a boy.

He peered around his bedroom, scanning for a threat. Nothing came at him out of the darkness. The inky black night outside his windows told him that it was still likely hours before dawn. The old grandfather clock down in the foyer was the only timepiece that they had in the house, so he couldn't be sure. He needed to respond to the alarm, regardless of the time of night.

He listened intently. The alarm no longer rang outside the house. Had he imagined them, he wondered. The sound of the clock's swinging pendulum permeated the darkness, but he thought he could hear movement outside. That wasn't right. At this hour, there shouldn't have been except the sentries awake on the perimeter walls.

Regardless of his tired, old body's protests, Aiden chose to listen to the little voice telling him that something was wrong. He sat up and pulled on his ancient denim jeans, which had been produced before the destruction of the old world almost eighty years ago and scavenged from abandoned stores in the former Republic of Texas less than five years before.

"What is it, dear?" Aiden's wife asked.

"The alarms," he answered, grunting as he pulled his boots on. "They woke me up."

He saw the outline of her jaw in the moonlight as she tilted her head to listen. "I don't hear anything. Maybe you were dreaming."

Aiden exhaled loudly and said, "Even if it was a dream, it's my responsibility to wake Blake and tell him what I thought I heard."

"Just come back to bed, you old fool! There's nothing out there. We're safe here."

He stood up and grabbed his sword with another sigh. He loved his wife dearly, but she'd become complacent behind the homestead's fence. Almost ten years younger than he was, she didn't remember the horror of San Angelo as almost thirty thousand people perished in less than a week. She'd only been an infant when her family escaped with the group that Aiden's father led to safety. Anna had grown up in a simpler world than young Aiden, who'd watched as his grandfather's flesh stripped from his body while he hid in the rubble of a partially-collapsed building. No, Anna didn't truly understand the depravity of the world that they lived in.

"I'm going out to check the perimeter, then I'll come back to bed. It will only be a few minutes."

His wife harrumphed and turned over on the threadbare mattress that had been a permanent part of their lives for as long as either could remember. Aiden shook his head and padded slowly across the floor to their door, opening it cautiously. A figure at the bottom of the stairs startled him.

"Blake?" Aiden called.

"Yeah, it's me, dad. You heard them too?"

Aiden's knees popped as he eased himself down the stairs. "The alarms?" he asked once he made it to the landing.

"Yeah. The alarms rang for a moment and then stopped," Blake stated as he shrugged into his greatcoat and strapped his sword belt around his waist. He also stuffed an antique pistol into his pocket.

"You sure that gun will even work?" Aiden asked, putting his own coat on. Guns were unreliable at best these days, usually more deadly to the user than their target since the years of ash and acid rain had wreaked havoc on most metals.

"Yes, sir. I've kept it clean and oiled like you taught me. I figured we might need the additional range if something made it past the perimeter.

"If something made it past our guards then that little pistol isn't going to be able to stop it," the old man muttered.

They went out through their front door into the family's central meeting area where they maintained a communal fire pit for roasting large animal carcasses. Aiden glanced wistfully at his old chair pulled near the pit's low brick wall. He was too old to be sneaking around in the darkness looking for intruders. The fire in the pit had burned down to small embers.

Just the night before, he'd sat in his chair and told his grandchildren about Aeric and Tyler's exploits in the beginning. As they stalked towards the wall's gate, he wondered if he'd ever have the chance to complete the story. His world was so much different than it had been as a child—and his grandfather used to tell him how different this world was from the one he'd grown up in, before the nuclear missiles.

What had caused the alarms to ring? Even more disconcerting for Aiden was the question of where were the other Traxx men? The alarms should have caused the courtyard to be filled with men and a few of the women who were not pregnant or not assigned the task of guarding the young. He looked around at the buildings, nothing seemed to move inside them.

Blake had noticed the lack of response as well. "Why is no one else awake?" he whispered. "The alarm only came from the west. The other two guards didn't answer the call with alarms of their own."

Aiden shook his head in confusion. "Something is not right here, Blake. We need to be careful."

The pistol glinted darkly in the moonlight as the younger Traxx pulled the weapon from his pocket. They began heading towards the western section of the perimeter fence when the scream of a woman broke the night's stillness. It had come from inside Luke's house and they turned towards the home.

The old man reacted slower than his son, who'd pulled his sword from its sheath as he raced towards the sound of the screams. He slammed through the front door and tumbled into the entryway. Blake had expected the door to be locked, or at the very least secured. The door had been ajar, not latched.

Aiden's sword felt comfortable in his hand as he took the porch steps two at a time, the aches and pains of his old body were temporarily forgotten. He arrived in time to see Blake sprinting up the stairs so he turned right into the family room to clear the bottom floor.

The Traxx family had found the abandoned homes fifty years ago. The fourteen houses had been the start of what his father called a "subdivision," centered around an open courtyard. They'd stumbled upon them in their wanderings and decided to settle the family in one location. They'd been high-end model homes that were never lived in until the Traxx clan took possession of them.

Aiden thought the homes were much too large and hard to heat, but they held a lot of people. The family had grown to over a hundred and there'd even been talk of building new homes within the compound to accommodate some of the younger couples. All that extra space in Luke's home smelled of death.

He wrinkled his nose at the metallic smell of blood and the acrid stench of loosened bowels. Aiden followed the scent towards Alex's room. His brother, Alex, lived with Luke and his family. His room was on the first floor in what was supposed to have been a home library.

The smell got stronger and more pronounced the deeper into the home that Aiden walked. The clash of steel of steel drifted from the stairwell, startling him. Blake had found someone upstairs and fought with them. He wasn't worried for Blake, every member of the Traxx family was trained to fight from the day they could walk. Whatever he'd encountered upstairs would soon be nothing more than a quivering mass of flesh.

He took a deep breath to steady his nerves and walked several steps towards the room where his brother stayed. There was a strange sound coming from around the corner. It was something that he'd heard before, he couldn't quite put his finger on it. There was a wet, sucking sound and then...was that chewing?

Aiden rushed around the corner with his sword held low. The darkness helped to hide a creature of some kind as it shrieked at him and charged. He had less than a second to lift the tip of his weapon, preparing to defend himself when the hilt jammed hard against his knuckles. The animal had ran into the blade, skewering itself.

It wasn't difficult to identify creature, even in the darkness. It was the nightmare of everyone's existence. The patchwork of black and gray fur mixed with hardened bone outcroppings made his bladder weak and the claws that flashed like sharpened steel in the moonlight promised a swift and painful death. It was a demonwolf—once called a badger in the old world before the radiation had changed them into the terrifying predator that they were today. Most wild animals in the area had died out once the food supply began to be depleted, but the badger was an omnivore, it ate plants, meat and insects. They'd survived the devastation of those first few years after the war and mutated into the largest threat to humanity in the wastes.

Too late, Aiden stepped back as the demonwolf's talons sliced through his coat and deep into his forearm. He screamed in pain. A lifetime of weapons training was the only reason he didn't drop the sword as his body rebelled against his mind to turn and run away. He knew that if he let go of the sword and allowed the creature to maneuver, he'd be dead in seconds. Somehow a demonwolf had gotten into the home without breaking the door down. Had it came in behind the person that Blake fought upstairs? What were the odds of an intruder *and* a demonwolf attack on the same night? If he survived the next few minutes, he'd have to puzzle it out.

The wolf jerked hard to the side, seemingly oblivious to the blade that had entered its chest and exited along its back. Aiden grunted as the damned thing pushed him hard into the wall and grabbed a handful of his coat. It pulled itself closer, its jaws opened and snapped shut on the empty space only inches from his face.

He pushed the sword outwards, using the crossguard to provide leverage against its chest. The demonwolf dragged itself backwards several inches and the tip of his sword disappeared inside the creature. It was trying to pull itself off of his blade so it could get around his defenses and attack.

Aiden laughed bitterly. All his efforts were simply delaying the inevitable. Demonwolves were the deadliest creatures that he knew of, next to man. He pushed forward, trying to reestablish control with the sword and the wolf yelped. The creature's back legs collapsed and it turned its head to snap at its backside. It turned back to him and slashed once again with the daggers on its forefeet.

The razor-sharp claws jarred hard against the bone in Aiden's forearm. This time, his body ignored his training and dropped the sword. He was able to keep his wits about him and staggered backwards. The demonwolf used its front legs to pull its unresponsive body forward towards him.

He allowed himself a moment's hope. When he thrust the sword in a second time, it must have severed the wolf's spine. He rushed backwards across the living room to the kitchen where Luke's wife, Skye, had knives sitting in an original chopping block. He pulled the cleaver from the top slot and turned in time to see the demonwolf scrabbling across the tile.

His left arm was virtually useless, so he swung the cleaver hard with his right across the front of the wolf's snout. The cleaver buried itself halfway through the side of its muzzle and it screamed like a woman. The creature fell to the ground, trying to claw the cleaver out of its face. In its desperation, it inadvertently stabbed itself through the eye with one of its eight-inch claws. The gelatinous orb oozed around its claw.

Aiden grabbed another knife and stabbed down through the demonwolf's ear into its brain. It shuddered once and died. He slid down against the cabinets and stared at his arm. The blood poured freely from multiple lacerations, the deepest had went all the way down to the bone.

He examined the wound with detached interest. His skin gaped wide as if it had been stretched across his arm too tight and the cut allowed it to spread open. Blood pooled inside the large injury so he tilted his arm and the dark fluid poured out. For half a second, he could see the light-colored bone inside, then the blood filled in again.

Aiden didn't know how long he sat in the kitchen. He was dimly aware of wetness under his ass, but he was unsure whether it was from the blood that he'd lost or if he'd pissed himself. He knew that he needed to stop the blood flow somehow, but he couldn't make his body respond. The injury to his arm was bad, and getting worse by the minute. He put his head down to think... He slapped himself in the face to stay awake.

The old man imagined being enveloped in a warm white glow. This must be the light that people speak of when they die, he thought. In all the years that he'd fought against scavengers, gangs and slavers he never imagined that he'd be killed by a demonwolf. The creatures were extremely dangerous, but they were easy to avoid as long as you didn't anger them. What had brought this one into his son's home?

"Easy, dad. I've got you," Blake said.

"Huh?" Aiden said and allowed his eyes to focus. Blake crouched before him, tying a length of rope around his forearm. Skye stood behind him, holding a large candle high, casting light across the kitchen.

"You killed a demonwolf, old man," Blake said as he continued with the tourniquet. "That's amazing."

Aiden's mind thought back to the battle and then he realized what his son was doing. "Hey! Don't put a tourniquet on me. I want that arm."

Blake gestured for Skye to bring the candle closer. He examined the wound before saying, "I don't know if we can save it."

"Bullshit. Get Luke. He's the best doctor we have."

Blake's lips thinned. "Luke is dead."

Aiden nodded his head, he'd expected as much. "Alex?"

Blake shook his head. "Dammit!" Aiden burst out. "What were they?"

"Slavers. They hit a few other houses. The adults are dead and the children are missing."

His heart broke. Not the children. Slavers were the most despicable creatures imaginable. "Tanya?" he asked, his voice betraying the secret that the little girl was his favorite grandchild.

Blake shook his head. "They didn't make it to Garrett's house. They're all safe."

"Why didn't anyone else respond to the alarm?" Aiden asked as his son wrapped strips of clean cloth around his arm and then loosened the rope incrementally to see if the blood flow was stopped.

"It looks like they came over the walls and killed all the sentries before they could raise the alarm. They went to the houses on the west side of the compound and grabbed the kids. Nathan was able to ring the alarm a couple of times before he died, but it wasn't loud enough for the family on the east to hear it."

"The west? Are Caleb and Varan safe?"

"No. They're missing."

"Humph," he grunted. "How'd that damn demonwolf get in here?"

Blake turned and picked up a device off the counter and held it up for Aiden to see. It was a long metal pole with a metal rope loop on one side. "They must have brought it with them and released it inside the camp. Probably to cause confusion."

Aiden tried to stand and his vision threatened to go black. "Sit down, father," Blake ordered. "I've already discussed it with the others. We're leaving at first light when our trackers can see. It doesn't do us any good to bumble around in the darkness outside of the walls."

"Good. That will give me time to make a cast for this arm," Aiden said, lifting his left arm.

"No. You're not going," Blake answered sternly. "Dad, you know that you'll just slow us down on the move. You're better suited to stay here and run the defense of the compound."

"I'm going after the children," he protested.

"Garrett and I have this, dad," Blake said with a comforting hand on his thigh. "You have to trust us now."

Aiden knew the accuracy of his son's words, but the truth hurt. For as long as he could remember, he'd been the leader of the Traxx family. Over time, the mantle of leadership had slowly been transitioning to Luke, but now he was dead and Aiden wasn't certain which of his two remaining sons was strong enough to lead the family. The world seemed to be sinking even further into depravity—if that was possible.

He was rocked hard as a small pair of hands clasped around his neck. "Oh, Grandad! I'm so happy you're safe," Tanya squealed in his ear as she buried her face in his hair. "You can't leave me. We need you here to defend us."

Aiden knew that he was stuck. His granddaughter had overheard him saying that he wanted to go on the search party. Now she'd requested that he stay. He reached across with his good hand and patted her head softly. "Of course little one. Grandad will stay here and fight off any more of the bad men."

Tanya pointed across the kitchen at the carcass. "Is that a demonwolf?"

"Yes, child," Aiden answered. "I told you and your cousins that they were very dangerous. Now do you believe me?"

She nodded her head, rubbing his scalp painfully as her forehead grated into the side of his head. "Can you tell me the rest of the story about Aeric?"

"Yes, of course," he said. "I'm going to try and get some rest tonight. Tomorrow, I'll tell you about my childhood and the first time I saw a demonwolf."

"Okay, thank you. I'll tell Caleb and Varan that you're gonna continue the story!" she said excitedly.

The tears welled up in his eyes and threatened to spill onto his cheeks. He composed himself, he was a Traxx. He had to be strong for the others. "Caleb and Varan will have to hear the story later. Tomorrow will be just for you, little one."

Tanya nodded her head once again. She understood what his unspoken words truly meant. Her cousins had been taken by the slavers. "Don't worry, Grandad. Daddy and Uncle Blake will find them and bring them home. They'll make those bad men pay for coming after the Traxx family."